NOWHERE TO HIDE

LYNDEE WALKER

Severn River
PUBLISHING

Severn River Publishing
www.SevernRiverPublishing.com

This is a work of fiction. Names, characters, businesses, places, events and
incidents are either the products of the author's imagination or used in a
fictitious manner. Any resemblance to actual persons, living or dead, or
actual events is purely coincidental.

ISBN: 978-1-64875-136-3 (Paperback)
ISBN: 978-1-64875-137-0 (Hardback)

ALSO BY LYNDEE WALKER

The Nichelle Clarke Series

Front Page Fatality

Buried Leads

Small Town Spin

Devil in the Deadline

Cover Shot

Lethal Lifestyles

Deadly Politics

Hidden Victims

Dangerous Intent

The Faith McClellan Series

Fear No Truth

Leave No Stone

No Sin Unpunished

Nowhere to Hide

No Love Lost

Never miss a new release!

Sign up to receive exclusive updates from author LynDee Walker.

LynDeeWalker.com

As a thank you for signing up, you'll receive a free copy of
Fatal Features: A Nichelle Clarke Crime Thriller Novella.

For Nichole Dwire

With much love and many thanks for being in my corner all these years.

"Hiding places there are innumerable, escape is only one, but possibilities of escape, again, are as many as hiding places."

—Franz Kafka

1

Murder is easy.

It's getting away with it that's the harder part. More on that later.

Most people—probably nine out of ten—kill because they feel it's necessary. Self- defense, revenge, greed—they can all push an average person over that line. But in the aftermath, most people regret what they've done. The mark of a true predator is lack of remorse.

Think of it this way: in the animal kingdom, survival of the fittest reigns supreme. Strength and cunning prevails, and life moves on.

Humans are different. Some say polite society has civilized the brutality out of folks, but you only have to look as far as the news to know that's bullshit. The real truth of it is, guilt is a powerful deterrent. The simple threat of that skin-shrinking, bile-in-the-back-of-the-throat feeling, imagining ghosts haunting dreams, reliving the screams, wondering who loved them, how that life has changed—it's enough to make even the cruelest person balk at the idea.

Because cruelty is a red herring.

Murder isn't about cruelty.

It's about power.

To take a life and go on about your day is a rare ability. But for those capable, there's nothing like it.

The adrenaline. The hunt. The absolute supremacy of looking a victim dead in the eyes as you land the fatal blow.

Fear lives in the eyes.

It has many markers for the prey—they may feel it in a racing heart, a queasy stomach, a dry mouth, or beading sweat. But a predator can always spot it in the eyes.

They widen first. That's the perception of danger registering in the amygdala region of the brain. The signal fires to the hypothalamus, activating the autonomic nervous system. There's a flicker, deep in the irises, maybe a slight dilation from the adrenaline rush the ANS sends out. Then the tears well as the cortisol hits. Nostrils flare as the heart rate speeds and breath quickens.

That's a common moment for a different sort of adrenaline to fuel the predator.

Because that's when they know. Those tears, that hastened breath, mean the prey understands the game that's afoot. Knows they're the hunted. That's when their necks start to twist and wobble, searching for a way out.

Cat and mouse. Lion and zebra. There's an art to it, make no mistake. It takes finesse, and every act provides learning opportunities.

From a moment of fury and passion, blurred red with cold violence and warm blood, to measured movements.

Slow steps punctuated by quick jerks will keep any prey unsettled. Carefully chosen weapons. Rooms scrutinized, plans laid to block escape routes. Angles and appearances considered.

Size matters, as does strength and speed. But a true

predator never lets a mismatch determine the outcome of the hunt. Cheetahs take down elephants. Hyenas attack wildebeests.

As it turns out, there's only one thing necessary to be at the top of the food chain, to be the strongest. To survive.

A predator's ability to banish guilt. That confidence makes the rest simple.

And then the real fun begins.

"Next time you're tempted to set something like this up, do me a favor." I paused, struggling to get air into my lungs and thrashing my arms above my head. "Drop me into a pit of rattlesnakes I can wrestle bare-handed instead."

My arms popped free and I shook my hair back out of my face, eyeing the half-dozen mounds of silk and organza scattered on the thick blue carpet.

"Yes, how dare I try to make my daughter's wedding memorable." I could hear the eye roll in Ruth McClellan's tone.

"Graham is what will make the day special," I said. "The rest of this is pomp and circumstance. Painfully constricting pomp and circumstance." I wriggled in vain against the unforgiving boning of the tightly laced corset pinching my waist.

Ruth sighed from a gilded white chair that so closely resembled a throne I wondered for a second if she'd had it delivered to the massive dressing room in advance of our appointment. "Faith Lorraine, you only get one ride on this carousel. The dress is the centerpiece. Until you choose one, we can't do anything else."

My teeth clamped down on my tongue. I didn't want to be doing any of this. As far as I was concerned, Graham and I could hop a plane tomorrow and get married barefoot on any beach. Give me two rings, some flowers, and a hotel with a bartender who could mix a good margarita over this circus any day.

As things stood, we had that on deck as our reward for putting up with this six-ring extravaganza. But right then, I was up to my knees in tradition—fluffy gowns and ecru embossed stationery—trying to forge some sort of overdue relationship with my mother by going along with her vision for my wedding.

"I love Archie a lot," I muttered.

"Pardon?" The reflection of Ruth's perfectly threaded eyebrow went up.

"Nothing." I swept an arm at the discarded gowns. "None of these. I really want something simple."

She opened her mouth, I assumed to tell me I was wrong, but a tap at the polished walnut door stopped the argument in her throat. "Mrs. McClellan? How are we doing in there?"

The smooth voice oozed fake adulation.

Ruth opened the door. "She rejected every one of them."

The shop's owner—her name was Nita—turned a dismayed face my way. "You don't love any of them?"

I didn't even like any of them. But she looked so crestfallen I couldn't bring myself to tell her that.

"I'm sure you have something I will adore." I flashed a bright smile, shifting my weight when the corset's boning dug into my hip. "These are all a bit..." I hunted for a word. "Much."

Sequins, frills, and lace abounded on every dress I'd seen in the past two hours. Hell, one even had a sort of breastplate armor-looking area made entirely out of Swarovski crystals.

Ruth huffed out a sigh so long it left me impressed with her lung capacity. "She wants simple."

The words swam in disdain that would make most people think I'd asked to get married wearing a garbage bag. A used one.

"Simple." Nita tipped her head to one side like she didn't understand. "Former Miss Texas, the governor's daughter..." Her eyes went to the piles on the floor that represented the pageant-worthy gowns I'd tried on and discarded.

"Think beach wedding," I said.

"Do not." Ruth's voice held a warning note as she half-rose from the chair.

"Mother, do you want me to be happy or do you want a ridiculous dress?" I blurted before I could consider the question carefully. "Never mind. Don't answer that."

I turned back to Nita. "Do you have something in silk, long, and slinky with a minimal train?"

Ruth's eyes narrowed, and I swear I felt a hole boring into the side of my head. "Maybe a few crystals?" I kept the smile in place.

Nita's head bobbed slowly, one finger going to her chin. "I have an idea."

She disappeared, shutting the door behind her.

"Faith." Ruth drew out the vowels in my name, a mark of irritation in her otherwise unflappable façade.

"I'm here," I said softly. "There was a time in the not too distant past when I wouldn't have been."

I bent to pick up gowns, shaking them out and returning them to heavy wooden hangers embossed with *Sempre*—the shop's Italian name shining in thick, metallic, rose gold lettering.

Ruth's jaw flexed in her reflection, her shoulders squaring

under her jade Donna Karan suit. She wanted to say some-thing. But she didn't.

It seemed she loved Archie, too. Which was at least a place we could start.

"I'm going to ask him tomorrow," I said, hooking two hangers over a brass rack on the only non-mirrored wall. "We're supposed to have lunch, he's going to be up here talking to Lieutenant Boone about something."

"He told me he'd be in Waco all day. I wondered if you had plans." She stood, offering a soft smile so out of character it looked almost painful. Or maybe that was the Botox. "It'll mean the world to him, Faith. You mean the world to him. And for the record, I am glad you're here."

I turned for the rack with another armload of gowns and stopped short when she hugged me. "Oh. Hi."

It was no less awkward for her, her arms dropping quickly back to her sides as she inspected my skin. "You're cold. I should ask her to turn up the heat."

"It's January. I'm fine." I put a hand on her arm. "I've never seen him happier, and I want you to know how much that means to me."

"He's a good man."

"The best one I've ever known. Next to the one I'm marrying."

"Not if you don't pick a gown."

Nita tapped the door again, rushing in with a white garment bag over one arm and two glasses of wine laced between the fingers of her other hand.

It was two-thirty. I downed the chardonnay in one gulp anyway.

"Thank you."

"I thought it might be a good time for beverages in here."

She flashed a small, knowing smile. A tiny spitfire of a woman who exuded class and elegance, she was tailor-made for the business of selling exorbitantly expensive dresses intended to be worn only for one evening—and it appeared we weren't her first dysfunctional family rodeo.

Ruth returned to her chair, half her wine already gone, and waved a hand at the bag. "Let's see it, then," she said.

Nita swept one arm up, and half a blink later, the garment bag was on the floor—I wasn't sure how she got it off so fast, but my eyes were locked on the dress in a way that made me fail to care.

"Oh." I reached out one hand, my feet moving toward the shimmering fabric with a mind of their own.

Nita stepped to the side, clasping ring-heavy hands under her chin and sighing. "There we go."

Perfection was a slinky satin charmeuse with a halter and sweetheart neckline, a skirt slightly raised in the front and trailing just six or so inches in the back, lone crystal dots scattered artfully over the entire thing in precisely the right quantity, glittering under the lights and sending rainbows dancing across every surface.

"It came yesterday. de la Renta," Nita said.

"You won't be able to wear the corset with it," Ruth said, standing to circle behind me and eyeball my slip-covered rear end. "You'll have to make sure you don't need it between now and March."

"Noted." I rolled my eyes, shaking my head slightly at Nita when shock flashed across her face.

"Could you excuse me while I slip it on?"

"Of course, of course," she said. "I have tape and fashion cups if you need them."

I nodded as she stepped out, holding the door for Ruth to follow. Some daughters probably don't mind their moms hanging out in bridal dressing rooms sans corsets and under-garments. We were not that mother and daughter.

I unlaced the corset with the expert fingers of a former pageant queen, shucking my strapless bra right behind it before I pulled the dress from the hanger.

The butter-soft fabric gave me goosebumps as it skated over my bare skin, the train fanning out behind me like Nita had it set for a portrait, the line from my slip so faint no one but Ruth would have noticed it. I twisted right and then left, staring at every angle of my reflection with a fascination I had never offered a mirror in my life.

The door opened, Ruth's breath catching as she stepped back into the room.

"Oh, Faith."

"It's perfect," I breathed. I had walked a hundred runways with tiaras on my head and my arms full of roses, and sat for portraits with the closest thing Texas had to royalty, and I had never in my life felt so much like a princess.

"You are beautiful," Ruth said.

"Oh my, yes ma'am," Nita marveled from the doorway. "If your marriage fits as well as that gown, you are headed for happily ever after, doll."

I couldn't look away from the mirror.

Maybe I was finally going to get the real deal fairy tale after a lifetime of the careful façade of one.

"We'll take it." Ruth moved to follow Nita out of the room. "Thank God. We're running out of time here."

I moved to pull the dress back over my head reluctantly as my phone buzzed on the table next to my wine glass.

Returning the silk masterpiece carefully to the hanger, I reached for my phone and the plush blue robe Nita had draped over the bench next to the table. It was cold in there.

I didn't recognize the number.

"McClellan." I shrugged into the robe and tied the sash.

"Faith, it's been a long time." The voice on the other end was female. Lilting. Familiar, but not familiar enough for me to place right away.

I let a pause stretch for a count of three before I spoke when she didn't. "I'm so sorry, my signal here isn't great. What can I help you with?"

"The TV tells me you're the best there is at investigating murders. I'm hoping you'll be willing to help out an old family friend."

Oh. My word.

"Mrs. Robbins, is that you?" The words tripped out of my face, memories of turning the crank handle on an ice cream machine, laughing at my sister, and warm summer twilight so strong I swear I could smell vanilla sugar tinged with mosquito repellent. "What on Earth has happened? Have you called the sheriff?"

"There've been two killings here in a week, and the sheriff can't climb out of a bottle long enough to know a murderer from a bottom-shelf vodka. I need help. I need you, Faith."

"Of course, ma'am." I grabbed my jeans, alternating hopping on each foot as I yanked them on. "I can be there in a little more than an hour."

"I'll put on the coffee," she said. "You'll have to ring the bell, though—the door is locked."

"Keep it that way." I clicked off the call and finished dressing, my brain running a thousand miles a minute.

Boots on and garment bag in hand, I touched Archie's name in my favorites list.

"Just let her buy you a dress, honey," he said by way of hello.

"I am," I said. "She's fine. Can you see if you can track

down files on recent murders in McCulloch County and who might be working them?"

"Murders, plural?" I could hear him pecking at his keyboard with two fingers as he asked. "I bet they don't get more than two a decade out there. Where'd you hear this?"

"Donette Robbins just called me. She says they had two this week, the sheriff is a booze hound, and she's locking her doors."

"Robbins, Robbins, Rob—oh hell." The pecking stopped. "You heading out there?"

"Right now. I'll be more than an hour getting to her even if I speed, can you send the files to my phone when you have them?"

"Will do. You drive safely, it's getting cold out there and the roads are still wet in some spots. They say it's going to snow tomorrow."

"Yes, sir." I'd believe any kind of significant snow in the Texas Hill Country when I felt the flakes on my nose.

I snatched the door open to Ruth's raised eyebrows.

"Here." I shoved the garment bag into her arms. "I love it. Thank you so much. And I'm sorry I have to leave, but I will call you later, I promise." I knew she didn't expect a hug, which made things easier for both of us.

"Mrs. Robbins just called me about a murder," I explained.

"You can't be serious. There are twelve head of livestock for every person out there."

"She asked me for help. I'm going."

I slid into my truck and blasted the heat, smiling when Graham's name appeared on my phone.

"Everyone there still breathing?" he asked.

"Ruth and I are fine. She's back at the shop, spending way too much of Chuck's not yet frozen assets on my gown. But I'm going to be a while yet—my granny's best friend just called me to report a murder."

3

The arching wrought iron gates were a little more rusted and a little less grand than I remembered, the concrete caps on the brick pillars stained and crumbling at the edges.

I parked my truck in front of the Homestead, a sprawling, clapboard-sided farmhouse with miles of porches and a half-dozen gorgeous stained glass windows.

Zipping my jacket against a biting wind, I jogged up the steps, pressing the doorbell.

Donnette Robbins pulled the thick oak door open, her smile softening the worry in her eyes. "My, I forgot how pretty you always were, sweetheart." She waved me inside, shooting a worried look around the yard before she slammed the door and threw the deadbolt.

"Thank you, Miss Donnie."

My eyes roamed the foyer. Everything, including Donnette, looked just a little more timeworn than I remembered. Dust dulled the prismatic effect of the crystals on the chandelier, the red and gold carpet had faded to more of a sickly orange and yellow.

"Come on in, make yourself at home." She shooed me

toward the parlor. "Don't think I don't appreciate you driving all the way out here at the drop of a hat."

I shrugged out of my coat when I crossed the threshold to a room that held so many childhood memories I had to catch my breath. The fireplace, nearly big enough for me to stand in even still, was home to a roaring blaze that practically dared the chill creeping through cracks in the old house to enter the cozy room.

I perched on the end of the same plastic-covered white velour sofa that had faced that fireplace my whole life, and Donnette sat next to me, her red apron flouncing over the clear vinyl. She reached for a silver tray on the claw-footed cherry coffee table, pouring two cups of coffee.

"Cream?" She lifted a tiny white pitcher.

"Just two sugars, thank you."

"Your granny would be so proud of you, Faith." She sat back and sipped her coffee, turning bright blue eyes on me. They had more wrinkles at the edges, but I'd bet she could still chop wood, make jam, and work a crossword all as well as she could twenty years ago.

"I hope so, yes ma'am." I let a pause stretch. "Miss Donnie, it is wonderful to see you."

"But you want to know why I called you out here?" She winked. "I'm not addled yet, sweet girl, don't worry."

"I'm a little confused," I said. "You told me there have been murders here lately, but my partner checked local files while I was driving out, and we can't find any information on them. Have you tried to report this to the sheriff?"

She snorted and waved one hand. "That old drunk wouldn't know a murderer if one walked up and bit him."

"So you didn't call him?"

"No point to it, honey."

I didn't know the local sheriff, but I could swing by and

introduce myself when I was done here. Archie said the department had three employees: the sheriff, a lone deputy, and a dispatcher. The last recorded homicide in the county was twelve years ago, and a retired B Company ranger had conducted the investigation at the invitation of local law enforcement.

"Can you tell me what you know?" I asked.

"Well, to tell you the truth, nobody thought much of the first killing. Clive was an ornery little cuss, and I suppose folks figured he had it coming."

I felt my eyes widen a touch with every word. My grand-parents had owned the next property over for sixty years, and I'd spent enough time there to know folks out here had a no-frills, pragmatic way of viewing the world that might seem cold. But this was a different level.

"But Samson was famous. And the killer took his head."

I raised one hand and pulled out my phone, turning on the voice recorder.

"Texas DPS Ranger Faith McClellan, today is Friday, January 28, and I'm interviewing Donnette Robbins on the Robbins family farm in McCulloch County about a suspected homicide.

"The victim was beheaded?" I asked. "Both of them, or just the second one?"

"Who would've wanted Clive's head?" Miss Donnie's tone was so matter of fact she might've been telling me about her favorite jam recipe or last summer's corn crop. "I mean, that's not the sort of thing you'd have mounted for the wall or anything. But he made for a damned fine Founder's Day barbecue."

Wait.

I coughed, setting my mug on the table. "You're not talking about a person."

"Prize-winning hog, took first place at the county fair in September. Over to the DeWitt place. You remember Marvin DeWitt, used to fancy himself the mayor?"

There wasn't any such thing as a mayor out here. There was barely a sheriff.

A murdered pig.

Archie would laugh for days, and I might never take another call without asking the species of the victim.

"And Samson? Was he human?"

"No, he's the star of *High on the Hog*," she said. "You know, on the internet. The my tube?"

"YouTube?" I clarified.

She pointed at me. "That's the one. My great-granddaughter says Samson has thirty-five million followers. Enough so that he was more valuable alive than at the stock show, I heard. Poor Kelsey Marie is beside herself."

"Is that his owner?"

"They were tacking up reward fliers all over town in this cold yesterday."

Did they call the sheriff? I didn't say it out loud. I wasn't sure what to do with this—I didn't want to hurt Miss Donnie's feelings, but this was not my idea of an emergency.

I sipped my coffee. "Dead livestock isn't my area of expertise, Miss Donnie."

She laughed. "Oh honey, I know that. But surely it can't be but so different. And we have nobody else to turn to."

"You just said the owner of the animal has posted a reward," I said. "In my experience, if it's enough money, people will rat out their friends. And someone has to know what happened to these pigs. I think they'll get to the bottom of it without intervention from me or the sheriff."

I stopped the recorder and moved to stand, pausing when I met her eyes.

She was scared.

Donnette Robbins had once run a bobcat out of her barn armed with nothing but a three-pronged rake and her stubborn streak, while my granny ran home for a 12-gauge. By the time Granny returned with the gun, the cat was gone and Donnette was calmly mucking out stalls.

Something else was wrong here.

"Miss Donnie, I need you to help me understand." I sat back down, laying the phone on the table. "Folks around here take care of their own. Hogs get slaughtered every winter. Why is this bothering you?"

"Because this was different," she said. "Samson, and Clive too, nobody killed them for bacon and ham—sure, old Marvin made the best of it, he's good at finding the bright side, but this was different. Somebody killed those animals for spite. My daddy always said a man who can be cruel to an animal will turn on a human in a hot minute. Maybe it's livestock to you, but murder is murder. And these were brutal. I can't hardly sleep, thinking there's somebody who could do something like that around these parts."

She fussed with the edges of her apron, her fingers plucking at a thread. "I can't lie to you, sweet girl. I called the sheriff. He thinks I'm crazy. I reckon from your face you probably do too. Hell, maybe I am. But whoever did this ain't right in the head. And there's nothing to say it stops with livestock just because that's where it started."

She took one of my hands in both of hers. "Do we really have to wait for some sicko to slaughter a person before anyone will take it seriously?"

I sighed.

Her point was well made. Criminal psychology is chock full of stories about murderers who started off with animal abuse. It serves as a gateway to inflicting injury to another person when you can learn to stomach inflicting it on any other living thing.

"Okay, Miss Donnie. Let me see what I can find out." I pulled a pad and pen from my hip pocket. "How do I get a hold of the folks who owned Samson? You said there was a YouTube channel?"

"Sure is. Kelsey Marie Sherman. She's the first young woman to ever be the president of the McCulloch County 4H. That pig would've brought a blue ribbon home from Fort Worth for sure if they hadn't pulled him from competing."

I jotted the name. "Where's their place?"

"Three drives down from your granny's." She squeezed my hand. "Thank you, darlin'. It is good to see you." She paused, looking down as she let go of my fingers. "Is that what I think it is?" Her eyes were on the simple solitaire engagement ring Graham had given me after I proposed to him in October. I tried to tell him I didn't need a ring but he wouldn't hear it. He said he'd already paid for it and my not wearing it was an insult.

I hadn't taken it off since he'd slipped it onto my hand that night.

"Yes, ma'am. His name is Graham Hardin; he's a commander at the Travis County Sheriff's Office."

"You know, there was a Graham Hardin who played base-ball at the university for a time," she said. "He was my Ernie's favorite pitcher. Tall fellow. Colored if I recall correctly."

"One and the same. He was quite an athlete, and he's a heck of a police investigator."

"And I bet your father is beside himself," she said.

I inhaled a cleansing breath. I didn't want to have to explain the offensive nature of casual racism to one of my grandmother's dearest friends, but that didn't mean I wouldn't.

Donnette blinked, leaning closer to my face and studying it. "Oh, honey—no need to fret over what folks think. Love is love. The heart doesn't see color—or anything else." She smiled. "Best wishes to you, and my congratulations to Graham. I hope you two have as many happy years as Ernie and I did. More, even. I just remember your fondness for annoying Chuck."

I blew out a relieved breath. "Thank you," I choked out, sniffling as I stood. "Please give Megan my love." Donnette's granddaughter was closer to my sister Charity's age than mine, but the three of us had passed many a summer day riding horses in the pastures and picking honeysuckle at dusk. "I hope she's doing well."

"She married her longtime girlfriend about three years ago and they just had a baby boy the week before Thanksgiving." Donnette beamed. "She's so happy. That's all anyone ever should want for their babies. I'm glad you are, too." She got up to walk me out, pulling her crocheted shawl tighter over her arthritis-hunched shoulders. "Thank you."

I squeezed her hand as I stepped out into the wind, which had picked up speed and chill while we talked. "Lock this door. And if you think of anything else I need to know, please call me."

"Sure thing, sweet girl."

I hustled over the ice-slicked red clay of the drive and swung up into my truck, eyeballing the sinking sun as I turned the heat up and took a right at the end of the dirt road, counting three driveways down from the farm that had been in the McClellan family for a century and a half. My father sold it after Granny died because "who in their right mind wants to live in this hellhole in the middle of nowhere?"

I had no idea how I was going to tell Lieutenant Boone or Archie—or maybe even Graham—that I was investigating a pork-icide, but I also figured it wouldn't take more than the weekend to get to the bottom of it. Plus, it got me out of spending the next 48 hours picking out china and flowers with Ruth, and it wasn't like my colleagues had never thought I was on a wild hog chase before.

They just hadn't ever been right in the literal sense.

4

The Sherman residence was less house than celebrity compound.

Set back a quarter mile down what might have been the only paved driveway in the county, the sprawling timber and stone ranch house probably took up nearly half an acre in its footprint. It was surrounded by two large, pristine barns, a pool house, and, past all that, a white metal building with a thirty-foot roofline and a Circle Double H brand outlined over an area the size of my truck between the bay doors.

These people had their own TV studio.

I tucked my notebook and my phone into my pocket and jogged to the porch, pulling a handbell rope dangling from the ceiling to one side of the twelve-foot oak double doors.

A uniformed housekeeper cracked the door. "Miss Kelsey no is giving interviews," she said with a heavy Eastern European accent.

I smiled. "I'm not a reporter." I pointed to my badge. "Faith McClellan, Texas Rangers."

She wrinkled a brow at the last words.

"Samson," I said.

She swung the door wide. "Mr. Sherman said the sheriff wouldn't help." Her accent was much lighter that time.

I wondered what the sheriff had to do that was more pressing than helping these folks, but filed that away for later.

"I'm not the sheriff." I stepped inside. "Donnette Robbins, just down the road, is an old friend of my family and she's worried. I'd like to speak to Mr. and Mrs. Sherman and their daughter, if you wouldn't mind getting them for me."

"Mrs. Sherman and her son are on holiday." The accent was heavier again, her eyes on the floor. "I will get Mr. Sherman."

I offered my best *I'm here to help* smile, and she scurried off into the cavernous house.

Clasping my hands behind my back, I turned a slow circle. Even the Governor wouldn't have called this place a hellhole. Part country cabin, part upscale ski chalet, the interior was all exposed timber beams, stone, warm paneling, and floor-to-ceiling windows lining the entire back wall of the family room. That space unfolded in both directions from the foyer, most of what I assumed was once a gorgeous view of the open plains blocked by the hulking TV building.

A pair of twenty-point bucks stared with glass eyes from their mounting spots on the walls of the foyer, and a bear skin rug decorated the center of the floor on the other side of a massive leather sectional at the end of the hall.

"These are the people who are running a program about caring for animals?" I muttered under my breath, my eyes on the Double-H brand decorating the side of the studio barn.

"Thirty-nine million followers and counting," a deep baritone came from behind me.

I spun on my heel. "No disrespect, Mr. Sherman."

"Call me Jeff, please," he said. "None taken, Miss...Marta said it's McClellan?"

"It is."

"Please come in." He pointed to my badge. "I have to admit I didn't quite believe Marta when she came in. I have called every cop for fifty miles and no one has been willing to do anything to help us. I thought the reward would be the only way we'd find out anything." He wrinkled his nose. "It's not going quite like I thought it would."

"Money brings the crazies out," I said. "I imagine you've gotten a couple dozen calls at least, ninety-nine to a hundred percent of which go absolutely nowhere." It hadn't been long enough for the reward offering to have time to sway anyone who might really know something.

"You have a sharp imagination there." He waved one arm in invitation to the family room.

Jeff Sherman was strikingly tall—towering probably four or five inches over my five-ten—and a lean brand of fit with thick, dark hair and a matching mustache that made it nearly impossible to guess his age.

He asked, "Who do I owe for getting your attention?"

"Donnette Robbins, a few miles down the road. She was my granny's closest friend."

"I will make it a point to thank her in person."

"Whatever happened to your daughter's pig has her scared, and I've known Miss Donnie all my life—she doesn't scare easily. I admit that animal slaughter is outside my normal wheelhouse, but I'm concerned because she is." I pulled out a notebook and pen. "Why don't you tell me what happened? When was the last time anyone saw Samson alive?"

"Tuesday evening, right about supper time. Kelsey Marie finished filming her video for the Friday drop, and she put him to bed right after. Wednesday morning, she went out to feed him at five-fifteen and he was dead."

A flat voice thick with sadness came from the doorway. "Worse than dead. Butchered. He wasn't just killed, he was, like, slashed up."

Kelsey Marie Sherman was probably five feet tall with her boots on, a tiny, thin girl with an angular face and a mop of curly brown hair tied messily on top of her head with a Lululemon scrunchie that matched her black leggings and three-sizes-too-big hoodie.

"Kelsey Marie, honey, the doctor said that medicine was supposed to make you sleepy." Her dad's face and voice softened.

"Marta said there was finally a cop here asking about Samson." She kept her eyes on mine. "You need to talk to me, right? I'm the one who found him."

"It's certainly helpful if you feel up to it," I said. "I'm Faith."

She padded across the floor in thick cable knit socks, curling herself onto half of the corner cushion at one end of the massive sofa. She tucked her feet underneath herself and let her sweatshirt sleeves swallow both of her hands.

"He was the sweetest boy." Her voice faded, tears strangling the last words. "He didn't deserve that. He wouldn't have hurt a fly. Everyone loved Samson."

"I understand Samson had quite a following on YouTube. Had you gotten any comments or messages from anyone threatening him?"

Kelsey Marie shook her head. "He was cute and funny. Why would anyone want to hurt him?" Her face crumpled. "Oh God, this is all my fault. I wanted to put videos of him on the internet because he was so sweet and fun. And I got him killed."

Her father stepped forward and laid a big hand on her bird-like shoulder.

"I'm not saying it was connected to your videos for sure," I said. "Just that I have to look at every possibility."

"Of course it was the channel," she shrieked. "Why else would anyone come looking to hurt him?"

"There was another pig killed a few days before Samson, on a farm near here," I said. "It is possible this was related. And even if it wasn't, it wasn't your fault."

She sobbed harder.

I put my notebook on the table and crossed the room, squatting in front of her seat and putting one hand on her knee. "Kelsey Marie, I need for you to understand something. I have worked and cleared a hundred and twenty-six homicide cases in my career. I have watched people beat themselves up every way you can imagine. And I can tell you for sure and certain that one thing I know about situations like this one is that it's not your fault. Sometimes, things just happen. You cannot let yourself get bogged down in wondering what if. There are a thousand ways to answer that, and not a one of them matters because it won't change what's already happened."

"I loved him." The words were halting, on hitching breaths between sniffles, every one as full of anguish as I'd ever heard. "I know it's dumb for a person to love a pig, but he was special. He wasn't food. He was my best friend."

"I'm so sorry for your loss," I said, my victims' family mode taking over on autopilot and somehow not feeling even a tiny bit ridiculous. "Let's see if we can figure out what happened to him."

Marta appeared at Kelsey Marie's elbow with a box of tissues and Kelsey Marie took one. Marta took the used Kleenex back without a word, setting the box on the sofa before leaving the room.

I stood. Kelsey Marie wiped her sunken, purple-hollowed eyes, sitting up straight.

"Whenever you're ready," I said. "Tell me about Samson."

It was weird, asking the same questions about a farm animal I usually asked about people, but one thing all those cases had taught me was that my edge comes from caring about the victims and the people they left behind. I was truly sorry the pig was dead—the young woman in front of me was downright heartbroken. I needed to understand why in order to do my best work helping her find closure.

"He was the runt of his litter," she said, plucking at the thread on the hem of her sweatshirt. "That's why Daddy let me keep him in the first place. Like Wilbur from *Charlotte's Web*. I almost named him that, but then he was just so strong and determined, I settled on Samson."

I flicked my eyes to Mr. Sherman. His gaze was locked on his daughter, his lips curving into a soft smile.

"Samson was the first interest Kelsey Marie ever showed in farming," he said. "And she took to it like a fish to water. My son has raised a hog for the stock show three times now, and we've never had an animal as healthy as what my baby girl turned that runt into. He took second place at the county fair last fall, and only by half a point."

I picked up my notebook and jotted that down, nodding along with Kelsey.

"Dustin kept telling me to go back to cheerleading. Like girls didn't belong in the 4H or something." She pursed her lips. "I'm president this year, and he's the one who's a senior."

"I know the feeling. But if you weren't interested in farming or 4H, why did you keep a pig?"

"That was actually on me, by accident," Jeff said. "She wandered out to the barn one morning spring before last, looking for a ride to school because she'd missed the bus. We had a new litter the night before and I was looking them over. Samson was half the size of his brothers, and weak."

"He was going to kill him!" Kelsey Marie's voice rose a full octave and then broke. "Way back then, he was going to kill him, just because he was small." She hugged her knees. "I'm small."

"I told her she'd have to feed him from a bottle and keep him under a heat lamp in a small pen in her room, thinking she'd lose interest real quick."

"He was my baby," she said, her arms tightening around her middle. "I kept his hay clean and got up in the middle of the night to feed him."

"Damn right you did," Jeff said. "I've never seen a kid take such good care of an animal. He was the most spoiled rotten pig in the history of pigs. She started letting him follow her around the house and the property, and damned if she didn't housebreak a pig. For a year, he lived in the house like a puppy."

"If he'd still been in the house, he'd still be alive," Kelsey Marie sniffled.

"He weighed almost a thousand pounds. You can't keep livestock indoors as a pet. Not forever, anyway."

Kelsey Marie just pulled on the thread some more.

"So how did you and Samson get started with YouTube?" I asked.

She snorted. "A dare from my stupid brother."

I waited. She didn't say anything else.

"Teenagers." Jeff huffed out a frustrated sigh. "Kelsey Marie, answer Ranger McClellan. And look at her while you do it."

Kelsey Marie rolled her eyes up until she was looking at me through a fringe of curlicue bangs, her face still pointed at her lap. "I did answer. Dustin told me I was stupid and worthless and that Samson was just a walking slab of bacon. And I proved him wrong." Her voice got soft. "Like always."

"Do you and your brother fight a lot?"

"Is a hog happy in slop?" She snorted, sitting up straight and letting her head flop back onto the leather cushion. "I will never know how we share even half our DNA. Dustin is a creep."

My eyes slid to Mr. Sherman, Marta's comment about his wife being away with "her" son flitting through my thoughts.

"Dustin is older than you?" I asked.

"Fourteen months."

"My wife...she was pregnant when we started dating. Just barely," Jeff said. "I've always taken care of him like my own."

I jotted notes. "And how is Dustin's relationship with his biological father?"

"We don't even know who that is. Mom never told us." She looked at her father. "At least, not that I know of."

Jeff shook his head.

That likely meant the boy's father didn't know he had a son, which meant he wasn't any of my concern.

"Mrs. Robbins told me that Samson was...um...that his..." I started the sentence with intent, but looking at Kelsey Marie's hollow eyes, I wasn't sure I could finish it.

"His head. She told you the bastard that did this took his head." Kelsey Marie's flat voice was so monotone it was obvious that she was trying to detach herself from the thought. "Because whoever killed him is a sick fuck."

"I'm so sorry," I said. "I just need to know if there might be some clue in that. Given Samson's relative fame." I turned, pointing to the mounted deer heads. "Would a collector somewhere pay for that?"

Kelsey Marie looked horrified, and Jeff laid a hand on her

shoulder, shaking his head. "It hasn't crossed my mind," he said, his voice a touch raspy.

I made a note. "I'm sorry to have to ask. It's my job for it to cross mine."

"Of course. Thank you, Officer," Jeff said.

Don't thank me yet, dude.

"Kelsey Marie, you found Samson that morning?" I kept my tone soft. If they wanted my help, I needed to know.

She sniffled. "There was so much blood. And the smell..." She shuddered. "It smelled so God-awful."

For a pigpen to smell worse than usual might be saying something, because there wasn't enough time in her story for decomp to begin in earnest.

"Mr. Sherman, how long have you lived here?" I asked.

"Sixteen years. We bought this place when Kelsey Marie was a baby."

"What does your wife do for a living?"

"She pretty much runs things around this place. I keep the books and handle the vendors, but she knows way more about the day-to-day of the animals and the land than I ever will," he said. "Randi always wanted to live on a farm as a kid. It was her dream, and it's been good to us." He squeezed Kelsey Marie's shoulder. "Really good."

I kept my hand moving at a normal pace as I jotted that note, my brain racing like a greyhound after a rabbit down that trail.

"And when will she be back?"

Jeff's eyes flicked to Kelsey Marie and he smiled. "Soon. They needed some time away."

"It may be important for me to talk to her if the animals are her area of expertise," I said. "Could I get her cell number at least?"

He glanced at Kelsey Marie and sighed. "They went hunting. We have a place about thirty miles west of here, which bothers my little vegetarian here. One of the best things about it is that it's out of cell signal range."

"Can I get the address then, please?"

"It's off 87 toward Eden," Kelsey Marie said. "Look for the double H brand on your right. If you get to town, you went too far." Every word was folded in sorrow. Was that because of her pig, or her mother? I couldn't tell, and a thousand of these interviews had taught me when to let well enough alone. I could circle back later if I had to know. When she trusted me more.

"Have y'all cleaned up the barn?"

"If you mean, is my child's pet still lying out there rotting, he is not," Jeff said. "He's in the cooler. Not slaughter time for a few weeks yet, so we had the room. We're going to get Kelsey Marie a new baby runt to raise."

"I don't want to replace him," she snapped, her bun falling loose as she whipped her head around. "He's not even in the ground. I won't do it. Not yet."

I cleared my throat. "I was actually more interested in the rest of the scene, Mr. Sherman."

"I took photos," Kelsey Marie whispered.

"Of?"

"Everything. I even got footprints outside the barn in the mud," she said. "Daddy said he was going to call the sheriff and I thought I could help before anyone could mess up the scene. I watch TV. The police always need pictures."

"We always do. Can I see those, Kelsey Marie?"

She pulled her phone from the pocket on the front of her hoodie and tapped the screen before she practically threw it at me, shuddering. "My poor baby."

I caught it and blinked hard at the screen. I've seen more dead bodies than anyone ever should. That was a lot of blood.

A lot.

I flipped through the photos, each more horrifying than the last. Blood on the white painted walls of the pen. Blood on the trough. Dark, spreading circles of blood soaking into the ground.

I swallowed hard. Kind of gave new meaning to the word slaughter. I wasn't even sure what kind of weapon a person would need for such a thing.

But I knew someone who might be able to tell me.

If he didn't laugh me right out of his lab for bringing him a dead pig.

The next image was of a muddy footprint. It was a close-up, with nothing to give reference for size, but better than nothing.

"Kelsey Marie, do you mind if I text myself some of these?" I asked.

"Sure, whatever."

I sent four bloody stall and carcass photos and one of the footprint to my phone.

"Where was this footprint?"

"Right outside the back entrance to Samson's barn."

"Mr. Sherman, do you have security cameras?"

His lips disappeared into a grim line. "Had them installed right before Thanksgiving. But they didn't get anything."

"Is there a camera on this door?"

"There is, but the feed was messed up. Like snowy," he said. "The damned thing was disconnected from Sunday until after we found Samson, apparently."

I made a note. "Could I get a copy of it anyway?" I asked. "I'm pretty handy with computers."

He shrugged. "Sure, I'll get it."

He stood, and I followed suit, squaring my shoulders for the harder ask. "And can I get Samson's remains? I will return them. But I have a friend who might be able to get us a lead by examining them."

"What?" That came from Kelsey Marie, high and strangled. "Daddy, you promised me a proper funeral."

"You'll get one," I assured her. "I promise to return him to you. But this could really help me figure out what happened to him."

"Okay, Officer. I hope you have a large vehicle," Jeff said.

"Daddy, I don't think—" Kelsey Marie's eyes welled back up and she sniffled, but fell quiet when Jeff raised one hand. "Okay," she whispered.

I glanced at the sun, sinking into a pool of red and orange on the western horizon, as I followed Jeff to the barn. This was a good start.

I could poke around and interview the locals and the sheriff another day. Having gotten a look at those photos, the first thing I needed was for Jim to tell me what happened to this pig.

5

No darkness is quite like Texas country darkness. It presses in, thick and impenetrable, only yielding a few inches at a time to any lumen count shy of a football stadium light.

By the time I got back to the interstate my shoulders ached from hunching over my steering wheel, trying to see to the limits of the piddly ten or so feet my high beams could pierce.

Relaxing back into the seat under the orange-yellow glow of freeway lights, I plucked my phone from the cupholder and hit the speed dial for Jim Prescott's cell phone with one hand.

"It's eight-thirty on a Thursday night, *Grey's Anatomy* is not on my TV, and my wife is still awake," he said by way of hello. "This better be a damned interesting dead guy."

"Oh, he's interesting all right," I said. "All nine hundred and forty-three pounds of him. Give or take one missing head."

"You have my attention." The edge of annoyance in his tone faded to one of curiosity. Sharon groaned in the background.

I bit the inside of my cheek. Jim and his wife didn't exactly have a lot of date nights to look back on in the past year. "But he'll also wait until morning if you could just let me into the lab to drop off the remains."

"I. I'm sorry?" The annoyance was back. "You don't *drop off* remains. Who worked the scene?"

"His owners?"

"I've only had half of one drink, so I know I'm hearing you right, but damned if I can figure out what you're talking about. What is it that you don't want to tell me, McClellan?"

"It's a pig. A murdered, internet-famous pig."

His breath went in for a lecture and I kept talking so he couldn't.

"I know it sounds dumb. I thought so too, when I first figured out what I was being asked to do. But Jim...whatever someone did to this poor animal...let's just say I hope I don't piss them off."

"Your odds are better than even on that if you go poking around where you're not wanted." He paused. Sighed. "That bad, huh?"

I smiled at the interest in his tone. We'd worked together too many years for me to not know right then that I'd won. "Come see. Tell Sharon I only need to borrow you for a half-hour tonight."

"Only you, McClellan," he said. "A pig. In my lab."

"I'll meet you there in fifteen minutes." I smiled. "Thanks, Jim."

"Yeah, yeah." He hung up.

"This is the weirdest thing I've ever had in here." Jim followed me out of the crime lab's cold storage, pulling his gloves off to toss them into the wastebasket. "And I have seen some weird shit in almost four decades at this gig, McClellan."

"I'm worried about who would do this and why," I said.

"And what that 'who' might do to a person, given the opportunity?"

Jim was a smart guy.

"That, too."

"We'll figure it out." He swung one arm wide in a *ladies first* and followed me out of the exam room. "Tomorrow."

I laughed. "I'm going, I'm going. Tell Sharon I said thank you. Y'all enjoy the evening, and I'll see you tomorrow."

He swung up into the driver's seat of his truck and waved. "You sure you know what you're getting into?"

"When do I ever really know? Mrs. Robbins was my grandmother's dearest friend. She's lived on that farm the vast majority of her days. I'm not inclined to let her spend her last ones locking her doors in fear of the pig-murdering boogeyman."

"Goodnight, McClellan." He put the window up and sped out of the lot, his taillights gone before I made it to the exit. I smiled. Good for them.

Graham texted that he had a pizza on the way.

I finally had a dress.

Not counting the dead hog in Jim's cold storage, everything was right in my world.

For the moment, anyway.

6

"I still can't believe somebody killed Samson the hog." Graham pulled a cinnamon donut from the bag in his lap Friday morning as I pointed the truck northwest toward McCulloch County.

"I still can't believe you've seen Kelsey Marie's channel."

"I clicked a link one of my 4H friends from high school posted on Facebook. It's funny. Samson is huge, and he acts more like a dog than a pig. Kid is bright, has a talent with the camera, and she's good about including relevant information for other 4H kids without it seeming boring."

"She was devastated." I took the glazed donut hole he passed me. "I've seen people less torn up over dead humans."

"We've met some humans with less pleasant personalities than Samson." Graham sipped his coffee, raising his eyebrows. "And they said the mom took her son hunting for a bonding thing?"

"I happen to know a woman who's a pretty damned good shot." That came out more defensive than I intended.

"Hold your fire." Graham raised both hands, cinnamon and sugar sprinkling down his starched uniform shirt. "No sexist undertones intended. I just thought it was an interesting choice in light of the daughter's pet being slaughtered in their backyard this week, that's all."

"Sorry." I flexed my fingers on the steering wheel, shaking my head. "I'm having trouble shaking off how scared my granny's friend sounded. Wondering if there's something I should've asked her that I didn't."

"Faith. It's a dead pig." Graham broke off a piece of a donut and handed it to me. "You hate spending time with your mother more than even I thought."

"That's a different conversation with a whole lot of therapy bills behind it. Make fun of me all you want, but this really is disturbing."

"I'm sure it is. And you still won't have to see your mother."

"I found a dress. She said that was all she needed to figure out the rest. Ruth is great at planning parties. She can handle whatever needs handling."

"You happy with the dress?" His voice softened. "This is our day, not hers."

"Wait until you see it and you tell me," I said.

"That good, huh? Okay. But I can wait. Momma says seeing your dress before the wedding is bad luck. We don't need any of that hanging around."

"I think that particular wives' tale involves seeing me *in* the dress, but I want to surprise you, anyway."

He squeezed my hand and flipped on the radio.

I had long ago given up hope that I'd ever find a man who could both tolerate my mountain of Louis Vuitton family baggage and make sparks skate from my hairline to my toes with the right look or the slightest touch. And then Graham Hardin walked back into my world and showed me I was wrong, and here we were.

Trying to solve a swine-icide on a frigid Friday morning.

We chewed in silence through three songs. Putting his coffee back into the cupholder, Graham cleared his throat.

"So now that you've had caffeine and sugar...you ought to call your mom." He threw both arms over his head in an exaggerated duck-and-cover stance.

I laughed. "It's not that bad."

"Have you met you?"

I sighed. I did have plans to meet Ruth for china shopping later—her idea, of course, but I had agreed and even taken the day off. She would see this as a calculated move to avoid that because she knew good and well I'd rather have my fingernails pulled out one by one than pick out fancy dishes Graham and I would never even unbox.

"Fine." I reached for my cell phone.

"I'll meet you at Saks at two," she said by way of hello. Ruth McClellan only made time for pleasantries with people who didn't know her well. "We can get coffee at the café and still have plenty of time to make your registry appointment."

"My what?"

"Registry appointment. There's more to choose than china and silver, after all."

"Graham and I both have our own independent households," I said. "It's not like we're just starting out and we need our friends to save us from paper plates. I think half the challenge of this will be deciding what to keep and what to get rid of."

"It's a show of respect to your guests to register for gifts, Faith." Exasperation dripped from the speaker. "People expect it. And it's nice for them to know they're getting you things you want."

"Except that's just it—I don't want any of this stuff. We're not hosting state dinners. We don't need china and silver. We like our Fiesta plates and our regular old flatware."

The sharp breath in would've made a passerby think I just told her I liked skinning babies alive for fun and profit.

"I see."

"The thing is that I'm working on something kind of urgent and I need to be out in McCulloch County today anyway," I said. "Can we talk more about this later? I'm sure there's a compromise we can come to."

"Is Donnette okay?"

"She's fine. But afraid there's a killer on the loose in her community. I'm going to see what I can find out since I'm not working today."

"We'll talk this weekend," Ruth said.

"Of course. Thank you for understanding."

I clicked the phone off and put it down.

"She didn't yell," Graham said.

"She did not." I was still trying to make sense of that, but I wasn't complaining.

"You told her we aren't hosting state dinners and you don't want china and she didn't yell at you." Graham spread his hands wide. "Archie has been good for her, I think."

"I'm afraid to think it," I said. "I don't know what's doing it or how long it's going to last, but I'll take it for now."

Archie. Damn. I grabbed the phone again. "Hey Siri," I said. When the *bing* sounded, I told the phone to text Archie. "I'm so sorry, I have to cancel lunch today. Rain check? Send."

The reply flashed up as I set the phone down.

"He says of course." Graham pointed to the exit sign ahead. "See? Everything is fine. It's got to be a good way to start the day, right?"

"I wish you wouldn't say that with no wood around to knock on."

"This is too easy for bad luck," he said. "I say we'll get something pertinent out of the girl's mother, because the moms always know everything, and then we'll stop in to chat with the local sheriff. We're home early for pizza and a movie while the sheriff tracks down your pig killer."

I pressed my foot a little harder on the gas, hoping he was right.

Frozen mud was the best description I had for the drive at the Shermans' hunting cabin.

"It hasn't rained in a week." I gripped the wheel tighter as the truck slid to the right. "Why the hell is it so wet?"

"Don't know. What I do know is I don't see any cars up there."

I scanned the property, which was probably a couple hundred yards wide. A small, ramshackle house clad in dirty gray clapboard siding just visible in patches through thick layers of ivy and moss sat to the left of the end of the dirt drive, with a carport-sized, metal-covered cleaning shack to the right. Gleaming, pointy tools for skinning animals decorated the one makeshift wall of the lean-to, a large rust-speckled table in the center of the space.

Beyond the structures, the woods loomed large and stretched as far as we could see.

But Graham was right; there wasn't a vehicle in sight.

I managed to get the truck stopped on the slick ground near the cabin and stepped down carefully, making sure my boot was planted before I tried to take a step. Graham met me at the front of the truck.

"Miranda Sherman?" I called before I even got to the porch. "Faith McClellan with the Texas Rangers. I have a few questions for you and Dustin if you can spare a few minutes."

We paused at the foot of the three concrete steps leading up to the door.

No answer.

"No bell," I said.

"Knock," Graham warned. "We're not up and walking into a place where people come specifically to shoot stuff."

"Of course."

I scaled the steps—which were dry as a bone—and rapped on the plywood door. "Mrs. Sherman? Dustin?"

Ten seconds ticked into thirty, then sixty.

I was tempted to try the knob, but Graham was right. It wasn't smart.

"It's after eight," he said. "Hunting parties usually set out early. Maybe they're in the woods already?"

I nodded, my eyes on a screenless window next to the door. "Well, we can't go into the woods looking for them. That's practically asking to get shot."

I stood on tiptoe and peered through glass that was probably last cleaned when Bush was president—though I couldn't say for sure which one.

"For someone who insists on such a tidy home, Miranda Sherman sure seems content to live...simply...here," I observed.

"Maybe their maid doesn't do hunting cabins," Graham posited. "You said they had a live-in housekeeper, right?"

"I don't think she lives there," I said. "But she does work for them full-time and she keeps a house Ruth McClellan would approve of."

I used the sleeve of my jacket, then my fingernails to chip some of the dirt off the outside of the window, then cupped my hands around my eyes, peering inside.

"Graham?" I stepped back, brushing my hands off on my jeans. "They're not here."

"How can you be sure?" He stepped to the window and assumed the same peeping-tom posture. "Oh."

Every piece of furniture was covered with drop cloth, the refrigerator was standing open—empty, and unlit—and the full-sized bed in the back room had a bare mattress.

I walked around the perimeter of the building carefully, sticking to parts of the grounds that weren't soaked and frozen.

There.

I pointed to the electric meter. "See? It's not spinning. The heat isn't even on."

"But the girl's father told you they came here?"

"Yep."

Graham twisted his lips to one side. "Huh. I'd bet she lied to him before him lying to you, because this is a dumb thing to lie to a cop about. It's too easy to check."

We picked our way back around front and across the drive to a pair of tire ruts in the mud.

I squatted next to them. "That's too narrow to be a pickup or SUV tire," I said. "And the wheelbase is narrow, too. Most people would take a truck if they were going hunting. You need the bed to haul the animals back out of the woods."

Graham knelt beside me, pointing to the depth of the tracks, which had a considerable drop at the back. "Whoever this was got stuck. The tires spun for a minute before they caught and went forward."

I leaned in. "But nobody pushed the car. That's a defined wheel, not one that slid forward."

I stood and pulled out my phone, walking around the ruts and snapping photos from several angles, squatting close and using my hand for a size reference.

"Small sedan?" Graham asked.

I touched one finger to my chin as I slid the phone back

into my pocket, pointing to the rectangles barely visible at the top of the ruts. "I don't think so, no. These are performance tire sidewall marks."

"Sports car?"

"Looks like it."

"Interesting."

"What's interesting is that it just got stuck right here." I turned to follow the ruts until they faded into the dirt and grabbed Graham's arm when my boot slid on the slick ground.

"And then it froze"—I pointed to my truck—"because we didn't put tracks in it coming in."

"And it wasn't wet over there around the house. Or on the steps," Graham added.

"So someone dumped water," I said. "A lot of water, right here." I pointed to where the tires got stuck. "And soon enough before the cold front came in Wednesday night that this didn't have time to dry out."

"Cleaning something?" Graham asked.

We surveyed the carcass-cleaning shack. I went straight for the back wall and checked every tool.

"Clean and dry as a bone," I said, pulling out a handheld blacklight and double-checking.

If Miranda and Dustin had used these, they were at least good at cleaning something—the tools were spotless. I leaned into a blade hanging at nose level and inhaled, and Graham coughed.

"Whatcha doing there, babe?"

"These have been soaked in some kind of disinfectant," I said. "And scrubbed totally clean."

"You think they were used on the pig?" he asked.

I shrugged, pulling my phone back out and taking a video of the tools under the blacklight beam. "Maybe. I'll say this: I'm a damned sight more interested in where Miranda

Sherman and her son are than I was when we left this morning."

The house held plenty of evidence that they had changed course somewhere between here and home. Or were never coming here in the first place. I laid one finger over a giant line on the paneled wall, shining the blacklight and following it up.

"An axe," Graham said. "They're missing an axe."

I pulled my phone out and shot a few photos of the outline on the wall, with and without the flash.

Tucking the phone back into my pocket, I flipped the blacklight around in my hand to click it off.

"Holy shit." Graham grabbed my arm, taking photos with his own phone.

The inside of the tin roof over the little lean-to glowed almost entirely purple with bloodstains.

7

"You're worried about blood under a blacklight on a cleaning shelter at someone's hunting lease?" The McCulloch County sheriff's dispatcher slid her glasses down her nose and tipped her head back so she could angle her eyeballs down and still see my face.

"No, I'm worried that two of your residents aren't where they said they would be when their pet was just savagely killed, and their property is missing a double-bladed axe." I struggled to keep my voice civil.

I didn't fool anyone.

"A grown woman is allowed to take her grown child on a vacation," the dispatcher said.

"No one is disputing that. What I am saying is that I'd like to speak with the sheriff at his earliest convenience concerning the safety and whereabouts of Miranda Sherman and her son Dustin."

"Have they been missing for 48 hours?" She raised one penciled-in eyebrow.

For fuck's sake. What was this woman, the dragon gatekeeper?

"Just in case we have some sort of a misunderstanding here"—I kept my voice low, the words measured—"I am not asking Sheriff..." I turned and checked the name under the framed photo on the wall behind me. "...Barnes for permission to search for this woman and her son. I am simply looking for his input, as the local law enforcement figure, on the situation. My jurisdiction stops at the state line, and I am more than capable of conducting a missing persons investigation on my own, should one prove to be warranted."

"Whatever you say, Miss. Have yourself a nice day, now." She picked up her pencil and turned her attention back to her Sudoku book.

Graham cleared his throat. "No one called in anything suspicious in the past three days from that sector? Noise complaint, animal in trouble, anything like that?"

Dragon lady turned her eyes on him, her face softening a touch. "If they had, I would've told y'all. Everybody around here knows the Shermans, and where their properties are located."

"Because of Kelsey Marie's YouTube Channel?" Graham asked, stepping closer to the desk as I slid behind him. Losing my temper with her was pointless, especially if he could charm her into saying anything helpful.

She shrugged. "I don't watch entertainment that's not professional," she said in a tone most people would use to describe something smelly they'd just stepped in.

"Everyone has their own taste," Graham agreed. "But she must have followers in the area."

"I suppose she does." The dispatcher sighed. "Listen, Commander, this is a small town. Nothing like Austin. Everyone around here knows everyone else's business practically down to what they had for dinner last night. If somebody's got a door locked, they're getting it on or they're up to no good. We help our neighbors. We work hard. We pray hard. And most folks don't have much patience for the kind of attention the Shermans have brought around with their nonsense."

"Do people come looking to meet Kelsey Marie?" Graham asked.

"Sometimes. Not like she's Marilyn Monroe or nothing, but we get the occasional bunch of kids from out of town or a reporter here and there asking after her. They always start at the diner. Like they all watched the same movie." She shook her head. "But I ain't talking about Kelsey Marie. She's a good girl. Helps out at the school, donates money to the Little League. Keeps her nose clean. That boy of theirs, though. Never far from trouble, that kid. Folks who want to be part of it know where to find him, and folks who don't know where to steer clear of."

Graham charmed the dispatcher right into promising to have the sheriff call him as soon as he was back in the office, and I leaned over and kissed his cheek as I buckled my seat belt and he started the truck.

"You're welcome." He flashed a smile.

"I don't hate the stepbrother as our killer here," I said. "But I'd like to stop off at the Sherman house and ask Kelsey Marie and her dad a few more questions."

I checked the clock. Almost two-thirty already. And Sheriff Barnes wasn't at work yet. "Let's see what else we can pull out of these folks and then we'll head home?"

"Deal."

My phone buzzed in the cupholder. Jim.

"Perfect timing," I said. "What've you got?"

"An apology," he replied. "I was in court all morning testifying and then Sharon had a check-up this afternoon with her oncologist, and I'm not going to get to your pig today. He's behind two humans in my queue."

"No worries," I said. "I appreciate you keeping me posted. Everything okay at the doctor?"

"Scans all clear, back in three months." I could see his grinning face like he was standing in front of me. "I'll come in tomorrow morning and work up your pig. Have you found anything special I ought to be looking for?"

"I'm not supposed to influence your findings," I protested.

"It's a hog, Faith. If there's something I ought to be looking for, let me know."

"I'd like to know what you think was used to cut him up like that," I said. "But that's as far as I'm going."

"I'll call you in the morning. Come by and see me if you feel like it, I'll be there by eight."

"Thanks, Jim, I'll see you then."

Graham turned out of the small municipal complex parking lot and pointed the truck toward the Sherman house. I opened the browser on my phone and logged into the DPS site. "Let's see what kind of trouble Dustin favors."

I searched his name and address.

No results.

"Huh. Nothing in the state database."

"Is he underage?"

"Kelsey Marie is seventeen and he's older, so...no."

"Try local records. Some smaller towns are pretty slow about uploading things to the state."

I found the McCulloch County page and searched local court records.

"Zip." I shifted in my seat, crossing my legs and hunching forward over the phone.

"Oh I know that pose." Graham laughed. "Look out, kid."

"That woman back there didn't want to tell anyone anything, and you pulled out of her that this kid is trouble. She acted like it was super common knowledge. And I can't find a single police report to back her up. So now I'm curious."

"She didn't like you because you're not from here," Graham began.

"Neither are you!"

"Yeah, but she seemed so protective of the sheriff, I wondered if she would be nicer to me because I'm a guy. It was a good hunch."

"She thought you were cute."

"I am."

I tapped at my phone screen with both thumbs, turning up a local newspaper. "Let's see if the local press knows him."

I searched.

Two results.

"Now we're getting somewhere," I muttered, clicking the first.

Or not. It was an article about Kelsey Marie's channel hitting five million followers, with Dustin mentioned in an aside about helping to run the cameras and mucking out the pigpen for extra cash.

"Ouch." I took a screenshot. "Can you imagine being a high school kid and having your name in the local paper for cleaning up your little sister's pig's shit?"

"I bet that got him picked on."

"I'd say."

Graham parked the car and I checked the second link. Traffic accident, serious damage, no fatalities. Dustin ran a pickup through a fence and into someone's garage—without benefit of an open door. I bookmarked that, too, and tucked the phone in my hip pocket as I hopped down to ring the doorbell.

I didn't want to have to tell Kelsey Marie that her brother killed her pig, but he was looking more and more like the easiest answer. And unless things here got complicated, the easy answer would be the right one.

———

Marta opened the door the second time I pulled the bell, her eyes on the floor before we could see her whole head.

"No one is here." Her accent was thicker when she was nervous. I'd noticed it the day before, too. What I couldn't tell was if it was my human lie detector going off, or just anxiety seeping through in her speech.

"Do you know when Mr. Sherman will be back?" I kept my voice soft, trying to coax her eyes up to meet ours.

She shook her head, her gaze not budging from the floor.

I put one hand on the door. "Could we wait for Kelsey Marie to get back from school?"

She looked up slowly, fear flashing in her eyes. "I'm not sure that's such a good idea." Her shoulders hitched with a halting breath. "She might be a little while yet. The other kids were gone to the stock show and she was going to stay late at school and catch up on work she missed when..." She pinched her lips shut.

When Samson died. I didn't need her to finish the sentence. I nodded, pressing just a little on the door. "We could also talk with her dad." I flashed a smile now that I had her attention. "This here is my partner, Commander Graham Hardin. We went out to the hunting lease where Mr. Sherman said yesterday I could find his wife and stepson, and it doesn't look like anyone has been there in quite a while." I tipped my head to one side. "Did either of them tell you they were going somewhere else at any point?"

"They didn't say."

I blinked. It definitely wasn't my imagination. Her accent was thicker sometimes. Just then, she sounded almost like a native Texan.

I needed her to talk more.

I kept the smile in place and stepped so close to her she had to step back to avoid awkward proximity, pushing the door wide and waving Graham into the house behind me.

"This place is gorgeous," he said.

"Isn't it?" I asked as Marta said, "Thank you."

She fussed with a towel poking out of the pocket on her yellow and blue apron.

The apron was stunning, the sapphire fabric an odd combination of sturdy and soft with intricate yellow flowers embroidered on it.

"Your apron is lovely," I said. "Did you make it?"

"My mama," she said. "She sent it for Christmas three years ago. I wear it every day."

"Where does she live?" I kept the tone friendly.

"Now in the Netherlands." She plucked at a thread on the edge of the apron. The words were still light on accent.

I moved toward the living room. "But you're not from the Netherlands."

She shook her head, her eyes back on the floor.

"Marta, we don't care about your immigration status," I said.

"I have a work visa," she said.

"I'm glad. But I'm also serious—that's not even on the list of reasons I'm here."

"Mr. Jeff and Ms. Miranda gave me a good job when no one else here wanted to let me try," she said. "I work hard for them. I can send money to my mother. Things are harder for her."

I perched on the edge of the sofa arm. "Where are you from?"

"Albania," she said. "You have heard of it?"

Criminals at every level of the government, an economy in ruins, a third of the young population out of work...yeah, I'd heard of it. People had fled at record rates in recent years, but it was hard for refugees to find asylum, and harder still to stay together or find work.

"I'm sorry for what happened to your family. You and your mom were separated?"

"There's no work. No money or food without work. I left first, came to America through England. By the time Mama decided she had to go, I couldn't find a way to get her here, because people..." She sighed. "They don't like us. Don't want us coming to their countries to try to make a life. Mr. Jeff watches it on the television and even he says people need to stay in their own countries and get rid of the corrupt government."

She folded her hands in front of her. "My country is tiny. Texas is much bigger. And the government, they just kill people who would try to resist. It's better to leave home than to stay and starve or be killed."

"We understand," Graham said. "I hope you get to see your mom again soon."

"I just need to know she's safe. That's enough for me."

"Marta, do you live here at the Sherman house?"

A genuine smile lit her face for the first time that I'd seen. "Not anymore. I used to have a small room in the barn. But now I have my own home. In Brady, just near here. My very own house, I rent from a nice lady in town."

"That's wonderful," I said. "What time do you usually get here for work in the morning?"

"Five o'clock. The farmhands are here early and I make Miss Kelsey Marie's breakfast while she tends to Samson."

"You didn't notice anything amiss on Wednesday morning?"

"It was very cold. I came straight into the house." Her accent dripped off every letter.

"Was Dustin awake yet when you came into the house?"

"I didn't see him that morning." Almost no accent. It was like a switch. I wondered if she even noticed it.

"And when Kelsey Marie came back from the barn?"

"She was so sad." Marta paused, clearing her throat. "When she came in. Crying, screaming for Mr. Jeff."

"Was her mother not here?" It struck me as odd for a distraught child to scream for her father, but maybe that was just because mine was the last person I'd ask for.

"Ms. Miranda was not in the house." I noticed that her words were halting, but the accent was barely noticeable, so I moved the conversation on.

"Had she and Dustin left before then?"

"The last time I saw Ms. Miranda was Sunday."

Well, shit.

If Miranda and Dustin left Sunday, he didn't kill the pig after bedtime on Tuesday.

The deeper we got into this, the more things leaned toward complicated.

My second cup of coffee was brewing Saturday morning when my phone rang.

"Tell Prescott he can let you finish breakfast," Graham said from his pancake-flipping post in front of the stove.

"Sure. He's working on a pig on a Saturday as a favor to

me. I'll be sure to get right on relaying that he should do it on my stomach's schedule." I winked as I stirred sugar into the coffee and reached for the phone. This wasn't Jim's number. "McClellan." I put the phone to my ear.

"You have to help me. Please." Young. Female. Absolutely batshit hysterical. I pulled the phone away from my head and winced.

Graham dropped his spatula and crossed the room, leaning in.

"Kelsey Marie, is that you?" I shouted over her sobs as my pulse picked up speed. Shit. What if Donnette had been more right than even I had given her credit for?

"Please, someone has to do something," she shrieked. "You said you were handy with computers when my dad was talking about the surveillance cameras."

Computer. Not bloodbath. I sucked in a calming breath. I wasn't used to hysterical phone calls over mundane things. I'd also never investigated the slaughter of a farm animal. It seemed not many folks connected to this case understood the prevailing definition of emergency.

"Sweetie, calm down," I said. "Tell me what's wrong, and I'll see if I can get someone to help you."

"There's footage," she shrieked. "There's footage of my Samson being hacked apart and whoever this sick fuck is fucking put it up on my channel and I can't get into my own account to get it down."

8

Graham closed his eyes four seconds into the most recent video on the *High on the Hog* page.

I stared as a cloaked and hooded shadow wielding an axe crept up on a sleeping Samson.

My God.

"Kelsey Marie, honey, don't you have a tech support person who can handle this?" My voice was too high as the figure on the screen raised the axe, which only had a single blade.

"It's Saturday. Even when the sun comes up on the west coast they won't be there today."

I took Graham's phone and laid it face down on the counter.

"Kelsey Marie, is your dad home?" I asked.

"No, he went to Forth Worth for a meeting. This is the last weekend of the stock show. He left yesterday morning, and he's gone until Monday."

"What about Marta?"

"She's off on Saturdays," she sobbed. "I don't understand this. Why would anyone do that?"

"Listen to me. Lock the doors. All the doors. Make sure the security cameras are running and do not open the doors for anyone. I have one stop to make and I'll be there as soon as I can get there."

I stopped short of asking her if her dad kept guns in the house, only because I didn't want to scare her.

Right then, I was scared enough for the both of us.

"What. The actual fuck?" Graham ran one hand over his close-cropped hair.

"Someone is messing with her. This isn't about Samson, it's about Kelsey Marie. And it's someone who might know she's alone in that house today."

I dumped my coffee into a travel cup and grabbed my keys. "I'm going to see if Jim is at the lab yet, and then I'm going to the Shermans' place."

He reached into the cabinet for a travel mug, too. "Not by yourself, you're not."

"It's your day off," I protested.

"And I choose to spend it with you."

Shit.

"I was hoping Miss Donnie was exaggerating. Maybe we just call Jim on the way?"

Graham nodded and opened the front door, waving me through. "I'm sure he'll understand."

Jim told me to drive fast and come by when Kelsey Marie was safe.

"This pig...well. You said there's a video of what happened

to him on the internet?" he asked over my speakerphone as Graham pointed the truck west.

"I'm not sure you want to watch it," I said.

"Oh, I definitely don't want to, but I think I may need to."

"How come?" Graham asked.

"I'll tell y'all when you get here if I find anything more."

"Thanks, Jim. I hope I didn't ruin your weekend."

"I can always count on you to keep my days interesting, McClellan."

"Glad to be useful." I clicked the end button and opened my laptop, connecting to the hot spot on my phone.

"You sure you want to watch it?" Graham turned the radio down.

"Hell no. But it's my job more than it is Jim's."

"I don't recall you saying anyone assigned you to this," he pointed out. "Does Boone even know you went out there?"

"No. But this." I brandished my phone. "Putting the video on her channel isn't a random act. Someone is terrorizing a teenage girl. I'm not stepping away now."

"I know. You think you can figure out how to take the video down?"

"Crack Google's security?" I snorted. "I'm good with this thing, but that's distinctly above my pay grade. I'm hoping I can find some clue to who managed to get around it to post this in the first place, but their security people are going to have to remove it if the hacker shut Kelsey Marie out of her account."

I found Kelsey Marie's page and clicked the video, swallowing hard and focusing on analysis, not emotion. In all the murder cases I've ever worked, none has been caught on film. At least not that I ever saw. There were clues to be found in this horror show, if I could ignore the gore long enough to see them.

Samson's paddock was posh—a hog version of a *Real Housewives* mansion, outfitted with toys and exercise apparatuses, a huge stainless steel trough, a concrete water fountain, and a wide, shallow pit in the floor fluffy with fresh straw for his bed.

The figure vaulted over the low fence easily, axe at their side.

I scribbled "*athletic*" on my notepad, my eyes not leaving the screen.

It was impossible to gauge height from the low camera angle. The attacker's build was slim, though just how slim was questionable thanks to the oversized cloak.

Damn.

I counted steps as the killer crossed the paddock. Nine. Rough stride length was something we could measure. I jotted it down.

Just before the figure reached Samson, the axe starting to come up, I paused the video.

Backed up four seconds.

"They walked in front of the light," I muttered.

"What's that, baby?"

I watched for the shadow to stretch and paused the frame. Took a screenshot.

That would tell us something.

"The camera is positioned such that I can't tell how tall this person is, backdropped against plain white walls." I looked up at Graham. "But then the killer stepped in front of a light."

"Whoops," he said.

"They always screw up somewhere."

"I have no doubt that Samson the Pig's killer is no match for you. Kind of starting to wonder if we'll have it wrapped up by dinner at this point."

"I'd like that. If it weren't for Marta's comment that Miranda left on Sunday, I'd believe it was Dustin. The easiest way for anyone to get into her YouTube account would be if they knew her password, and it would be easy for him to swipe it."

"Maybe the parents know he did it and the quick trip with mom is an invented alibi. The maid seemed extraordinarily grateful to them for hiring her. Not much chance she'd challenge the story they put up for you."

"I don't think her father knows who did it. It's too big a show, the reward fliers and trying to get the police involved...if they wanted it kept quiet because they knew it was the other kid, why do all that?"

"You do know a mind-boggling level of complication in parent-child relationships from the inside out," Graham conceded. "What do you think?"

I sighed.

"I suppose I can't rule it out. All I can say for sure is that if Dustin was the culprit, Kelsey Marie doesn't know it. There was clearly no love lost there—if she thought he did this"—I waved a hand at the computer screen—"she would've told me Thursday. Plus, Kelsey Marie's financial independence would be a factor in any tension between her and her parents, I bet. How much can they tell her what to do if she has her own fortune at her disposal?"

I jotted a note. "You ever stop to think about how different the world is just since we were her age?"

"Not often. But when I do, it's alarming."

"No kidding."

I woke the computer and clicked play.

The axe went up. Came down and sank to just shy of the handle into Samson's side.

I took another screenshot and made a note.

Play.

Blood splattered, gushing when the axe was pulled free. Jesus. I swallowed hard.

Samson never moved. Didn't know what hit him, quite literally.

The figure paused, just for an instant, the axe faltering toward the ground. Then it went back up. I noted that.

Another blow to the torso. Blood splattered. The figure moved to the side and squared up to Samson's back, raising the axe again. The posture was familiar, the same one Granddaddy had used for splitting logs for the fireplace.

One to the neck. More blood. Two to the neck. Three. Four.

It took seven blows to completely sever the hog's head.

The figure let the axe fall, shoulders heaving with deep, tired breaths, and bent to retrieve it.

I waited for them to retreat.

They didn't.

Turning to the trough, the figure bent, back to the camera.

They stood and turned back with a bucket in hand.

My fingers tightened around the pen, the plastic biting into my skin.

The figure moved to Samson's bed and dipped the bucket into the hay, holding it there for a five count before they stood, moved to the center of the paddock, and spun in a circle while holding the bucket on its side. Blood flung outward in a spiral pattern like a spin art paint machine of gore.

Upending the bucket, the killer dumped a large splat of blood in the center of the floor.

"Jesus H. Christ on toast." I muttered my grandmother's favorite quasi-swear, shaking my head as the bucket fell to the dirt. The killer retrieved the axe and Samson's head, placing them on the other side of the pen's fence one at a time before hopping it again. The screen went black five seconds later.

I checked the bottom of the screen. Four million views in three hours.

"That bad, huh?" Graham put one hand on my knee and squeezed.

"I have some stuff we can look at here. I'm sure I'm going to find this fucker. But my God, Graham, who does something like this? And who the hell are these four million people and counting watching it?"

"We see the worst. It's part of the job."

He was right. I stared out the window at the stark, leafless trees blurring by in front of a low, gray winter sky. "I guess I think of it a little differently, because humans are complicated creatures. Jealousy, rage, misunderstandings, revenge, psychosis...there are always reasons. Or almost always. Even when we don't understand or agree. Who hacks up a defense-less animal?"

"Statistically speaking, often someone who's trying to see if they can stomach doing the same to a person. Maybe we get in front of that this time?"

"Gotta say, if this shit was the prequel, I sure as hell hope we get in front of it before the headliner. I can't imagine how someone could make murder more grotesque and disturbing."

"We will."

I reached for my phone. "I'm going to check on Kelsey Marie. Just in case."

I touched the last number in my recents.

"Hello?" She picked up on the fourth ring.

"Kelsey Marie, it's Faith McClellan. You hanging in there?"

"Oh hi. It's the Texas Ranger who's going to find this fucker, y'all."

"Kelsey Marie? Is someone there with you?"

"I'm on TikTok," she said. "Live. I figured if someone was coming for me, they might not with three hundred thousand people watching."

Smart. Though maybe not the part where she told those three hundred thousand people she was home alone.

"Good thinking, Kelsey Marie. Keep talking to your followers and we'll be there as soon as we can get there. About another half hour."

I leaned my head back against the seat and turned up the radio, staring at the flat, dormant fields lining the road to keep from seeing the cloaked figure on the backs of my eyelids.

Graham was right. Just the next thing, which right now was making sure Kelsey Marie Sherman was safe—and getting a closer look at Samson's paddock.

I had a place to start. I just had to get to the finish before anyone else died.

9

I took my seatbelt off before Graham stopped the truck at the foot of the Shermans' front steps, taking the stone stairs two at a time and yanking the bell. I gave it five seconds before I knocked. "Kelsey Marie, it's Faith McClellan," I called.

Footsteps came from the back side of the door. She paused, probably looking through the brass peep hole, before I heard the locks disengage. I sighed. She was okay.

She threw the door wide and held up her phone. "Smile, Ranger!" she said, a fake brightness in her voice that didn't come close to reaching her eyes, still swollen and red—and dull.

I blinked at my face on the screen of her phone, a cascade of smiley faces and hearts drifting over the image. "It's time to sign off for a while, Kelsey Marie."

"But everyone wants to know what happened to Samson." She stuck out her bottom lip in what had to be a practiced-in-front-of-a-mirror pout.

"That will be a lot easier for me to find out without an audience of hundreds of thousands." I kept my tone polite, but there was enough of an edge for her to notice. Graham plucked her phone from her hand and closed her app, shooting me a what-are-we-getting-into-here look over the top of her head.

I honestly wasn't sure. The young woman in front of me didn't match the panicked cries that had gotten me to drag Graham speeding a hundred miles across the plains on a Saturday morning. She looked sad. But also...energetic. Like the attention was feeding something she desperately needed to nourish.

I could unpack that later.

I gestured to the door. "May we come in?"

She was too busy staring at her phone, almost invisible in Graham's big baseball-player hand, to notice that I was speaking to her.

"Kelsey Marie." I touched her shoulder. She flinched, shaking her head.

"What?" Irritation was plain in her voice, her eyes still on her phone.

Do you want our help or not? That's what I wanted to say. But I didn't. Because she was a teenage YouTube star, and she didn't get to decide what I investigated and what I didn't. I wasn't dropping this until I was satisfied that no one was in danger.

I fixed a practiced, patient half smile on my face. *Trust me. I'm here to help*, it said without me opening my mouth. "May we come inside?"

"Oh." She backed up a step. "Yes. Of course."

Graham closed the door and locked it, and Kelsey Marie led us to the big, open family room before she spun, one hand on her hip and the other outstretched. "Can I have my phone back now?"

Graham handed it to her. "No video," he said. "This is a police investigation, not a reality show."

I wasn't sure how I expected her to react to that, but I would've been wrong.

Her eyes welled with fresh tears that spilled over before I could blink.

"How am I supposed to keep everything up if Samson is dead and you two won't go on camera?" she sobbed. "I've been sick for days over this, and then you showed up yesterday like God had actually answered my prayers, and then this morning I thought we could do the investigation—not live, I'd want to edit it—but the viewers would be in the millions, maybe tens of millions. People loved Samson. And now you say no cameras."

She pulled in a hitching breath, sniffling snot back into her nose and wiping it with the back of her hand.

"Keep what up?" I asked.

"The money," she snapped. "I have almost forty million subscribers. Every video is monetized down to the last pixel. Without Samson, what am I going to do?"

"People watch the channel because they like you," Graham said. "You're smart. You teach people things about animals and country life in such a fun way that they don't even realize they're learning anything. Like the *Sesame Street* of ranch life. You'll be fine."

I recognized the tone in his voice; it was the one he always used with distraught witnesses. Slow speech in his deep baritone, with the barest soft inflections. Calming. Soothing.

"How would you know?"

"I've seen some of your stuff," Graham said.

She sniffled again, tipping her head back. "You watch my channel?"

"I grew up in the country. Maybe not this far in the country, but it wasn't city by any stretch. I raised a few goats in my meemaw's backyard, one for the stock show. An old friend posted a link to one of your videos that I clicked one day, and I came back to check in several times after that, too. Your personality is genuine on camera. Stop selling yourself short."

Kelsey Marie furrowed her forehead, holding Graham's gaze. "Okay. Thank you, Officer..." She trailed off, turning to me.

"This is Commander Graham Hardin from the Travis County Sheriff's Office," I said.

"Travis? What do you care about what happened to Samson?" she asked.

"He's also my fiancé. Today is Saturday."

"Oh." She flashed a smile. "Well congratulations. And thanks for coming." She turned back to me, her voice calmer and more polite. "I didn't know who else to call."

"You have no idea who put that video on your site?" I asked.

She tucked herself into the same corner of the couch she'd occupied the day before. "I can't even figure out why anyone would take a video of something like that. But I can't get into my own account to see what happened. My password doesn't work, and when I try to reset it, it doesn't send the email like it's supposed to." She pointed to the shiny silver MacBook on the coffee table. "See?"

I picked up her computer and sat across from her, balancing it on my knees. The screen showed a failed login page, with a pop up note saying password reset instructions had been emailed to the address on file. "So someone changed the email associated with the account and changed the password." I bit my lip. "This might be easier than I thought."

"What do you mean?" she asked.

"Well, depending on how smart—or not—the person who hurt Samson is, we might be an email address away from locating them," I said. "Do you have an account person at YouTube we can call?"

"Not until Monday. I do have a guy, but he's off on the weekends."

"Customer service center?"

She shook her head. "They don't staff a call center. People with less popular channels email in their issues and get an answer when someone gets to them in the queue. Which will be a heck of a lot longer than Monday."

Damn.

"Well. Then we'll just go forward knowing we have that as a possible ace in the hole if we don't figure this out before then."

"But in the meantime, millions of people are watching my poor baby be slaughtered in his sleep," she said, the tears welling again.

"And while I can understand your distress, that video might be the very thing that helps us give you some closure here." I stood. "Can we go out to the paddock again, please?"

"Sure."

I pulled out my notes. "Do you have a tape measure, Kelsey Marie?"

"Sure. My dad has them on his workbench." She waved for us to follow her.

Graham stood to one side and let me walk ahead of him.

It's nice, knowing someone always has your back. Literally and figuratively.

I pulled my coat tighter as the icy wind blew in when Kelsey Marie cracked the door. She hugged herself, clad in

Victoria's Secret sweatpants and a long-sleeved henley, and charged out into the cold, stopping to pull the nearest barn door open. "There," she said between chattering teeth, pointing to the ten-foot workbench spanning half the length of one wall. I retrieved a metal tape from a pegboard hook before we headed for Samson's studio building.

"Let's get out of this wind," Graham said, sliding the heavy white metal door back.

We filed in the person-sized opening and Graham threw the door shut behind us. The wind howled around the corners of the building, a high, keening whistle filling the cavernous space.

Kelsey Marie stopped short just inside the door.

"I haven't. I can't."

I laid one hand on her arm. "I got it."

She sniffled. "Thank you. It's so weird. For so long now I've felt more at home out here than in the house, and now I don't even want to be near this building."

I surveyed the paddock, the dark stains on the floor still telling a story of what had happened here to anyone who knew what to look for. "Graham? Your phone?"

He touched the screen. "Getting it now."

I concentrated on what we came here to do. She needed our help, not our sympathy. She had hundreds of thousands of fans who felt sorry for her. We could get her an answer. Maybe keep her alive if the dead pig was indeed just the opening act.

I ran the video—now up to five-point-two million views—to the part where the shadow crossed the camera, looking for a marker in the paddock.

Bingo.

It stretched almost exactly to the end of the trough.

Phone and tape measure in hand, I crossed the paddock,

Graham on my heels. "Can you find the lights and see if there's a night mode?" I kept my voice low. "The killer crossed in front of some sort of a night light and cast a shadow here." I stopped at the end of the trough.

He crossed back to the doors, searching the walls on both sides for light switches before he turned back to me and shrugged.

I tipped my head toward Kelsey Marie, curled into a beach-ball-sized lump, face buried in her knees.

He sighed big enough for me to see it from thirty feet away and knelt next to her on the dirt floor. "Where are the light switches, Kelsey Marie?" he asked.

"There aren't any." She raised her head. "It's all automated. Motion sensors and programming." She pointed to a closet in the far corner. "In there."

I glanced at Graham's phone screen and tapped a foot, crossing back to the fencing around the paddock. "No lights came on with the person in the video moving around."

"The motion sensors are off between ten and five," Kelsey Marie explained. "So the lights wouldn't come on and confuse Samson if he got up in the middle of the night."

I noted the times. A seven-hour window. "When did you go to bed Tuesday night?" I asked.

"Probably about eleven-thirty," she said. "I had a trig test on Wednesday and I was studying late."

"You didn't hear a car or anything?" Graham asked, waving me over from the door of the closet where the lighting controls lived.

"No." She tipped her head to one side. "I guess whoever did it would have to drive, huh? We're pretty far from everyone."

"Doesn't mean someone couldn't have parked nearby and walked up, though," I said. "But we'll check everything. Kelsey

Marie, when did your mom and your stepbrother leave? Were they here that night?" I flashed a tight smile, hopping the fence and crossing to Graham. "I'd just need to know if they saw or heard anything unusual. Even a small thing they might have dismissed as nothing at the time could be important."

"She left on Sunday." Her voice was dull.

Damn. Probably time to look beyond Dustin, then.

I met Graham's wide eyes with a raised brow. "I don't have my notes handy—when did your dad say they were due back, again?"

"Not sure. Probably not until Monday at least." She drew a circle in the dirt floor with one finger, etching triangular pig ears above it. "She's never been great about sticking to a schedule. Probably will depend on how the hunting's going and whether Dustin is being an asshole or not."

I bit my tongue to keep from telling her they weren't at the hunting cabin until I knew more. No sense in upsetting her further.

"Weird," Graham muttered when I stopped in front of him.

"Sounds like maybe someone needed some cooling off."

"Sounds to me like we need to find him. Soon."

"Without letting on to the dad that he's a suspect," I agreed. "I'm working on a plan if you have suggestions."

I turned to survey the pen, the smell—or lack of one, to be more precise. "There's no...um..." I waved a hand. "There's no poop."

"Good?" Graham raised his eyebrows.

"No, I mean, remember that thing I saw in the paper about Kelsey Marie? It said Dustin mucked this all out. If they left Monday and the pig was killed Wednesday, who cleaned it up?"

Graham shrugged. "Her dad, probably. Or someone who works for him." He pointed to an iPad on a long, narrow console inside the closet. "Pretty sure we have to get into that to be able to do anything to override the lighting scheme that's programmed for this time of the day."

"Passcode required?" I asked.

"Naturally."

I touched the screen. Six digits.

So what would Jeff Sherman use?

"Kelsey Marie, when is your birthday?"

"October twenty-eighth."

"Year?"

"Oh five."

I punched it in.

Nope.

"What about your mom?" I asked. Ninety five percent of people use significant dates for six-figure passwords.

Over the next three minutes, we tried everyone's birthday including Samson's, with no dice.

"What else is important to your dad?" I asked. "Anniversary? The day he bought this place?"

"Their anniversary is in May, but I'm not sure what day to tell the truth. We moved here in the summer, but I was little and the only thing I remember is that we didn't have a TV."

"Can you think of anything else he might have used?" I asked.

She shook her head slowly, biting her lip. "Try oh nine eighteen oh four."

I touched the numbers and the screen filled with a black background, the *High on the Hog* logo branded across it in blue and red.

"Wonder whose birthday that is?" Graham whispered.

Me too. But I couldn't just outright ask, especially since she was visibly upset by the idea. Hell, she looked so fragile I didn't even want to tell her that worked.

"That was it, huh?" she called, her voice a little too high, when we were quiet for longer than we'd been in a bit.

"It was." I kept my voice even, touching the lone app and choosing "bedtime" from a list in the center of the screen.

The room dropped into pitch-black nothing for a split second before the small lights flashed to life, dotting the perimeter just above the ground, offering a soft white glow.

"Now we're in business." I whirled for the paddock.

Graham followed, looking over my shoulder at the video still when I stopped in front of the light. He put both hands on my shoulders. "Turn. Okay, now back up two big steps."

I did. He surveyed the scene, his eyes darting between the image on his phone and me. "Tiny step forward. Pinch your knees together."

I followed the instructions. We wouldn't get it exact, because the two-dimensional aspect of video would alter the perception we were trying to recreate. But a ballpark was better than nothing.

"Yep," Graham said. "There. Tape?"

I pulled it from my jacket pocket, dragging my toe in the dirt to make a line where I was standing. I pulled enough tape free to measure from there to the edge of the trough.

"Eight feet four inches," I said, laying the tape down and walking over to check the alignment.

Graham followed. "You know what else is weird?"

I looked up at him, brows up.

"He didn't move. Pigs have super sensitive ears, and someone walked up on him in his sleep, and he didn't stir."

"I mean, he's a star. Spoiled, right? He probably didn't ever have a need to be skittish." I walked the pen, continuing my measurements: from the line and the trough to the light, and from the part of the fence the killer hopped to the edge of

Samson's hay bed. Thirty-eight feet, which would put the stride length at slightly shorter than average.

"What's all that for?" Kelsey Marie's voice came from close enough to startle me.

"The angle of the camera makes it impossible to tell how tall the assailant is," I said. "But they walked in front of the light. So this will help me calculate at least a ballpark height."

"Oh, like the triangle stuff in geometry." She nodded. "So there actually are some jobs where people use that mess?"

I laughed. "Some. Depends on what you want to do. Honestly? I've studied a lot of different things, and I've pretty much found that I use them all in my line of work."

"And you like, catch murderers for a living? Like ones who kill people?" She looked more animated, turning to Graham. "You too?"

"We do," I said.

"And you met at work, and you're getting married?" Her eyes raked Graham in an entirely different way.

"Correct." He shoved his hands into his pockets.

"That sounds pretty badass, altogether," she said. "Decent career. Hot guys who stay in shape for work. What do you have to know to do this?"

"You don't want to be a rancher like your dad?" I couldn't keep the surprise out of my voice. "Sorry, not that I'm not happy to talk to you about career options for women in law enforcement—"

"Of which we could use more," Graham interjected, eyes still on the floor.

"Right," I said. "I just...Miss Donnie said you were the first young woman to be president of the 4H, Graham says you know your stuff about animals, and you seem to love Samson. I'm surprised, that's all."

"That's the problem. I do love the animals. And we raise them to be food." She pursed her lips. "Samson ate a vegan diet just like me. But people would just fry him up for breakfast and not think twice about it if I sold him. So I don't know what I want to do. It's kind of fun, being famous, but it's work. And people keep threatening to kill me. I don't think that part is so cool."

10

I dropped the measuring tape on my toe. Pain flared, but I was too fixated on Kelsey Marie to notice.

"People keep threatening to what?"

She shrugged. "Every day. I get probably a hundred dick pics for every death threat, but they're always there. Save the animals, don't profit off the animals, ranchers are evil, Google is evil...name the manifesto and I'm sure there's copy in my DMs."

I swiveled my head to Graham, whose jaw was loose.

"I asked about this yesterday and you said 'never,'" I reminded her.

"You asked if Samson got threats. He didn't. They're only ever written to me."

"I sure wish your dad had led with this yesterday." I paused. "Your dad does know about this, right, Kelsey Marie? Does the sheriff?"

"The sheriff doesn't like us, so I don't know why he'd care. My dad knows, sure, but the money the channel rakes in is more important to him than just about anything."

"How much money are we talking about here?" Graham asked.

It was a fair question that could have bearing on the case. But I was more interested in why her dad cared so much. This place didn't belie a man hurting for money enough to need to rely on his teenage daughter. Certainly not at the possible expense of her safety.

"Last month my check was like two hundred, I think?" Kelsey Marie tipped her head to one side. "I don't even look at them anymore."

"You have millions of viewers and you get paid two hundred dollars a month?" I asked. "I made more than that scooping ice cream after school at your age." Much to Ruth's chagrin.

"Two hundred thousand, McClellan." Graham tried to hold back a chuckle. Didn't quite manage it.

"In a month?" I blinked.

Kelsey Marie shrugged. "Whatever. It was just supposed to be a thing to get people interested in 4H. Girls don't join as much as boys do, especially not to raise animals, and I wanted friends in the club. I put the videos on my TikTok at first, and then I started getting all these likes and follows and it went viral, and so I started my YouTube so I could post longer videos. People loved watching him." Her eyes drifted to the empty paddock. "He was so funny. Like a puppy, when I came in the door, he would lumber over to the fence and wait for me to say hello." She pointed to a rubber ball. "He loved toys, and he really loved the mud. His favorite thing was to get dirty and then come over and wait for me to spray him off."

Her voice seemed sadder with every word.

"I'm so sorry for your loss, Kelsey Marie," I said. "But when we're done with these measurements, I'm going to need to have a look at these DMs you mentioned."

She dropped her chin back to her chest. "Sure. Whatever will help."

I stopped on the line in the dirt I'd used to mark the killer's spot, pulling the video back up on Graham's phone and retrieving the tape measure.

"Can you take this to the other side of the light spray?"

"Why does that matter?" Graham reached for the end of the tape.

"I need the differential distance and the spread of the beam to get as close to accurate as I can."

He took the tape that way. "Three feet seven inches," he said, letting the tape go.

I jotted that down and joined him, measuring the height of the beam spill of the light before I handed him the tape measure and wrote the other figures down.

"That's all I need from out here," I said.

"Creepo messages?" he asked.

"Let's have a look." I turned back to Kelsey Marie.

Who wasn't there.

"Kelsey Marie?" Graham's booming baritone reverberated off the high metal walls in the cavernous space, almost echoing.

I crossed the paddock, hopping the fence and prompting the lights back on.

"Kelsey Marie," I called, stepping back out of the closet. It was just a big rectangular room with a dirt floor dotted with camera riggings. There wasn't much of anywhere for her to hide.

Graham passed me on his way to the door, which was cracked. I'd been so focused on my measurements I didn't notice the extra chill in the air until I saw it. I turned and took off for the house, calling her name.

"I'm going to check the drive." Graham's long, muscular legs gobbled up the yards of dormant lawn between him and the side of the house.

I paused just inside the back door and unsnapped the safety on my holster, keeping one hand on my Sig as I moved through the house, peeking into rooms. The kitchen was a chef's dream, all gleaming mahogany cabinets and polished stone counters with top-of-the-line professional appliances and an espresso machine built right into the wall.

I crossed a threshold into a hallway, the only sounds the ticking of a massive grandfather clock and my boots on the polished hardwood floor.

Heavy, dark wood doors lined both sides of the hall, all closed. Except one at the end. Hand still on my weapon, I moved toward it.

And almost jumped out of my skin when the nearest door on my left opened. A gangly young man in Wranglers and Ostrich Laredos pulled up short when he saw me. His eyes went to my sidearm.

"Uh. Hey." He took a step backward into the room, which held a rumpled bed with a red comforter and plush gray carpet littered with clothes.

I sucked in a deep breath. This must be Dustin, which meant Kelsey Marie's mom had to be here somewhere, too. I was glad to see the kid; them coming home would save me some time.

I buttoned my holster and offered a hand. "Faith McClellan, Texas Rangers. I'm looking for Kelsey Marie. Do you know where she went?"

"She came outside when she heard my truck pull in, but I needed to hit the head so she said I could come in the house."

"You're not Dustin?" I asked.

"Naw, I'm Sam. The boyfriend? Kelsey Marie knows you're lurking around in here?"

"She knows I'm—"

"There you are!" Kelsey Marie's voice came from the end of the hallway.

I spun to face her, flashing a smile. "Back at you."

"Sam said he was running by to pick up something." Her eyes flashed annoyance at him. "I just went to run it out to him so he could get on with his day, but then he insisted on coming inside."

I looked back at Sam, expecting him to argue.

He looked at his boots and mumbled an apology.

"You good now, boo?" Kelsey Marie's voice had a hard edge I hadn't heard in it before.

Sam nodded. He aimed a vague peck at her cheek as he passed her on his way out.

"Hi—" Graham appeared at the end of the hallway, slightly winded.

Sam didn't look at him as he continued to the front door. "What was that?" Graham asked, watching him go and then turning back to us.

"Kelsey Marie's boyfriend?" I didn't quite intend for it to be a question, but it came out that way anyway.

She snorted and broke into a coughing fit. "Is that what that asshole told you?"

Graham's eyebrows went up behind Kelsey Marie as I nodded.

"Not even in his dreams," she said. "He's a buddy of my buttface brother. Been following me around for the better part of a year." She held up her phone. "He texted me, said he needed something Dusty left for him. I went out to head him off 'cause I didn't want him interrupting you guys and your investigation."

I relaxed against the closed door behind me, folding my arms across my chest and nodding. "Is that Dusty's room?" I pointed.

"Yep. Why?"

"Because the kid told me he had to go to the bathroom, but he came out of there. You mind if I have a look around?"

She shook her head. "Help yourself. But if you find something you can arrest the little prick for, I call dibs on telling him. Deal?"

This family had some deep chasms of dysfunction. Finally, a part of this case I could relate to.

"Technically I have to tell him, too, but whatever makes you happy."

Graham followed me into the room and we started with the bureau in the front corner and worked our way across and back systematically, checking drawers to no avail.

"Nope," Graham said, shaking his head as he closed the bottom drawer on the far nightstand. He looked behind a plaque on the wall from the high school theatre program, replacing it carefully. It was much easier to search a room when we knew what we were looking for.

"Nothing under the mattress, either." I paused to pick up a framed photo from the dresser. Dustin, I assumed, sliding Bo Duke-style across the hood of a black Mustang with orange racing stripes. "Looks like he's pretty into his car," Graham noted.

"Car with sport performance tires," I replied, pointing out the rectangles on the sidewalls. So they went to the hunting cabin. They just didn't go inside. I flipped the frame over, but all it held was the picture.

"He drives that thing way too fast," Kelsey Marie said from

the doorway. "My dad said he couldn't have it because he'd get himself killed, but Dusty just went and bought it with his own money. Found it on some auction site. You'd think the damned thing lived and breathed the way he treats it."

I put the photo back and looked down a short hallway at the far left corner of the room, flanked by doors on both sides and emptying into another room, my eyes flicking to Graham. "The kid did say he was in the bathroom."

Graham waved an *after you* as I started for the hallway.

The bathroom was exquisite, if you could look past the clothes littering the Mojave tile floor and the open tube of toothpaste surrounded by aqua blue blobs on the granite countertop.

"Wow." Graham poked his head in before he continued into the bonus room at the other end of the hallway. "It's a video game paradise in here. He even has his own pinball machine. This kid's bedroom suite is nicer than my apartment."

"Something tells me your apartment is warmer in the people department," I murmured, standing in the center of the bathroom and turning a slow circle.

Nothing about Dustin's suite matched the rest of the house.

"Kelsey Marie?" I called.

She appeared in the doorway, wrinkling her nose. "He's so gross."

"But why?" I asked. "Today is Marta's day off, but he's been gone a few days now. Why isn't his room as clean as the rest of the house?"

She bit her lip and shaded her wide eyes with long, thick lashes, casting her gaze at the floor. "I love Marta."

"I know the feeling." My parents' longtime housekeeper was one of my only happy links to my formative years. "I can tell she takes a lot of pride in her work. Even the baseboards in this house sparkle. So what happened here?"

"Dusty said she stole something. A baseball card that was supposed to be worth money that belonged to my grand-daddy. Meanwhile, my room is full of shit worth more than Dustin's whole life, and she's never touched any of it except to dust it. She would never. But Dusty had a hissy fit and my dad said she couldn't come into this room anymore."

I tapped one foot, locking eyes with Graham over the top of Kelsey Marie's head. The car. It had to have been expensive.

"Dustin hasn't struck me so far as the strong work ethic type," Graham said.

Kelsey Marie backed up a step. "No shit. He'd live in bed if my parents would let him." She waved one arm at the bath-room. "So he just lets it look like this. Like a pig wallowing in the mud."

I tried the medicine cabinet first, because teenagers. All I found was a can of shaving cream and a bottle of vitamins.

Graham slid in under me, rifled through the drawers in the vanity, kneeling to look under and behind them, too. Nothing.

I turned to the toilet, wishing for the tenth time that I'd thought to bring gloves.

Nothing in the tank. I crouched, peering under and behind the fixture.

"Strike three." I stood, turning to the linen closet.

Graham and I sifted systematically through every shelf, checking inside folded sheets that smelled a whole lot better than the crusty ones on the bed.

Nothing.

"Wait." Graham dropped to his knees when I went to return a pair of navy towels to the bottom shelf. He pointed to the corner of the closet, then poked at the wall, and a small section of it popped loose.

"How did you see that?" Kelsey Marie asked from behind me.

"His sight is like 20/13 or something crazy," I said. "Part of what made him such a good pitcher."

"You were a ballplayer?" she asked.

"I never made it to the majors," he said absently, pulling on a small tab the same color ivory as the wall and removing the square of sheetrock, setting it carefully aside. "But I'm a good enough cop to know this kid doesn't have a hole in the wall for hiding school supplies." He reached inside.

And came out with a gallon-sized freezer bag of small, round white pills.

"Holy shit, what's that?" Kelsey Marie jumped backward so fast she almost fell. "Is he taking steroids or something?"

"By looking at it, I'd say it's some variety of opioid." I took the bag from Graham's outstretched hand. It was heavy. I'd guess there were a couple of thousand pills there. "And not for recreational use." I swiped a tissue from the holder on the counter and wrapped a pill in it, tucking it into my pocket until I could get an evidence bag from the truck.

"He's selling this shit?" Kelsey Marie's voice went up three octaves.

Her comment about her father forbidding Marta access to the room—but not firing her—was practically burning my ears. "Kelsey Marie, we need to have an honest talk about your family."

11

One kid happening into crazy success via a viral internet video could be random. A second one selling large quantities of prescription drugs means it's time to talk money.

Or maybe money problems.

I hate it when a case involves financial motives. In my experience, if I can get someone to trust me, and I usually can, they'll spill their guts after a few hours of questioning at the most.

Affairs, fights, neighborhood feuds, health problems, insecurities...I've heard it all in nearly twenty years behind a badge.

But ask about debt or finances, and folks who are embarrassed by the truth will lie every damned time.

Leading Kelsey Marie to the kitchen, I hoped she didn't know enough to be embarrassed, but at the same time, I needed her to have enough information to give us an idea of whether or not we needed to try to get a judge to issue a warrant for a financial data search on her parents. We'd need evidence that there was something material to the case. We also might need more than a dead pig, regardless of how many followers he had.

I took a seat at the kitchen table and pointed to her computer. There was nuance to this sort of questioning, and plenty of psychological skill to be tested. Step one, start with the easier stuff to get her talking.

I pointed to her computer as she sat down across from me. "First off, can I see the DMs you were talking about outside?"

She shrugged, flipping the computer open and tapping keys before she spun the screen to face me. "There's hours of reading there. I try not to delete them, just in case one of these sickos shows up. We save screenshots, too. My mom says we have to keep evidence because we never know when we might need it."

"Is your mom a lawyer or something?"

Kelsey Marie snorted. "As if. I don't even really know if she graduated high school. She just watches a shit ton of *CSI* and *Law & Order*."

Graham rounded the table and took the chair next to mine, leaning over my shoulder.

I clicked the first message, which had a little green dot indicating whoever sent it was online.

A new window opened—to a full-screen photo of a penis. I diverted my eyes to the type beneath it. *Do you know what to do with this, Kelsey Marie?*

"Jesus," I muttered, closing it.

"Which one?" Kelsey Marie asked.

"It was a...uh...a picture." Graham cleared his throat twice between the words, a frustrated edge to them that I knew him well enough to discern. Graham has no use for men who assault women, be it virtually or otherwise.

"Oh." Kelsey Marie rolled her eyes. "One of those. I mean, I've studied animal anatomy for two years, but there are definitely some creeps who have provided me a working knowledge of human anatomy this past year."

"Do you report these things?" I asked.

"If I did I'd literally spend my entire life emailing social media security people," she said. "All so these shitheads could open new accounts and start threatening me instead. I have better things to do, and these dudes are all bluster, my dad says."

Graham's jaw flexed. I got it. Was it fair that people could just send her bullshit like that and she thought it was her job to shrug it off and let them get away with it because she was afraid of pissing them off? No.

Did I understand where she was coming from? Absolutely.

"I usually delete those. You must've found a fresh one. Sorry."

"It's not you who owes anyone an apology for that," Graham said.

I clicked the next message down, which didn't have a green dot. Sent today at 5:31 a.m.

Trash like you profiteering off gentle animals makes me sick. As sick as the video of Samson's untimely death, which rests squarely on your shoulders, you greedy little bitch. Prepare to meet your maker. It won't be long now. And before you breathe your last, you'll wish I was as kind to you as this monster was to poor Samson.

"The one from this morning, right?" Kelsey Marie's voice hitched. "He's not wrong, you know. I did get greedy. And it did kill him. I didn't mean to."

"Kelsey Marie, when did you notice that the video of Samson's death was posted on your page?"

"After I saw that," she said. "I still wake up at five-fifteen every morning like I have to go out and feed him, and since I don't have anything to do, I check my phone. I saw the message and I went to Google."

"Why?" Graham asked.

"I never said, not to the audience, that he was..." She swallowed a sob. "I just said he passed away and asked them to give me a little time. That's why I went live too this morning after I talked to you. I couldn't get into my channel on YouTube to take the goddamn video down, so I went to TikTok to tell people what happened and beg them not to watch if they hadn't already clicked their notification."

The video had gotten a million views in the time it took us to drive here. I didn't want to tell her that plan had backfired. The fastest way to make a human look at something horrifying is to tell them there's something horrifying and ask them to not look at it.

I tapped one finger on the edge of the computer, my eyes still on the message. I clicked to the next one.

Do you want to know if he screamed?

I poked Graham, nodding to the screen.

He read the line and sat back in his chair. "Who did know what happened to Samson, Kelsey Marie?"

She shook her head. "Just us, I'm telling you."

"But it wasn't just you, because Donnette Robbins sent me to talk to you. If you kept it to yourself, how did she know?"

"Well, I mean, she doesn't count. This is a small town. Everyone knows everyone else's business. My dad called the sheriff. He didn't actually help, but I'm sure he blabbered to someone about it from his regular stool at the White Elephant, and whoever that was told someone else, and whoever that was told someone else. All it had to do was get to the church for Miss Donnette to hear about it."

I made a note, also noting the screen handle of the message I'd just read—WildBillRedux.

I tapped the pen on the paper. "Do you know anyone named Bill or William?"

Kelsey Marie thought on it. "I mean, my English teacher's name is William Ward, but Mr. Ward is like the most chill, nicest little old man ever."

"I'm sure he is. I know it's a lot to ask, but can I borrow your computer? I'm pretty handy with them when I have time to work, and it seems there might be some important evidence in here."

"Sure. Damned thing hasn't caused me anything but trouble for a while now, anyway."

"Thanks. I'll keep it safe. And I won't snoop."

"Snoop away, I don't have anything to hide," she said.

I pushed the paper and pen across the table. "Can you write down your password for me?"

"It's Samson's name and birthday." She scribbled on the page.

I took the pen back carefully by the end and laid it on top of the computer. "Thanks." I looked around. It was a beautiful house. My mother would approve.

"It's been a long time since I've been on a working farm," I said. "My grandfather owned the place three down from here toward Miss Donnie's—she was my granny's best friend—they bred cattle. I assume your dad does pigs from everything I've seen and heard, but what else do y'all raise? I always loved being at my grandparents' house because of the peace in the country."

"We have a few head of cattle at all times, but that's mostly because my mother is exceedingly picky about meat," she said. "We don't sell them or anything. Most of the profit comes from the pork operations. And my dad is talking about getting into breeding quarter horses. That's why he went up to Fort Worth this weekend. To look at a couple of mares."

"How many farmhands do y'all have to manage operations?"

"Two. Just day labor, they don't live here or anything. On Saturdays they're here before sunup and gone quick after. Pigs are a relatively self-sufficient stock."

"Did they know what happened to Samson?" Graham asked.

"Well sure," Kelsey Marie said. "Ricky was the first to get to me when I found him."

I picked up my pen. "Can I have their names?"

"Ricky Tester and Bobby Yager."

"Do you know where they live?"

"They share a trailer on the other end of town. West Meadows trailer park. Right past the cemetery."

I jotted it all down.

"Has this been a good year for the farm?" I asked.

She shrugged. "As good a year as any farm has."

I noted the way her shoulders tightened as her eyes went to the table.

Graham did, too.

"Kelsey Marie, is your dad having money problems? It could be important." A man desperate enough to take money from his daughter was likely getting it other places, too. Places where people might, say, murder a pet over a late payment.

"My dad has never been good with money." She was still talking to the table.

I waved a hand. "He had to have done something right somewhere," I said.

She raised her eyes to mine, blinking. "I paid for this," she said. "The house I grew up in was about the size of this room."

12

Everything but the barns looked brand new because it was.

Kelsey Marie had only been an internet sensation for a little over two years. Looking around, I guessed that she didn't have much of a savings account to show for it, either.

Which meant Jeff Sherman was suddenly suspect number one. His comments about Kelsey Marie's weekly views, the hits on the slasher film of Samson's death, and their bickering over her raising a new baby pig the day before collided in my head, dripping with more greed than empathy on rewind. But I had to get out of here without letting that on to his only daughter.

I flashed a toothy, the-judges-are-watching pageant queen smile and patted her hand. "Real estate is always a wise investment. Or at least it always has been for my father and his associates," I said.

"Your dad used to be the governor, huh?" she said. "We learned them all in seventh grade. And I saw something on the news about you putting him in prison last year."

"My relationship with my father is complicated." I held the smile at half wattage.

"That must be hard," she said softly, tracing a pattern on the granite tabletop with one finger.

"It has its moments."

"What about your mom, Kelsey Marie?" Graham got up from the table and checked the lock on the kitchen door before he moved to the living room and did the same with the patio doors. "Are you two close?"

She snorted. "I mean, I guess."

Less than convincing. "It's normal for there to be friction between teenage girls and their mothers."

"She's fine. She just has trouble caring about anyone else as much as she cares about herself."

Boy howdy, I knew that song by heart.

"That's the nicest way I've ever heard of calling someone selfish," I said.

"Being polite is pretty much in our DNA around these parts."

"Did your folks grow up here?" I asked. Her dad was a little older than me, from looking at him, but I found myself wondering if anyone who knew my sister might've known him, too.

"Oh totally. Like a corny country song, you know? Quarterback. Homecoming queen. Except they split up after high school and she went and got knocked up by someone else before they got back together."

My pen started moving across the paper again as Graham resumed his seat at the table.

"And how did they get back together?"

"Ran into each other at the gas station." She shook her head. "Of all the dumb things. Went to dinner that night, and four months later they were married. Three months after that, Dustin was born. Then me the next year. People used to make jokes about rabbits that I never understood when we were little."

"Kelsey Marie, does your dad have an office in the house somewhere?"

What I really wanted was a couple of hours alone with his computer, but I wasn't pressing my luck. Anything I could see with a quick look around was better than nothing.

"Sure, it's right back there." She pointed to a short hallway off the other end of the kitchen. "My mom is forever griping at him for the state of it, he's messy as all get out."

So also off limits to the housekeeper. Noted.

I stood and prodded Graham back toward the bar, hoping he got the keep-her-entertained vibe.

"My favorite video was the one where you tried to teach Samson to jump through hoops." He took the seat across from her.

Lord, I love this man.

I squeezed his shoulder and lit out for Jeff Sherman's office, trying to keep my steps slow enough to avoid raising Kelsey Marie's suspicions.

The first door I tried led to the most gorgeous powder room I'd ever seen. I kept going and found Jeff's study behind door number two.

It was big but windowless, and it took me a second of fumbling with the light switch to be able to see anything.

This was a mess Miranda Sherman complained about?

While the desktop did have a couple of organizers and trays full of papers, the rest of the room was what even Ruth McClellan would call tidy.

And Jeff Sherman had an old-fashioned ledger book on his desk blotter where most folks would keep a laptop.

I skirted the big wooden desk and flipped the book open, scanning columns of cramped lettering and numbers.

From last October, so the beginning of the fiscal year.

He spent twenty thousand on hay and fifty on feed. I snapped a photo of the page, wondering if that was a monthly expense or a less frequent one.

The next line was a payment to Sherman for five hundred head of stock, from a slaughterhouse I was pretty sure was near the stockyards in Fort Worth. Fifteen thousand.

I kept going.

Kelsey Marie's YouTube income was noted on the fourteenth, a hundred and seventy thousand. That brought everything back into the black.

It paid the salaries of the two farmhands, paid Marta, paid the mortgage—six grand a month on the house, and another three for the outbuildings and land. On the twenty-fifth, a line item marked "HotH merch" added another twelve grand to the plus side of the balance sheet.

I kept scanning. Four car payments, the amounts suggesting that the Shermans liked very nice vehicles, plus almost five hundred dollars a month for cell service, the same for high speed internet and cable. Sherman didn't keep separate books for his business and his home, which was a little odd, but I wasn't complaining—or asking why.

I snapped photos of every page through the current one and closed the ledger, opening drawers in the desk. Pens, paperclips, markers, rubber bands.

In the bottom right drawer I found a fat envelope from an attorney in Austin.

I pulled a sheaf of papers out and unfolded them, smoothing them out and reading.

Hot damn.

Three years ago this month, Jeff Sherman had been on the verge of losing everything he owned to foreclosure—before, according to Kelsey Marie, he had this showplace of a house to lose. Or the mortgage on it to pay.

I snapped more photos, tucked the papers back exactly like I found them, and kept hunting.

In the middle right drawer I found a stack of Visa statements with Miranda's name on them. She used this card for everything. Which meant it could likely tell me where she'd been this week. I opened a real-time tracing app that would spit out an automated government order for any cop with a half-decent excuse and entered details. Ninety seconds later I had an authorization email. Fifteen more and I had her recent card history on my screen.

The last charge was Sunday morning at the diner in town.

Damn.

Nothing else in the desk.

I moved to the cabinets under the bookshelves behind the desk and knelt, expecting them to be locked.

The door opened easily when I pulled.

Nobody out here locked anything, apparently.

Pay dirt: stacks of ledger books matching the one on the desk, organized by year according to the stickers on the spines.

I pulled the ones for the most recent two years and rifled through, taking photos of the pages to examine later when I hadn't already been absent for a conspicuously long time.

An envelope fell out of the back of the one from two years ago as I went to return it to the shelf.

I grabbed it from the floor and went to put it back, the type in the top left corner catching my eye.

Dennis LaVeaux Enterprises.

Holy shit.

I snapped a shot of the envelope and the sheet inside, which appeared to be a loan agreement, shoving everything back into the cabinet and pausing to slow my breathing before I shut off the lights.

"I only said how much he loved bananas once, and we get every kind of banana anything you can think of on the daily." Kelsey Marie grew more animated than I'd seen her yet, leaning over her computer, showing Graham photos.

I caught his eye over the top of the screen, hooking a subtle thumb toward the door.

"He was a great pet, Kelsey Marie. I'm so sorry for your loss." Graham stood. "I checked all the windows and doors. You're locked in safe." He paused and waited until she looked up at him. "I'd like for you to stay that way until your parents get back. Don't go anywhere, and if anyone comes to your door, ignore them."

"What about my friends?" she asked. "Could I invite someone to stay over?"

"I don't think that's a good idea."

"And don't let your brother's friend back into the house," I said. "Will Marta be here tomorrow?"

"She's off all weekend."

Her phone binged and she pulled it out and touched the screen, her face stretching into a smile. "Finally. The damn bots took that horrid video down because people kept reporting it after I asked them to on TikTok this morning. Thank God."

I leaned to read over her shoulder. "Warning?"

"It's just because the bots flagged that video. I'd warn me, too. Perry will fix it for me, and he'll get me back into my account." She sighed. "I suppose I have work to do. I should have a video ready to go Monday explaining to my subscribers what happened to Samson. I have way more followers on YouTube than I do on TikTok."

"Could I get his contact information from you? Perry, your person at YouTube?" I asked.

She bit her lip. "I'm not supposed to give out proprietary information from the company," she said. "They're pretty strict about that. I know someone who lost her channel because she was trying to help out a friend who was getting started." She drummed her fingers on the table. "Can I give you his name and you can talk to their, like lawyers or whatever? That way I didn't break my contract."

"Sure." She was supporting her family at seventeen with the money she made from the videos. And I could probably get what I needed somewhere else if I couldn't find my way through Google's customer service to her guy.

"Perry Gardener."

I jotted it down.

"Can I see your phone?" I asked.

She pulled it out and handed it over. I added my number to her favorites list. "You call me if anyone bothers you. The sheriff may not be worth much for investigating, but if anyone threatens you, I can put him on guard duty."

She scrunched her brow. "If you say so." Biting her lip, she sucked in a deep breath as she took the phone back. "I need to go get the small camera from Samson's barn. It's time to explain all this to my viewers."

Graham unlocked the mudroom door and waved an arm. "I'll walk you out."

I stood, picking up her computer and the pen she'd used to write down the password. "Kelsey Marie, how many acres do y'all have here, do you know?"

"Two hundred and fifty." She didn't miss a beat.

I jotted that down, wandering the house myself to check door locks until she and Graham blew back in on a gust of icy wind, the camera in her hand.

"Take Graham's advice, stay inside. Do your video." I paused. "Are you sure I can borrow this?" I gestured to the laptop. I wanted to take it, but I didn't want to interfere with her ability to do what she felt like she needed to do, either.

"I'll use my dad's computer to upload the video."

She walked us to the door. "You think I'm going to be safe here?"

"I think as long as you keep the doors locked as a precaution, you're perfectly safe," I replied. "We'd just rather be too careful than not careful enough until we figure out what's going on here, that's all. But you call me if you feel like you need to."

She shut the door, and I waited for the deadbolt to slide home before I followed Graham to the truck.

"What did you find in the study?"

I watched the house shrink in the rearview as he drove up the driveway, hoping we were right to leave her here.

"That she might just be safer with her dad out of town. Her parents' finances were a mess before she saved them with videos of her pig," I said. "To the tune of Jeff Sherman borrowing a hundred grand from the Dixie Mafia."

13

Hiding a body is way harder than most folks would think.

In the majority of murder cases in the United States, it's people fucking up this step that gets them caught. Dead bodies are gross—once a heart stops pumping and the blood isn't flowing anymore, the body begins to break down—actually digesting itself—starting in a matter of only minutes. All the bacteria—from what's on the skin to what thrives in the gut—uses the disintegration of cells to grow and travel, moving to the brain and other places bacteria usually doesn't reach. Blood cells leak out of broken vessels and collect under the skin, causing it to look blue or purple.

But all of that is just the preshow for the biggest problem a dead body poses.

Once the cells are digesting each other and the bacteria can run amok, sugars that the bacteria excrete in the body make gases like methane and ammonia.

That's what makes a body stink. It also makes it puff up full of gas.

This means you can't hide them in a closet or a car trunk, because the smell would give the hiding place away. And you can't dump them in the lake or the river, because the gasses will bring them to the surface. Weighting them down doesn't work except in the movies, because eventually enough of the corpse would decompose to slip whatever secured it to the weights, and it would float to the top.

Digging hands in, removing tissue, burying bones...the true predator does what's necessary. Because once the police have a body, it's much easier for them to figure out what happened to it.

But some bodies are too big to get rid of.

A cheetah can take down an elephant, but the cat isn't taking that prey home for dinner.

When the victim is too big to move, a predator has to be crafty about hiding things in plain sight. Getting away with murder is in the details.

The very second the life has gone out of the victim's eyes, right after the heart beats for the last time, split the gut open and let it spill out. Smelly and gross, but effective. It'll both stop the bloating and let evidence degrade quicker than it would on its own.

The more horrifying the scene, the better. Distraction is a powerful smokescreen. When police officers are appropriately horrified, they miss little things.

True predators leave true carnage.

And the hunt continues.

14

Ninety minutes of poking through Kelsey Marie's DMs later, I had a list of possibly psychotic creeps longer than my legs. And that was just Instagram.

"How can so many people be so vile?" I asked Graham. "Surely this level of online harassment is criminal in and of itself. She's getting dozens of messages like this every day, from different accounts. Listen to this one: 'Have you ever imagined being gutted like the pig you are? How loud will you scream when I get to you?' She's a kid, for fuck's sake. What could possibly push someone to do this?"

He put one hand on my knee. "We'll figure it out, babe. Someone snuck into a barn in the middle of nowhere and killed a pig. It's not like that takes a master criminal." He waved a hand at the computer. "Odds are even in our favor that everything you're looking at there is just pontification. Far more likely it was someone she knows."

He was right about that. I'd gone back two weeks before Samson's death in Kelsey Marie's DMs and I had a list of the handles behind the most disturbing messages. But that was a big haystack, and finding the right needle would be a long labor. It was far more likely that the actual culprit here—and any danger to Kelsey Marie herself—was someone much closer to her than the other side of a computer screen.

I flipped to a clean page in my notebook and opened her email.

Two hundred and thirty unread marketing messages, interrupted only by notes asking for Kelsey Marie's approval of designs for various *High on the Hog* t-shirts, mugs, socks, and—the latest addition to the merchandise line—belt buckles. "Don't young people use email to communicate anymore?"

Graham shook his head. "No, I think that one is firmly relegated to us old-timers. Check her messages."

I clicked the icon for her texts.

The most recent ones were from her dad and Sam Harris, the kid we'd met in the hallway outside Dustin's room. "He told us he was her boyfriend," I murmured.

"Yeah, and then she was emphatically against that whole idea," Graham said. "What can we find out about that kid?"

I copied his phone number and ran it through a reverse lookup database on my phone. Clicking the address up in my map, I tapped a finger on the edge of Kelsey Marie's laptop. "He's a farm kid," I said.

"Odds are good out there," Graham said.

"But that means maybe killing the pig wouldn't be such a stretch for him if he's upset with her," I said.

Graham turned into the parking lot at the crime lab, where Jim's truck was still parked in front of the door.

"Let's go see if more about how Samson died helps us with anything."

"We saw him die in full color video," I pointed out. "I'm not sure how much more help we get with method than that. But sure. Let's see what Jim has to say." I texted him that we were here and watched the door until he opened it and waved us inside.

We followed him to the body room, where Samson's remains were splayed over the table, Jim's computer on a nearby counter with a screenshot from the beginning of the video on his screen.

"You have a habit of bringing me strange shit, McClellan." He waved for me to follow him to the table. Graham lingered near the doorway. The lab wasn't his favorite place.

I stopped, swallowing hard at the curling flesh around the edges of the wounds.

"And the species isn't even the weirdest part. Your pig was sedated when the axe hit him," Jim said. "With enough OxyContin that an elephant wouldn't have felt a blow."

"That's why he didn't move." Graham edged further into the room. "Someone tranked him?"

"Well, someone overdosed him on narcotics, anyway. But not to the point that it stopped his heart; he lost too much blood for that. His blood showed high enough concentrations of Oxy that I'm pretty sure it had to have been administered close to when he was attacked." He pointed to his screen. "And I'm betting the same person who drugged him killed him, because they were deliberate and unhurried about approaching him. They knew he wasn't going to move."

"Yeah but he was in a pen, anyway," I said. "It's not like whoever that is wasn't going to kill him whether he moved or not."

"Maybe they didn't want him to make noise and alert Kelsey Marie and her family?" Graham mused.

"Plus, to be so big, hogs are hard to catch if you spook

them," Jim said, pushing his glasses up his nose and leaning back against the counter. "And one this size can actually be a formidable foe if you corner him."

I blinked. "And you know this because?"

"I paid attention in my 4H meetings as a kid?"

"You were in the 4H? I feel left out all of a sudden."

"When I was a teenager everyone who was anyone was in 4H." Jim laughed. "Including all the prettiest girls."

"And you still paid attention in the meetings?" Graham asked.

"Well. Mostly." Jim winked.

I flipped back through my notes. "I know we've had two people tell us Dustin and Miranda left on Sunday, but come on. First this video shows up on YouTube and now the animal was drugged with the very thing we found a stash of in Dustin's bathroom? Maybe he doubled back."

"Why do I feel like I'm missing a crucial bit of information?" Jim asked.

"Kelsey Marie, the girl who raised Samson here, has a brother."

"Half-brother. In what seems like dysfunctional family city," Graham interjected.

"We found a gallon-size freezer bag of pills inside the wall of the linen closet in his private bath. Kelsey Marie had no explanation for them. There's major friction between the two of them, though." I started pacing the length of the room, hands clasped behind my back. The more I thought about the brother, the more sense it made. "She even kind of told me yesterday that she ran for president of the 4H this year to keep Dustin from winning. She wanted to show him up. And he wanted her out of his club. It sounds like pretty standard sibling rivalry stuff until pets start getting chopped up on video."

Jim let out a low whistle.

"I mean, who's to say some of those hateful DMs weren't coming from cover accounts?" Graham said. "Like, hey babysitter, the phone call is coming from inside the house."

"I don't hate this. But we need more evidence. If it was Dustin, the family is intent on protecting him."

"I'm about wrapped up here, but I'll holler if I find anything else."

"Thanks, Jim. We're going to hunt down Kelsey Marie's absentee family."

"And how exactly are we going to do that?" Graham asked. "You find a new source for that information since yesterday?"

"Sure did." I flashed a grin. "If they're not at the hunting cabin out of cell range, Kelsey Marie's laptop can tell us a lot more than just how many sickos live in her DMs."

15

Miranda Sherman and her son were flat ass off the grid.

Thirty minutes of sitting with Kelsey Marie's computer trying to call, text, and track their cell phones, it seemed like they had fallen off the edge of the Earth. The constantly-connected one most folks inhabit nowadays, anyway.

I slapped the silver computer shut and stuck out my lower lip, blowing a stray hair out of my face as Graham looked up from his laptop on the other side of the coffeehouse table. "Still nothing, huh?"

"If this woman got a teenage boy to give up his phone, she's probably qualified to be running some sort of nuclear secrets program. I can't find either one of them."

Graham checked his watch. "You up for another road trip today? It's only 1:30, and I've got her dad, he's at the Worthington. Let's go ask him how to get a hold of the wife and stepson."

"He told me they were at the cabin," I said.

"But maybe he knows different now—or maybe, if he was lying to you, mentioning those pills we found in the kid's room will persuade him to tell the truth."

I grabbed my coffee and Kelsey Marie's computer, following him to the door. "I don't like this," I said.

"That her jealous brother probably murdered her pet?" Graham opened the passenger door on the truck for me. "I mean, that sucks, but it's probably right. There's not a big mystery here. He was dealing narcotics, Jim found narcotics in the pig's blood. All we really need to do is get a look at how tall the kid is and put him in an interrogation room with you and Archie for ten minutes. Case closed. Maybe Kelsey Marie will get a new pig. Maybe she'll get off that farm and make her parents pay their own bills. But none of that is our concern."

"Something feels off to me," I said. "I can't shake the idea that Kelsey Marie is in trouble. Or danger. Or both."

"I would be more inclined to agree if we weren't talking about a farm kid." Graham steered the truck toward 35 and got on the northbound ramp. "Killing a pig isn't a big deal when you grow up on a pork farm. At least, in theory it's not. Sure, this was brutal and the video was gross, but is it all that different than shooting a metal rod into an animal's brain?"

"I guess not. It just seems like a perfect storm. The pig was slaughtered days ago, but the video just went up on her channel overnight, when she was waking up alone in the house."

"Well sure, her brother didn't kill her pig for fun, he's trying to freak her out. But how much do you want to bet our man Dustin has Kelsey Marie's login information for her channel? The story works—he drugged and killed her pig, skipped town with mom, got up early and logged into her channel, posted the video as her, changed her password so she couldn't take it down...and he did it all in a timeframe when he knew she wouldn't be able to get anyone at their headquarters on the west coast to take it down before her subscribers all got a notification that she'd posted something. The kid might be homicidal, might not. But he is smart. How many nasty comments did she get both on her page and in her DMs this morning? The object of this isn't to kill Kelsey Marie, Faith, it's to destroy her. We've just worked too many homicides." He patted my knee. "Relax. This isn't that complicated. We'll be done and you'll be back to being annoyed with your mother's need to control our wedding before coffee is ready on Monday."

He was probably right. When you spend your waking hours dealing with the worst humanity has to offer, it's damned easy to jump to the worst-case scenario. Kelsey Marie had seemed genuinely frightened when she called this morning, but she was young, she was grieving her pet, and—it seemed—worried about her income and her celebrity status.

Graham had an excellent point—maybe some of those awful messages were coming from inside the house. I dug my own computer out from under the seat, opening an IP trace as I checked my notes for the password to Kelsey Marie's Instagram.

I clicked to her DMs and copied the user handles from the most disturbing messages, populating the right fields on my IP tracer. A nifty little tool I'd found on the dark web, the hacker who created it took advantage of big tech's obscenely long terms and conditions to link a profile to the email address listed for it, and then used the email to ping over an html coded message that looks like gibberish to most people, but actually prompts the computer to autoreply to the email with the last saved autoreply in the mail program. From there, an IP address in a place like Brady, where internet service providers were still stuck in the 1990s, was easy to pilfer. Took about 45 seconds.

Hot damn. Of the nine accounts I'd noted, four of them originated from the same IP address.

I clicked back to the tracer and typed in Kelsey Marie's Instagram handle.

It was not the same.

"Several of these nasty DMs going to her from different accounts do appear to be coming from the same place, but it's not from the same IP Kelsey Marie uses," I said. "So that's not the brother."

Graham wobbled his head from side to side. "Maybe. Maybe not. That's one point of data. Let's reserve judgment until we talk to the dad and see what else Jim finds." He drummed three fingers on the wheel. "What about the other kid? The brother's friend who thinks she's his fantasy girlfriend?"

I turned the notebook page and found his address.

"They use AT&T for internet," I said, clicking back to the tracer window and finding the right fields to enter the information.

"Got him." My stomach lurched when I looked up from my screen, downtown Cowtown looming on the horizon. "Well. Sort of. His home IP is a match for one of these accounts."

"But it's not the one sending her stuff from several profiles?"

"Not from what I have here." I clicked her iCloud. Password protected. I tried the one she used for Instagram.

Nope. I picked my phone up and opened a text.

"Let's see if Cyber can get into her cloud and check for some of those screenshots she mentioned—if we can get a bonafide threat, we can get a warrant." I double-checked the IP before I clicked send.

Graham took the Belknap exit off the freeway and hung a left on Taylor between the jail and the courthouse.

"These might not be the most threatening messages she's

getting, but they're enough to pick Sam up for questioning. Especially since he knows her in the real world," I said as a line of sheriff's patrol cars flicked by the window.

"If he has any sense, he's scared shitless right about now," Graham said.

"Kind of what I was thinking."

"Think he'll run, now that he knows she's talking to the cops?"

I shook my head. "Run where? There's nowhere to hide out there."

"Let's see what we find here. If we have to, we can call the local sheriff to pick the kid up for questioning. If he stews for a while at the station and it was his buddy Dustin and not him, he might rat out his friend." Graham stopped the truck under the covered portico at the Worthington, and a navy-uniformed bellman swept forward to open my door before Graham got the engine shut off.

"Welcome to Fort Worth, ma'am." He waved one arm toward the revolving glass door leading to a clean, modern, and minimal lobby that held no remaining trace of the brass-and-flash memories I had of this place. Sunday brunch at the Worthington when we were in Fort Worth was one of the governor's can't-miss things throughout my childhood.

I took his gloved hand and hopped down. "Thank you so much. We're not staying, just visiting a guest of yours while he's in town."

The bellhop—his little silver name tag read Scott—nodded. "Make yourself at home. And enjoy the rodeo." His eyes flicked to my boots and back up. "If you're going."

We were barely three steps past Scott when I spotted Jeff Sherman—slipping out a door twenty paces to our right. Hands in his pockets, head down.

I tapped one elbow into Graham's ribs and jerked my head

toward Jeff. "Looks like he's headed out." I was way more inclined to follow him than call out to him.

We stepped out of the foot traffic that overwhelms the city's most storied hotel during the stock show and watched Sherman until he had a half-block lead.

Graham aimed an index finger surreptitiously at the camera over the front door. "Figure that doesn't pick up the service entrance he used," he said.

"Nope." I started walking. Wherever Kelsey Marie's dad was headed, he didn't want any record of him setting out for it.

Three blocks west of the hotel, Sherman ducked into the parking garage at the county office building that was once home to Tandy Center.

"It's four forty-five," Graham muttered, starting across the street.

I flicked the safety strap on my holster open as we strode across the sidewalk, unease creeping over me like a prickly, itchy blanket.

"On Saturday. Whatever he's up to, it's shady."

"At best."

We fell quiet, both lifting and deliberately placing our feet in soft steps on the polished concrete as we turned back-to-back, eyes going opposite directions and scanning the area in the underground garage.

I spotted Sherman leaning one shoulder on a thick, purple-painted pillar about halfway down the second row to my left. I swung one arm back and tapped Graham. Sherman couldn't see us from where he was, and since I wasn't sure who he was meeting or what he was up to, I wanted it to stay that way.

We crept into a niche between the elevator and the stairs and watched.

He was talking to someone, gesturing with his left hand. But his broad shoulders and the angle of his head obscured all but a sliver of forehead and a shock of white-blonde hair.

Graham rested a hand on my arm. "Nope," he whispered.

"I'm not moving." Hand to God, the man could read my mind on occasion. I wanted to creep closer, but right then I was more focused on staying out of sight. Years of experience had taught me it's not always wise to jump in with both feet—there's a time in this job for the quick chase. There're far more where waiting both gets to the same goal and keeps everyone safer.

Sherman's hands came up, gesturing in jerky motions. His voice got louder, but I still couldn't make out much of what he was saying.

I moved one hand to the butt of my Sig, cold under my already frigid fingers.

"There's only one way out of here," Graham murmured out of the corner of his mouth.

"Unless he gets into the building, yes," I hissed.

"Let's hope he just comes this way, the—" Graham didn't get the word out before Sherman hauled one arm back and smashed his fist into whoever he'd been talking to.

I took one step forward.

Sherman's arm dropped to his side, his hand flexing. "You piece of shit. Stay away from me. Stay away from my family." The words came out in a roar, ringing off the concrete rafters and walls.

I paused.

Graham tugged on my shirt, pulling me back to him. He was right: we needed a look at who had pissed Kelsey Marie's dad off so much, and—maybe more importantly, because

Kelsey Marie was a minor—we needed to not piss him off ourselves. At least not until we could arrest him, if he needed arresting.

He kicked the pile of overcoat attached to the white-blonde hair and hustled for the stairs in the far left corner.

"You had to go and remember the doors to the building," Graham said under his breath.

"Yep. Me mentioning they were there definitely made him bolt that way."

"Coin flip?"

"You take him, you're bigger and your legs are longer."

"I'm not grabbing him, just following, right? He'll kill our access to the kid if we piss him off."

"Yep. I'll get a look at whoever's over there bleeding and be right behind you."

Graham took off across the garage, crossing the space in a matter of seconds. My eyes caught on his graceful, loping form for a split second before I pulled them away. I don't regret many things about my life, but damn, I wish I'd been able to see him play.

The rumpled khaki coat hadn't moved.

I ran toward it, slowing and quieting my steps as I encroached.

Squatting, I looked for a purse or wallet that might contain identification. Because of the large, shapeless tarp of a coat, it was impossible to tell much except that there was a person breathing under there. Size, gender, and age were all still guesses.

I lifted the hair out of a trickle of blood, catching a sharp breath. It was a girl.

Not a woman. A girl. Probably Kelsey Marie's age.

What the hell drove Jeff Sherman to cold-cock a teenage girl?

Maybe a certain dead pig, if this young woman was in town for the stock show, too.

I shook her shoulder gently. "Miss?"

A grunt issued from her throat, but her eyes didn't budge.

I pulled my phone from my back pocket and stood, eyes scanning the garage as I dialed 911 and gave my badge number to the dispatcher.

"I have an unconscious female in the garage in the old Tandy Center," I said. "Breathing, no signs of overexposure to cold. Request EMS."

"On their way, Ranger," she said. "Can you remain with her until they arrive?"

"I will," I said, not quite getting the words out before I heard something that sounded a hell of a lot like gunfire from inside the building.

16

"Scratch that," I said, running for the door Graham had disappeared through.

"Was that gunfire?" The dispatcher's voice was calmer than Lake Travis on a still summer afternoon. "Should I send backup?"

"It came from inside the building. I think. And yes, please. Advise that Travis County Commander Graham Hardin is also on scene, out of uniform. He's six foot four, African American, muscular build and green eyes, wearing a blue shirt and a brown leather jacket."

"Got it."

I didn't break stride as I stuffed the phone back into my pocket and threw the door wide, my boots echoing off the pockmarked white tile, down a wide hallway, toward the old mall.

I was almost to the well that used to be an ice rink when I spotted Graham, sprinting toward a corridor leading to the Tower Two office elevators.

He wasn't bleeding, thank God, but I couldn't see Sherman.

Or where the gunshot noise had come from. Graham's weapon wasn't in his hand.

I kicked up my speed, my calves burning as Graham rounded the corner into the hallway.

Jeff Sherman must be in better shape than I thought— Graham and I clock a six-minute mile on even terrain, not because we like to run, but because not many criminals can beat that.

I hurdled the furniture in the lobby, which shaved a few seconds off my chase, and spotted Sherman at the other end of the hallway, just in time for him to disappear up a set of stairs.

Graham had gained, reaching the staircase about ten seconds behind Sherman and pulling a door open at the top. Before he stopped.

Turning back, he paused at the bottom of the staircase and doubled over, leaning his elbows on his knees and sucking wind.

He was still bent over when I caught up. "Why'd you let him go?"

"It's a public building. Looks like a library," Graham said. "I'm not causing a panic chasing him through a crowded public building just to lose him on the street when all he did was deck someone, and we don't even know why."

"Didn't he shoot at you?"

"Shoot?" His brow furrowed. He lifted his jacket to show his snapped holster. "Definitely not. Sorry if something scared you, though."

"You didn't hear gunfire?"

Graham shook his head and I dropped mine to my hands. I didn't imagine it; the dispatcher heard it, too. So what now? Where the hell had those shots come from?

"Well, he decked a teenage girl." I paused for a deep

breath, trying to focus only on facts we had in that moment. "Or a very young woman who has exceptional skin. And why'd he run if he wasn't guilty of something?"

Graham shrugged. "In a weird way that actually makes me feel better. I mean, it was a girl he seemed pretty angry with days after his daughter's prize pet was murdered. And if we keep up pursuit, we'll blow our chance to get anything else out of Kelsey Marie if he sees you—I haven't met him, and I'm not in uniform. Hell, for all I know, he thought I was trying to hurt him."

I leaned back against the cool marble slab of the wall and sighed. "I suppose." I didn't care for losing a pursuit, but his points were all valid. Especially the possible link between the unconscious girl in the garage and Samson's death. "Let's go see who he was mad at?"

Graham nodded. "You call EMS?"

I opened my mouth to answer just as I heard the sirens.

We kicked it back up to a run, staying clear of the lobby furniture and ice rink this time. Graham pulled the door to the garage wide just as the ambulance turned in.

I gritted my teeth at the sirens echoing off the walls until the driver turned them off, jogging over to meet him and flashing my badge.

"Nice to meet you," he said. "Brent McAulay." He glanced around. "What can we do for you, Ranger?"

"Faith..."

That was Graham, from behind me. I turned, already knowing what I was going to find by his tone.

She was gone.

Dammit.

Graham handed me a cup of coffee and took another from the cart attendant as I surveyed the crowded midway.

"How are you at popping balloons with darts?" I sipped my coffee and pointed to a booth. "Want to see who can win a bigger stuffed unicorn?"

"How about this: coffee while we walk, then a game?" He offered an elbow that I threaded my free arm through and we set off at a pace just shy of ambling.

"So in one day we have a variety pack of random internet sickos—one of whom goes to the trouble to make ghost accounts—the girl's own competitive and likely dope-dealing brother, and a teenager her dad calls a rather harsh name before he punches her out and she disappears. Now what?"

"While I can't say yet that one thing is for sure more likely than another, statistics fall on the side of someone Kelsey Marie knows. So I say we focus on finding Jeff Sherman, locating our mystery young woman from the garage, and trying to track down the brother. Especially given that the pig was drugged."

I shivered at a stiff wind gust, the lights and shouts of the stock show carnival carrying on around us like it was sixty degrees and not twenty-five.

Graham pulled me in closer. "Getting lab results back on those pills we found will help that case if it matches what Jim found on the hog's tox screen."

"But Jim can probably empty his stomach faster than the lab will get pills broken down for us." I sighed. "I want to know who the girl was that Sherman punched."

"So do I, but if you ask him, you're going to piss him off."

"That would definitely not be a first resort for me. We'll figure it out, I got a good look at her face."

We fell into the easy silence that was my single favorite thing about us—Graham was the only person I'd ever known in my life that I didn't feel a need to entertain or impress constantly. I could just be myself, and we could just be—and that was just fine.

Scanning the faces of the crowded midway, half expecting to light on Jeff Sherman or the young woman he'd decked, I spotted a Brady High 4H ball cap on a lanky kid in starched Wranglers and a thick canvas jacket covered with bright red and blue patches. Touching Graham's elbow, I nodded in the direction of the boy, who was penned between a tangle of rowdy cowboys and a wall of women waiting in line to get into one of the two port-a-johns stuck discreetly between the ring toss and the basketball free throw game.

"You're up." Graham took my coffee cup and faded into the crowd as I started for the bathroom line.

Poor kid. He almost looked resigned to spending the rest of the evening there.

I joined the back of the line and caught his eye.

His cheeks flamed red and he tucked his hands into the pockets of his coat. The line moved, and I stepped up in front of him, holding his gaze. "I couldn't help but notice your cap," I said. "My grandparents owned a ranch outside Brady for more than fifty years. Glad to see the 4H there is still thriving."

He blinked, his mouth gaping and closing for three cycles before he managed to make words come out of it. "Yes ma'am, we have a bigger group this year than we ever have."

"Is that a fact?" I widened my eyes. "That's so refreshing, that y'all can still get so many young people away from their screens and out into the barn. My granddaddy would be proud." Up close, I could see his name, embroidered on the chest of his jacket. "So, Colter, what did you raise for the stock show?"

"A Hereford bull." He smiled. "He took second place in the

preliminary rounds of judging in the county last month, and he's up seventy-three pounds since."

"Wow. Well, I wish you both good luck. My cousin raised a prizewinning hog when I was a little younger than you, I remember how much work went into it." I heard my voice tighten as the lie rolled through my lips and hoped he was too distracted to catch it. Even after years of Archie's coaching, most of the time I suck at lying. But since he didn't bring up pigs, I needed a way to.

His face darkened for half a second. "My family has had quite a few of those over the years," he said. "But this year..." He shook his head hard enough to knock the cap askew. "Well. Nobody was allowed to raise a hog this year. But me and Hidalgo, we had a shot at a ribbon, anyway."

My brow scrunched, genuine curiosity creeping back into my voice. "Nobody was allowed? Why on Earth not?" My gut said Kelsey Marie and Samson had something to do with that, but especially since she hadn't mentioned it, I needed him to explain.

His eyes shot to the restroom line, which had snaked around me and moved on when I stopped to chat with him. "You're going to miss your turn."

"I'll get back in line. My grandparents raised hogs for a generation. I'm curious."

He shrugged, scuffing the toe of one worn work boot on the floor. "Rich people get what they want. Especially when they're the teacher's special pet," he muttered. "If queen Kelsey didn't get to show her hog, nobody else could bring one either."

"I, uh." I paused. "I'm sorry."

He tipped his hat and gestured to a lull in the line when the cowboys collected their stuffed gorilla from the ring toss and moseyed on. "It's just that swine is a smaller category, so statistically, you have a better chance at a champion. But, it is what it is, my daddy says. You have a nice evening, ma'am."

I stepped back and let him pass, moving to the end of the line mostly to keep up my charade of an accidental chat in case he turned around.

Kelsey Marie had sounded downright contemptuous of the school's 4H sponsor, yet her schoolmate said "special pet" in a way that didn't go unnoticed.

17

It took three desk clerks, two managers, and both badges to get Jeff Sherman's room number out of the Worthington's staff —which raised my eyebrows clear off my forehead. I was used to dragging room numbers for celebrities and politicians out of hotel employees, but this was a new one. Sherman was at best famous-adjacent, and Kelsey Marie wasn't even there.

"Okay." I offered a saccharine smile to the general manager, a stout man with a hairline that had retreated farther than Santa Anna at the Alamo. "I'll just knock on doors and flash my badge at your guests until I find the one I need to speak with."

That did it. He couldn't write the suite on a Post-it fast enough.

"Glad we could come to an understanding." I glanced at the paper and stuffed it in my pocket.

"That was weird," Graham said.

"He's in the Johnson Suite," I said. "That's the Governor's preferred room. So they probably just think Sherman is a VIP." I squeezed his hand and pointed to the bar. "I'll be back. Grab a drink and watch the college highlight reel."

He waved as I stepped into the elevator before he made a beeline for the bar.

I rapped on the right-hand door of the Johnson Suite just as the sun vanished fully behind the horizon outside the hallway window.

I kept my eyes on the peephole, a soft smile in place as I listened for signs of life on the other side.

I counted to thirty and knocked again.

Two halting footsteps, followed by a crash—glass breaking. I knocked again, harder. "Mr. Sherman? It's Faith McClellan with the Texas Rangers. Please open the door."

It sounded like he stumbled into the other side of the door, but I heard the lock slide back.

Great. Was I about to go into a hotel suite with a large, stumbling drunk man who I'd watched punch out a tiny girl only a few hours ago?

When the door cracked open, a single red-rimmed, squinting eyeball peering out said I was indeed.

"Sorry," Sherman breathed, shaking his head. I hoped it kept him from noticing that I recoiled from the whiskey on his breath. "I wasn't expecting company." The slur said he was probably half a bottle or more into his evening.

I didn't know Jeff Sherman at all. Maybe this was an everyday thing. But there was a good chance that him being plastered by sundown had something to do with the altercation, or his daughter's pet being slaughtered, or both.

"Don't give it a second thought," I said. "I know it's terribly rude to drop in this way and I apologize, but I saw you in the lobby earlier by chance and wanted to ask you a few questions without Kelsey Marie being present. I wondered if there might have been things you didn't want to tell me with her there for fear of scaring her." I kept my voice breezy and even. It was Saturday. Lots of folks go to Fort Worth on January Saturdays from all over the state. He had no reason to suspect I was there looking for him.

He dragged one hand down his face before he held up a finger and turned for the mini bar, pivoting back with a bottle of water in his hand. I watched the red Ozarka label shrink in with the plastic as he sucked the contents dry. "Kelsey Marie has had a rough year," he said. "She's tough, but there's only so much a daddy can watch his little girl go through, you know?"

Not from experience. But I wasn't telling him that. "Of course."

Sherman waved a hand at a long black leather sofa in the middle of the floor, backed by windows that overlooked the city, the neon lights of the stockyards saloons glowing softly in the distance. "Have a seat."

I obliged, settling into the near corner of the sofa. He sprawled across an armchair opposite me in a flail of long arms and legs. "She needs some downtime," he said. "A quiet weekend to herself. I'm hoping she'll just rest with everyone out of the house."

"As soon as she makes sure that awful video is gone from her channel, I'm sure she will," I said in commiseration.

His wide forehead scrunched into a dozen folds. "Awful video?"

Oh hell. I widened my eyes, groping for words. Why would Kelsey Marie not have told her dad what happened?

Because he was out of town and she didn't want him to worry. She took care of him in more ways than financial ones, it seemed.

"She's perfectly safe," I said. "She called me for help this morning and I drove out and we got it all straight."

"Got what all straight?" He fumbled with his pocket, brandishing his phone. "She's alone, in the middle of nowhere, for the whole damned weekend."

"Someone hacked her channel early this morning. Mr. Sherman, you have my word, she's fine." I caught his scotch-bleary gaze and held it. "However, I saw some things when I was out at your place this morning helping her, and I'm going to need to talk to your wife and her son. Do you have any idea how to reach them? Kelsey Marie tried, and they aren't answering their phones."

"They were going away, just the two of them." His eyes went to the plush navy carpet. "The note she left didn't say where."

His voice broke and tears streamed down his face.

Oh, shit. It wasn't a getaway. It was a gone for good.

I leaned forward, though it wasn't far enough to reach him. "I'm so sorry." I let five beats go by.

"I'll live."

"Does Kelsey Marie know? That she's not coming back?" The giant bag of Oxy didn't track as a thing most people would leave behind, but hell, for all I knew Miranda hadn't told her son they were leaving for good, either.

Sherman dropped his chin to his chest. "I'll find a way to get her back. Somehow. Always do."

I wondered if any of the other times she'd left had involved her leaving him a note and taking her son, but I wasn't sure how far I could push without irritating him, and I wanted him to keep talking.

"Mr. Sherman, how well do you know Dustin's friend Sam?"

He stuck out his bottom lip and wobbled one hand side to side. "I mean, as well as you know a kid's friends, I guess. He spends a lot of time in our house. Eats a lot of our food."

He raised his head from the arm of the chair and swiveled it to me. "You don't think he killed Samson?" His head was shaking before he got the words out of his mouth.

"Nah. Not a kid we've hosted in our home, taken care of, helped out."

I shook my head. I didn't know if I thought that, but I wasn't there to argue with him, I was there to get as much information as I possibly could. "No, no." I leaned my elbows on my knees. "It seemed like he made Kelsey Marie uncomfortable, and she said she thought he took something from Dustin's room."

I would've bet my gorgeous wedding gown he wouldn't remember enough details tomorrow to ask Kelsey Marie about that, and I needed a way to test the waters for what he knew about Dustin without asking outright.

"Prolly pills," Sherman slurred.

So that much, then.

I popped my eyes wide and pursed my lips like I didn't already know that. "I suppose that would've upset Kelsey Marie, especially if she thought it was medicine Dustin needed."

Sherman squinted at me. Let his head drop back to the arm of the chair. And sighed.

"He's been selling them."

"Opioids?"

"Yeah, them." Sherman waved his hand. "He didn't think I knew. Didn't think anybody knew, pompous little shit. The sheriff is about as worthless as you can get at detecting anything, and even he knew who the local dealer was. Cost me ten grand to get him to look the other goddamn way, and for what? So she could leave." He kicked the lamp on the table next to the chair and watched with a flat stare as it teetered and fell to the carpet. "Pfft. I been thinking for months now eventually somebody would up and croak. I watch the news, that shit kills people every day. Then I wouldn't be able to protect him. But now he's not my problem anymore. I guess that's what you call a silver lining, right there." He stuck one finger straight up in the air as he mumbled the last words, his heavy eyelids finally dragging shut. I waited a full minute for him to pop back up and keep going. A snuffly, obnoxious snore told me I had overstayed my welcome.

Punching the button to call the elevator, I checked my watch. Seven-fifteen. Graham and I could be back in Waco in time for a late dinner and sleep at my house, then head back to see Jim in the morning before he left for church. Provided the roads would cooperate with that. Glancing out the window, I saw flakes falling, and the Channel Two weather was almost never wrong about snow—their chief meteorologist had been there my whole life, and if he'd ever called one wrong, I couldn't remember it.

I stepped into the elevator and drummed my fingers on my thigh as it crept toward the lobby. On one hand, we'd come up here trying to find the rest of Kelsey Marie's family, and it didn't look like this trip would get us there. On the other, I'd picked up a truckload of new information and leads I didn't know to look for this morning, so I could call the day a win on that front. Especially if one of them led to the truth at the bottom of this mess.

If there's one thing I've learned over the course of my career, it's that there's no such thing as a family without secrets. I'd seen them rip apart folks in every socioeconomic and racial demographic. They're the lone constant in my world.

The trick is always figuring out which one somebody would be willing to kill to keep hidden—or to expose.

And it doesn't get easier with experience.

"So the local sheriff took a payoff to turn a blind eye to one kid dealing dope, but couldn't be bothered to help out when the other one's prize, internet-famous pet got slaughtered?" Graham hunched over the steering wheel, the wipers working overtime to keep flakes off the windshield. "Damn, have we ever had a blizzard in Texas? Because I'm going to have to pull over if this doesn't let up or we're going to crash the damned truck."

"Give me a good old-fashioned soupy hill country fog to drive through any day," I agreed, watching the deepening winter wonderland roll by the windows. "Though, it is so pretty. I love snow. Just not as much when I have things to do and Monday looming." I sighed. "I didn't find what I went there today to find."

"But maybe we found something better." Graham wasn't even blinking, his eyes were so stuck to the road. "I haven't heard great things about the sheriff out there. But if he's willing to take kickbacks to allow opioid sales in his town, what other shady shit might he be into?"

"You think the sheriff killed Kelsey Marie's pig?" It sounded a little absurd when I said it out loud, but I also didn't completely hate it. Which was probably a mark of how desperate I was for a lead.

"I'm not sure I'd go that far, but what her dad let slip to you makes me wonder if he knows who did."

"I would kiss you if you weren't concentrating so hard on the road," I said. "So just consider yourself properly rewarded."

"Oh, I can think of better rewards." He wriggled his eyebrows, gaze staying on the windshield, and I laughed.

"Yeah. Me too. So who do we know who could give us insight into the McCulloch County sheriff?"

"Besides Google?" Graham asked, finally putting the signal

on for the exit near my house and relaxing his shoulders a touch. "Archie."

"He does know everyone." I checked the clock. Not quite nine. "How has it only been fifteen hours since we left your place this morning?" I touched Archie's name in my favorites list.

He answered on the first ring. "I was just about to call you," he said. "Are you already out there?"

"Out...where?"

"McCulloch County," Archie said. "You said you were headed out there yesterday to investigate a murder and I just got a formal request from the sheriff for assistance with a homicide. Slow on the uptake, that guy. Wanted to make sure you were already on it so I could ignore it and go back to bed."

"The sheriff made an official request for help from the Rangers," I said. "Did it come with a case file? Because what I went to check on yesterday was a pig."

"I'm sorry?" To his credit, he tried hard not to laugh.

I sighed. "You can make fun of me later. Was this call about Samson the pig, or something else?"

Graham let the truck roll to a stop at a red light, the tires slipping a little even with the four-wheel drive.

"Hang on." Archie pulled the phone away from his head. I could hear him muttering about everyone losing their damned minds as he opened his email.

"Marta Milosevic, twenty-seven, found in her home at seven-twelve p.m. after a neighbor called in a welfare check." He paused. "This says today. What—"

"Archie, thanks, tell him the Rangers are happy to help, but I gotta go. I'll call you as soon as I can."

I touched the end button and scrolled through my recent calls for Kelsey Marie's number.

"I'm getting back on the goddamn freeway, aren't I?" Graham asked.

"No, from here take 84 west out of town. The maid. She was murdered tonight."

I touched Kelsey Marie's cell number and crossed my fingers.

Voicemail.

I tried again as Graham steered the truck back to an on-ramp for 35W.

Voicemail.

I opened my TikTok app and went to her account to see if she was live-streaming.

Nothing since morning.

Staring out the window into the first honest-to-God blinding snow I'd ever seen in my life, I dug my fingernails into my palms to keep from feeling quite so helpless.

18

"I told her dad she was safe," I said for probably the fiftieth time since I hung up with Archie.

"You didn't know at the time that she wasn't." Graham's words slid through clenched teeth as he gripped the steering wheel tighter when the truck slid on an icy patch of Highway 190. "Or have any idea that she might not be."

At that point it was only the occasional sign and our turtle-level speed that had me convinced we were still on the road and not in someone's dormant hay field. Everything was covered in a thick, fluffy blanket of sparkling white, the moon reflecting silvery rays off it until it was half as bright as a cloudy afternoon outside at nearly eleven o'clock.

I had called the sheriff to tell him we were on our way a few minutes after nine. Or rather, I left a message with a dispatcher —more helpful than the one we'd met yesterday—who promised to call his cell and ask him to both send someone to check on Kelsey Marie and call me back. I hadn't heard from him, and the dispatcher wasn't answering now, either.

"How can they just ignore a welfare check on a minor with

a murderer on the loose and a once-in-a-century snowstorm going on?" I asked.

"I'm sure he sent somebody," Graham said. "I'm also sure they're not used to working homicide, they're freaked out, and we shouldn't make any snap judgments until we get out there and see what's going on."

"We're stopping at Kelsey Marie's house first."

"You're supposed to be assisting with the investigation of the maid's death."

"It's on the way, and I need to know she's okay, Graham." My voice cracked a little at the end of that sentence. Kelsey Marie wasn't my sister, of course, but the dread sitting heavy in my chest was one I hadn't felt since I sat, bare feet tucked under my rose nightgown, in the back corner of my closet, hands pressed tight over my ears trying not to listen to Charity scream as she was dragged from her bed in the middle of the night two days before they found her mangled body on the shores of Lake Travis.

I couldn't have helped my sister. Years of therapy had taught me that it was okay to accept that all I would've done was get myself killed.

But I walked out of that house this morning and left Kelsey Marie there alone, confident she'd be safe. Two decades of turning myself into a bonafide badass, and I might as well have been stuck back in my closet floor, trying to muffle the screams.

I pinched my eyes shut and tried to shake the ghosts of Charity's last minutes in our house out of my head.

"That's it, right?" Graham asked.

I looked over to see him tip his head toward my side of the car. Cursing my wipers, which were dragging under the weight of the snow, I put my window down and stuck my head out. Squinting into the storm, I could just barely make out the outline for the hulking barn in the distance.

"This is it," I yelled. "I think the driveway is right here past this fence post."

Graham turned and the truck sank into the drift of soft snow, the tires spinning. He let the truck float to a stop and then eased his foot back onto the gas.

We didn't move.

"Shit," he said.

I was already sideways in the seat, shoving with my legs to open the door. "I'm sure they have a shovel, we can dig it out. After we find Kelsey Marie. Come on." I heard the shrill note of urgency in my voice and Graham did too, scrambling to the ground and shuffling through the snow to meet me at the front of the truck.

I'd never seen snow in Texas that your feet would actually sink into. We weren't halfway up the drive before I stopped being able to feel anything below my ankles, but I didn't give one damn. The wind and snow had nothing on the dread sending chills from my hairline to my boots.

The house was pitch-dark, and it wasn't yet midnight.

I tried to run for the house, cursing snow for the first time in my life. It was like being stuck in a bad dream, the ones where you need to run and can't move faster than a snail scrunching through cold molasses, no matter how hard your legs pump.

It seemed like an eternity before we made it to the porch. I banged on the door with both fists, shouting Kelsey Marie's name and stomping snow off my frozen legs at the same time.

Five seconds became twenty. I glanced at Graham and he yanked on the doorbell, banging with a fist at the same time.

"Why don't they have a dog?" Graham asked.

"Huh?"

"A dog. They're farm folks. I'm not sure I ever knew a 4H kid who didn't have a dog."

I shrugged. "Maybe someone is allergic." I pounded the door again. They had pigs and cows and horses. Why didn't they have a dog?

I sighed, sagging against the brick lining the entry alcove, shivering and shaking my hand, sore from pounding the door. "She's not in there."

"Or she's sleeping with headphones on. Or she took something to help her sleep." Graham's voice oozed calm. "No jumping to conclusions."

He was right. Facts, not supposition. Just move to the next step.

I backed up, looking around for a sign from an alarm company. I didn't see one, and couldn't recall spotting a keypad inside. While that would be weird for a house this big in the city, out here, it wasn't.

Miss Donnie had gotten me out here in the first place by telling me she'd taken to locking her doors. I'd told Kelsey Marie to lock up behind us this morning, but would she have kept the doors locked all day and night?

I tried the latch.

The door swung open.

Stooping, I examined the edges of the frame where the massive double doors came together. "It hasn't been forced."

I could lecture Kelsey Marie about leaving the door unlocked with a murderer on the loose after we found her.

"Kelsey Marie?" My voice was impressively calm and flat given the anxiety thrumming through me like a drum beat at a Metallica concert. "It's Faith McClellan. Where are you?" I clicked my cell phone flashlight on and shone it around the house. Graham kept slow stride beside me, the two of us falling right and left to check around every corner in a way that only partners who've worked together long enough to know each other's every move can.

This house was big, and the kind of dark that made it hard to see my hand in front of my face without the little LED light shining from the back of my phone. But I wasn't scared—not for me, anyway. Graham and I, we had each other's backs.

I moved into the hallway that led to Kelsey Marie's room. My Sig was strapped securely into the holster, which was the safer-for-someone-else side of a sticky decision—we now had a dead human on top of the dead pig, and an unresponsive resident of this house. There might be a bad actor in here; that's part of why I'd tried the door and come inside. But it was also dark, I was on edge, and while I didn't want to think I had the kind of jumpy trigger finger that might accidentally shoot Kelsey Marie, or Miranda or Dustin back to retrieve belongings (like maybe a giant bag of opioids), that didn't mean it was impossible. So my sidearm stayed where it was, my ears on high alert for anything that might be moving in the house.

The oiled bronze doorknob was cool in my hand as I turned it, sending up a silent prayer as her bedroom door swung wide. A softly glowing orb on the night table projected a blue and yellow Milky Way on her vaulted ceiling. Covers bunched and folded on the king-sized bed, but none of them appeared to be covering a Kelsey Marie-shaped lump. I stepped closer. "Kelsey Marie?"

She wasn't in the bed.

Graham pivoted to check the bathroom while I went to the closet.

I flipped the light switch inside the door and caught a sharp breath. Ruth McClellan's closet in the master suite at the Ranch was the biggest, most over-the-top closet I'd ever seen.

Until tonight.

Roughly the size of my living room and kitchen put together, Kelsey Marie's dressing room—because really, closet was too plain a word for what stretched out before me—held three horseshoe-shaped sections of white-painted wood cabinetry with rods and drawers at various intervals. A full section was nothing but shelves of jeans organized by wash that would make a Gap manager jealous; to the far right, a wall full of sundresses hung by color. Directly opposite the door, with its own lighting, stood a glass-fronted cabinet housing probably thirty grand worth of Louis Vuitton, surrounded on both sides by floor-to-ceiling shelves showcasing boots in every style and hide I could name.

Overhead, a cut crystal chandelier threw little rainbows on the shelving and clothes.

I moved through each section, moving clothing and opening cabinets. No Kelsey Marie.

"She's not here," Graham said from behind me. "But there're water droplets lining the walls in the shower, and the clothes she—" He let out a low whistle as he looked around the closet. "Damn. I'm kind of surprised she put them in the hamper instead of just throwing them in the trash."

I opened drawers, looking around and under neat stacks of panties and bras that rivaled any Victoria's Secret I'd ever shopped at.

Nothing.

I wasn't even sure what I was looking for, but after my conversation with Jeff in Fort Worth and the giant bag of pills we'd found in Dustin's room, I'd be foolish to think Kelsey Marie didn't have a few secrets of her own. Whatever they were, she didn't hide them in her underwear drawer like I had at her age.

Back in the bedroom, we turned on the lights. "No signs of struggle," Graham said.

I stepped to the bathroom. The mirrors weren't fogged, but Graham was right, the shower had a few water droplets clinging to the tile. "But where did she go, especially in this weather?"

"And why did she go?"

I touched one index finger to the end of my nose and pointed the other at Graham. "Million-dollar question."

We shut off the lights and walked back through the house. I checked every bedroom along the hallway, just in case.

"Faith." Graham walked out of the elder Shermans' closet, crooking a beckoning finger.

I followed him back inside to find a slightly smaller, mahogany-lined version of Kelsey Marie's closet. Except instead of a handbag showroom, Jeff Sherman had a gun safe.

A gun safe that was missing three large pieces of machinery.

Shit.

We crossed the hardwood floor, boot strikes echoing off the lined walls, and peered through the glass. Each gun rested in a custom molded foam casing.

"An AR, a 12-gauge, and a pistol." I pointed to the empty slots, glancing around. "Did you turn these lights on when you came in?"

"Nope."

I checked the lock embedded in the side panel of the gun cabinet. The key, small and silver, was still stuck in it, a mate dangling from a small copper ring.

"So did he leave the key in it, or did she know where to find it?"

"Or did someone take her out of the house using her dad's private arsenal?" Graham posited.

It wasn't an invalid scenario. Just one I didn't want to believe.

I paced a circle around the middle of the closet. "I don't think so. She locked that front door behind us this morning when we left, I heard it. It wasn't forced open. The whole house is dark, except this closet and the nightlight in her room. She showered not that long ago. Certainly not long enough to fall deeply asleep, get kidnapped, and have us get down the drive and into the house without seeing her and her attacker on our way in. She took these guns and went somewhere. The immediate question is where, but the more important one, like you said before, is why?"

19

As we moved toward the garage, I scoured every corner of my brain for a mention of what kind of car Kelsey Marie drove. I pulled open the door and pressed the rocker switch on the wall next to it.

A row of what must've been close to twenty fluorescents flickered to life, revealing two Ducati motorcycles with matching helmets resting on the leather seats in the nearest bay, a silver Cadillac SUV in the middle, and a small, sporty BMW convertible in the last bay. The three between the Cadillac and the BMW were empty.

I reached for my phone, but Graham already had his in his hand.

"Huh." He scrunched his brow. "Jeffrey with a J, Sherman conventional spelling, right?"

"Yep."

"I can't find anything registered in his name except a 1988 Datsun hatchback."

"There's got to be more than one Jeff Sherman in Texas."

Graham shrugged. "It's all that's here."

"Kelsey Marie can't own cars; she's not eighteen." I peered over his shoulder. "Maybe they're all leased?"

I walked to the empty bays in the center of the garage, pointing out slight moisture stains in the concrete where cars had been parked. "There are three missing vehicles. If we assume Dustin and Miranda are in his prized Mustang, and Jeff has his car in Fort Worth, then Kelsey Marie's is gone, too. She left. Though why she'd take off in this weather is still the looming question."

"I think given the sheriff's report about the maid, what we saw earlier, and the missing firearms, we can safely assume she's scared."

"I wish we knew what she was driving."

Graham pecked at his phone screen; he flipped it around. "A blue Porsche Cayenne SUV. It's here in a video from last fall. Plate number VRF-479." He clicked the buttons for a screenshot.

I snapped a photo of the other cars and the bikes with my phone, turning for the front of the house. "Excellent. Let's go see where she went."

The wind had died down considerably while we were in the house, snowflakes whispering softly onto already-high drifts as we stepped back onto the porch. Pulling my gloves on, I sucked in a deep breath and scanned the silvery, snow-lit yard.

A pair of evenly spaced depressions in the snow rounding the side of the house caught my eye.

"There. Tire tracks." I pulled my hood up and slogged back through the snow to the trails, just dips in the seven or so inches that must be on the ground by now.

"So she left when there was probably an inch or so on the

ground," I said. The further into the storm it was when Kelsey Marie left, the deeper the difference would've been between her tire marks and the snow that filled them in afterward.

Reaching under my coat, I unsnapped the safety strap on my holster. "That does put a damper on the mood. I'm guessing Kelsey Marie took off because she thought someone was coming after her. So we ought to watch ourselves getting out of here."

Whoever Kelsey Marie was afraid of might've come and gone before we got there, or might not be coming for her at all yet—but there was no way to know for sure.

Graham watched the left and I took the right, the snow crunching under our boots the only noise for what seemed like miles around. Nobody spoke again until we got within sight of the road.

Absent the blinding snow flying in our faces, we could see the highway and both shoulders for several miles thanks to the silvery reflection of the full moon's light shining back off the fresh snow.

A blue Porsche Cayenne was half-buried in a drift about a half-mile from the end of the Shermans' driveway. And my truck was gone.

Still couldn't run in the high drifts, but it didn't stop me from trying. Breathing hard and sweating by the time I got to Kelsey Marie's SUV, I brushed stray flakes from her windows and shone my wimpy cell phone flashlight into the passenger side, banging on the glass with the other fist. "Kelsey Marie?"

The car was empty.

Graham and I checked it back to front, using our hands to

scoop snow away from the doors so we could get the driver's side open.

Opening the console with frozen, gloved fingers, I found a bottle of water and a box of granola bars. "She prepared to get stuck somewhere when she left," I mused. "But she was too scared to stay in her own home."

"I don't see the guns."

We backed up, looking in all directions around the car for depressions that might've been footprints from around the same time the tire tracks came out of the Shermans' garage.

"We've walked around this vehicle too much, stirred up the snow." I pursed my lips, looking down the long, empty stretch of snowy highway that led toward town, then swiveling my head back toward the Sherman place.

"If I were seventeen, I wouldn't take the dark, open road full of large truck traffic when I'd just put my car into a snow-bank," I said, pointing to the barn. "She said she felt more at home in the barn than she did in the house, remember? Maybe that means she feels safer there, too."

Graham shrugged his broad shoulders and started back that way. "Certainly worth a shot."

"Would've been nice if I'd remembered that before we came all the way out here."

"You mean if you'd somehow known clairvoyantly that her car was out here, and not parked safely at a friend's house in town?" Graham shook his head. "You're too hard on yourself sometimes, you know it?"

"Who has the truck, Graham?" The thought chilled me.

"No conclusions there, either. Could have been towed by motorist assistance. When we get to the barn I'll make a call."

The only thing I knew right then was that I wanted to find Kelsey Marie. And no matter how hard I pushed with my legs, slogging back through the snow all the way to the barn felt like it would take a hundred years.

It actually took about twelve minutes. I shoved the door to the side and tumbled through, snow falling off my boots and darkening the floor.

Graham followed me in, both of us shining our flashlights around the cavernous space.

Nothing. Stomping my feet off, I crossed to the low fence around Samson's pen and checked behind the hay feeder. Still no Kelsey Marie.

There wasn't anywhere to hide in here. Except...

Slipping between the rails of the fences and standing, I crossed to the little closet that housed the fancy TV lighting controls.

She couldn't be gone. I couldn't have let that happen.

Pushing open the door, I met resistance. Oh, please God.

I poked my head through the crack and craned my neck around it before my shoulders dropped with the sigh that *whooshed* out of my chest.

Kelsey Marie was asleep on the floor, both arms curled around a well-loved, matted brown teddy bear.

I backed up and pulled the door shut, nodding to Graham. "She's in there on the floor asleep."

He crossed to meet me, the two of us leaning on opposite sides of the fence.

I checked my watch. "It's after midnight."

"The truck is still gone."

"We can't go to the murder scene without a vehicle. If there's even still anyone there."

He wriggled his eyebrows at me. "Can I interest you in some clean hay and maybe a blanket if I can scrounge one up?"

I laughed, leaning my head on his shoulder. "What in the blue hell have I gotten us into here, Hardin?"

One of his big hands brushed gently over my hair before he dropped a kiss on the crown of my head and extracted himself to look for makeshift bedding. "No idea, baby. But I'm always happy to be along for the ride."

Hand resting on the butt of my gun, I faced the door, which didn't even have a lock out here in the outskirts of real-live Mayberry. At least Kelsey Marie had us on the door in lieu of Barney Fife. I scanned the area around the pen until I spotted what I was looking for—extra fence rail piled in a corner. Picking a piece that looked roughly the right length, I dropped it in the sliding track behind the door and tested it.

I couldn't even fit through the opening it allowed if I turned to the side.

"Jackpot. I found a stash of camping gear back there." Graham jerked his head in the direction of the rear reaches of the building, his arms full of sleeping bags and bedding rolls.

"I made a way to lock this door." I tapped the wood rail with my boot before I met him halfway, helping him spread the rolls and bags on the floor.

He shut off the lights when everything was set and I was comfortably warm in my mountain camping rated outdoor bag. I felt him slide into the bag next to me, his arm going around me. Both sidearms lay on the ground near our heads.

"Something scared her, Graham. She tried to leave and when the car went off the road, she came out here instead of going back in the house."

"But she's fine. And we'll get to the bottom of it. But we'll do a better job by her if we get some sleep first, and you know it."

He was right. Kelsey Marie was safe for tonight. And tomorrow, we'd go see the sheriff about Marta.

My hand went to my gun before my eyes opened.

"Texas Rangers. Stop where you are." The words were thick and heavy with sleep as they rolled off my tongue, less forceful than usual, but they got the message across.

"Ranger McClellan?" Kelsey Marie's voice was just as sleepy, but smaller and much more confused.

I let go of my Sig and sat up, pushing my hair out of my face and flicking a quick glance at Graham, curled on his side and still snoring softly with every other breath. He could've slept through the siege of the Alamo, hand to God.

"Good morning."

"How did you get here?"

Rising and stretching my arms over my head, I holstered my sidearm and shivered, motioning for the door. "If there's coffee in the house, I have some things to talk with you about."

The sun was barely up, weak rays casting a silvery sheen on the snow piled high all around us, every last cloud gone from a wide indigo sky. The air was still reminiscent of stepping into a subzero, though. I hugged myself even with my coat on, tucking my head down and setting out for the house.

"Wow." Kelsey Marie stepped out of the barn and sank in the snow halfway to her knee. "I've never seen anything like this."

"It's got to be a record for these parts, that's for sure."

"But you know, climate change isn't a real thing." She rolled her eyes and waded toward her house.

Inside the back door, Kelsey Marie stopped in the mudroom and slipped bare feet out of worn barn boots. She waved a hand at me. "Don't worry about your boots. Let's get that coffee."

I stomped as much snow off as I could on the tile floor before I followed her to the kitchen, where she was attaching a milk container to the sleek, fancy espresso machine recessed into the far wall. "Latte, macchiato, flat white? I'll make whatever you want."

"A macchiato would be fantastic, thanks." I checked the clock on the microwave.

Five-forty. "Maybe with an extra shot?"

"Syrup?" she asked.

"No, thanks."

She stuck a cup under the spigot and pressed two buttons, and the machine roared to life. As it hummed and buzzed, I noted her puffy eyes and looked around the room. A mutilated iPhone with a shattered screen and a bent frame rested on the island.

"What happened to your phone?"

She handed me my drink when the machine quieted. "I threw it."

"Oh?"

"The sheriff called last night looking for my parents. I told him they weren't here and he told me to tell them he needed to speak to them because Marta is dead." She fluttered her lashes over tears shining in her eyes, waving one hand in front of her face. "Like, I just can't take anything else right now. I didn't even wait for him to finish talking. The screen shattered and it wouldn't come back on. So I left it there. I just wanted to sleep, you know? I figured maybe with you having my computer and my phone being broken, I'd get some peace."

"You don't know what happened to her?"

Kelsey Marie shook her head, tears spilling over. "All that matters is that she's gone. And I feel like I've done something to offend God at this point."

"I know the feeling. But I don't believe you did, for the record."

Her small shoulders hitched. "Thanks. I think."

I took a sip of my drink. "Holy coffee gods, this is amazing." We needed a lighter subject. She was verging on shutting down on me, and I needed her to keep talking.

"My mom brought the beans back from Jamaica last month," she said. "They're like, the best in the world or something."

I could go with that. Focused on the coffee, I sipped half of the steaming drink before I spoke again. "So—what happened last night?"

She was busy sipping her own latte by then. "What do you mean?"

"I'm wondering how you ended up sleeping in a closet in the barn in the middle of the closest thing we've ever had to a blizzard around here."

She put her cup on the counter. Toyed with it, using the handle to pivot it back and forth. "I was all alone. My mom and Dusty, well, I kind of think from the way Dad has been acting that maybe they're not even coming back. But he won't say and I'm afraid to ask. And he's gone. And then the sheriff called and said Marta was dead, and I just felt like, more utterly alone than I ever have in my whole life. And so I got in my car and tried to leave, but it slid right off the road." Her teeth closed over her lower lip. "I was scared. I figured nobody would look for me out there."

I laid a hand on her arm. "It's going to be okay." I fished my own phone out of my pocket. "Do you have a charger I can borrow?"

"Sure."

"Where were you going?" I asked. "When you tried to leave last night?"

A sad half smile twisted her lips. "I don't even know. Sad, right? Millions of people who adore me on the internet, and when I was scared for my life I couldn't think of anyone to run to. So, just anywhere but here. Kind of messed up, isn't it?"

"It may well have been good instinct."

While my phone charged on the counter, I finished my latte and set the cup down just as a knock sounded from the back door. Kelsey Marie started for it and I grabbed her shoulder, shaking my head and putting my hand on my weapon. I knew it was probably Graham. I also knew I wasn't taking chances.

I hurried through the mudroom to the door and knocked twice on my side of it.

"It's me, baby." Graham's melted-honey baritone came through the wood.

I pulled the door open and waved him inside, locking it when I shut it.

"There's a Starbucks on the kitchen counter in there." I pointed.

Graham ambled through the door to investigate. "Morning, Kelsey Marie," he said. "Are you okay?"

I perched on a barstool. She nodded, putting her mug down and pulling a clean one from the cabinet. "It hasn't been the best week ever. But I'm hanging in there. How do you like your coffee?"

Graham eyed the sleek espresso maker. "Can you do a latte?"

She pointed to the syrup. "Caramel okay?"

"That's great," he said.

She pumped syrup into his cup and poked at buttons, and Graham took the stool next to mine.

My phone buzzed on the counter. "McClellan," I answered.

"Sheriff Milton P. Barnes here, Miss McClellan." His voice was sandpaper on gravel, ravaged by years of booze if his reputation was to be believed, and definitely some smokes thrown in for good measure.

Jeff Sherman's words about the sheriff's willingness to accept bribery floated through my head. "Just the man I was about to be looking for. How can I help you this morning, sir?" I asked.

"Like I told Baxter last night, I'm at a damned loss for what to do here. I've never seen so much blood in my life, and I grew up three lots down from the slaughterhouse. My men, our county...we're not equipped for this. I know our roads aren't passable right now, but I'd sure like to see you at the crime scene when they are."

"I actually think someone with McCulloch County might've towed my truck last night. It was out near the highway in front of the Sherman place, stuck in the snow. Figured motorist assistance or rescue picked it up."

"You've gotta be fucking kidding me," he said. A few more choice words came out under his breath. "We don't have a motorist assistance unit."

My eyes widened. "Any idea where my truck got off to, then?"

"Oh, I'm sure it was Cleetus. Jackass riles folks up every weekend towing vehicles parked at the bar after closing, and at the city park after dark. Takes 'em to his shop and charges a seventy-five-dollar ransom to get them back."

I blinked. "Um. Can't you put a stop to that?"

"He's the county judge's baby brother. He does as he pleases."

Huh. And he was out here sometime right after we arrived last night.

"I'll take care of it. Thank you, Sheriff."

"So there's really no way for you to get to the murder scene right now?"

I cupped one hand over the receiver. "Kelsey Marie, honey, do you have a vehicle in the garage with four-wheel drive?"

"My mom's Escalade has that. You have to push a button to turn it on."

"I always wanted to drive a bus when I was a kid." Graham stood. "Keys?"

"Sheriff, send me the address, we'll be there as soon as we can."

"WE? No, you can't bring a minor into this. I was serious when I said I've never seen anything like it."

While I was quite sure Kelsey Marie watching her beloved pet hacked to death on replay yesterday morning beat anything Sheriff Milton had ever seen, I agreed with him that she couldn't go. "Of course not. I'm bringing my..." I let the words trail off when fear flared in Kelsey Marie's eyes and she reached for Graham's arm. He patted her hand and nodded to me.

"Just me, then," I said to the sheriff. "I'm leaving the Sherman place now."

"Thank you, little lady," he said.

I let it go and hung up. I learned my fourth day as a new

deputy that if I barked back at every old geezer who referenced my gender in addressing me, I'd never get anything else
done. I picked my battles, and they usually involved words
that started with a B or a C. Mostly because this kind of bullshit usually dispensed with itself after I'd been on a crime
scene for an hour or so.

"Where are the guns?" I asked Kelsey Marie when I hung
up the phone.

Her brow furrowed. "Uh. What?"

"We came in last night when we found you'd left the door
open, and we saw the empty storage racks in your dad's gun
cabinet," I said. "Where'd you take them?"

"I don't touch those damned death machines," she said. "I
wouldn't know how to shoot one if my life depended on it.
And I didn't leave the fucking door open. Are you kidding?"
She jingled her keys, a frantic, scared gaze bouncing around
the open living area. "I always lock it, and I double-checked
last night."

My stomach turned a slow somersault as my gaze followed
hers.

"I got things here," Graham said. "We'll be fine. You stay in
touch and watch yourself."

I nodded. He knew he didn't have to say it. But it was one
of the few superstitions we shared as a team. The words when
one of us headed to work functioned like verbal talismans,
warding off the very danger we warned each other against.

"Always." I held his gaze. "Back at you."

I took the Escalade keys from the pegboard on the wall
next to the garage door, venturing out with my hand on my
gun again as Graham started moving room to room through
the house with Kelsey Marie on his heels.

This was stupid. While I didn't think our killer had the
patience or cunning to lie in wait inside the house, I couldn't

make out geckos from rattlers in what the actual hell was happening here.

"Y'all just come with me," I called. "Kelsey Marie, throw some stuff in a bag."

Graham stood in the door to her room while she packed. He could be her bodyguard while I went into Barnes's crime scene. And this way I could work said scene without a chunk of my headspace worrying that our mad slasher was waiting in this massive house to carve up Kelsey Marie and my fiancé while I was looking at blood stains with Sheriff Bourbon.

We were halfway to town, the car handling the roads well enough to keep us moving forward and finally starting to heat up when Graham slammed his fist down on the leather console, his phone in his other hand.

I couldn't look, but I knew Graham well enough to hazard a guess that he'd checked Kelsey Marie's YouTube page.

I swallowed hard and breathed deep to keep my churning stomach from rejecting the coffee, eyes on the road and hands on the wheel.

We could watch the video of Marta's murder with Barnes when we got to the scene.

21

We didn't pass a single other vehicle until we turned onto Marta's street, where a pair of sheriff's patrol cars and an ambulance nearly had the road blocked, yellow tape strung haphazardly between two low, scrubby Texas trees in the yard warning neighbors not to gawk from too nearby.

And gawk they did. The modest residential lane was lined with folks in multiple layers of pants and jackets, but nobody was playing in the mounds of snow—they were all standing in clumps, whispering among themselves.

I parked nose-to-nose with a cruiser and checked the mirror. Kelsey Marie was sleeping.

I waved Graham out of the car and met him at the hood.

"You want to chat up the nosy neighbors while I pop inside?" I nodded to a group about ten feet away.

"I'll keep an eye on the car. If she wakes up, I'll keep her out here." He let out a shuddering breath. "Probably good her phone is busted."

"You reported the video?"

"There was a box to check if you're in law enforcement, so

I used my credentials. But like a million people already saw it."

"Hopefully they'll take it down before too many more can." I squeezed his hand and rounded for the door.

The house itself wasn't much different than mine, small and tidy with a pair of shutter-flanked windows framing a red front door. It opened as I put my foot on the lowest step of the little brick stoop.

"Miss McClellan?" I'd have pegged Sheriff Barnes's three packs and ten scotches a day growl even without the nameplate on his uniform.

"Ranger." I met his eyes with a friendly smile that softened the edge in my tone. "Ranger McClellan."

"No disrespect, ma'am." He tipped his ten-gallon Stetson and backed up, raising an arm to welcome me into Marta's home.

I glanced around. "Do we have gear?"

"I'm sorry?"

"Booties, hair nets, gloves?" You know, stuff to keep our people from contaminating the crime scene? I didn't say that last part out loud. This man had been the sheriff here for nearly two decades and he'd only ever seen one other murder. And that one was outside, with half a dozen witnesses.

His wide forehead furrowed under his hat, drawing unruly white brows to a point over his nose. "Nope."

Since he wasn't the only person who'd been inside, the scene was contaminated anyway. I sighed and stepped into the house, my nose stinging from the coppery tang of blood, though blessedly missing the sickly-sweet stench of decomposing human. She hadn't been dead long enough for that, thank God.

A young deputy, snow dripping off his caked boots, followed a tall woman in a quilted jacket with a Texas Justice of the Peace patch on one arm around the living room, taking notes as the JP pointed things out. And picked things up. With her bare hands.

I blew out a slow breath. Odds weren't in my favor that forensics were getting us across the finish line of this one, anyway. So what could I control here?

Get the facts.

I stepped closer to the body.

Her stomach had been slit open, and her intestines were... well. What was left of them was in her lap. I swallowed hard and stepped backward.

"Shit turns your stomach, don't it?" Sheriff Barnes said. "I mean, what kind of sicko can gut a human being like a deer?"

"In this case, the same kind who wants to preserve the experience on video."

I pulled out my phone and opened my YouTube app. Touched Kelsey Marie's channel in the list. And gritted my teeth. "Hoping the angle of the sun through those windows will help us with time of death." And narrow the suspect pool.

This one started with a setup shot of the outside of the house, from the back. It was dark, so no help with a time estimate. Dammit.

My eyes were glued to the shaky camera work, unblinking. I swallowed hard when the killer just turned the handle and walked right into the house. There are definitely drawbacks to feeling like bad things don't happen in your community. Because in still relatively isolated places like this, they don't happen until they do, and offenders take full advantage of small-town, feel-safe habits like leaving doors unlocked and being kind to strangers.

On my screen, the killer moved through the kitchen, plucked a stainless steel-handled butcher knife from Marta's block, and crept toward the doorway to my right. Light flickered from the other side on my screen, the TV probably on. A deputy and the JP wandered over to see what Sheriff Barnes and I were staring so intently at when there was a dead woman five feet from us.

"Holy shit, is that—" The deputy cut his question off when Barnes shushed him.

I just nodded.

Placing the camera carefully on the floor at the same up angle we'd seen on the video of Samson, the killer moved in front of it, a long, dark hooded robe cloaking even the most basic understanding of clothing, size, or gender.

Behind them, we could see Marta, her head lolling back and jaw slack, napping in the chair in front of the TV.

"My God, what are we about to watch?" That was the JP—they stand in for the medical examiner when there's not one available—a tall, buxom woman with short, poofy red hair that reminded me of the way Ruth McClellan wore her blonde hair when my father was in the governor's mansion.

"Hopefully something helpful."

The robed figure approached slowly, tossing the knife back and forth between black-gloved hands.

Stopping on the left hand, the right one going to the side of their face, the killer raised the blade. Pointing it first at Marta's heart, then her throat, the killer moved it back and forth in a strangely familiar rhythm.

"My God, is he playing eeny meeny miny moe?" the deputy asked.

"Nice observation."

The knife stopped over the heart. Pulled up. Plunged down. The killer held it for three seconds and then ripped down and up, and blood sprayed and spurted three different directions. In a flash of bright steel, Marta's throat was slashed from one ear to the other. Her heart tried to beat twice more, each sending a successively weaker fountain of blood into the air and onto the walls.

She never moved.

The killer wasn't done, though. Moving to her hip, they stabbed into her belly and ripped the knife across, letting her intestines spill into her lap.

The knife hit the carpet, the killer grabbing handfuls of Marta's insides and smearing them across her pale green and blue walls.

Barnes turned and scrambled for the door, retching quietly into the snow-covered bushes next to the steps.

I flicked my eyes toward the chair where the body still lay. I couldn't see her lap over the arm of the recliner.

"That's what I picked out of the carpet," the deputy said, looking a little green himself when I glanced at him.

"You picked it up?"

"I didn't know what it was. I thought it might have a clue. It's in a plastic baggie in my cruiser."

My attention was riveted on the screen. All visible walls coated in blood and gore, with a thin trickle of blood trailing from Marta's open mouth. The killer picked up the knife and moved toward the camera. I pulled the phone closer, searching for an eye color or a shadow. Some small detail that would break this case.

My screen went black.

I clicked the back button.

Page not found.

I touched the logo to go to YouTube's main page and searched for *High on the Hog*.

No results.

They killed the video and suspended Kelsey Marie's page. She was going to freak right the hell out.

But the fallout would be a million times worse if she saw

that video. Hell, I was more than a little freaked out myself. Not that I could show it.

Stepping back to the side of the chair, I looked down at Marta's lifeless, mutilated body. I had spoken with her less than seventy-two hours before. She'd seemed to want to protect Kelsey Marie and her family.

"I'm so sorry," I whispered to her.

"For what?" the deputy asked.

I ignored him. I know it's a little weird that I talk to dead people. But keeping them human and vital in my brain is how I make myself push through actual horror movie scenes and chase the monsters other people run away from.

To keep myself from panicking at the thought of what havoc this killer might wreak before we figured this mess out, I focused on what little I currently had control over.

Until this was done, Kelsey Marie would be lucky if I let her pee alone.

I turned to Barnes, now pale and sweaty but back in the room. "Has someone called her family?"

"None we can find," Barnes said. "Not on this side of the ocean at least."

The sour twist to his lips as he said that spiked my temper.

"And God forbid you climb out of your scotch long enough to do some real police work and locate next of kin when they don't live up the road."

He hooked both thumbs in his belt loops and rocked up on his toes, staring daggers way sharper than the knife that had done this to poor Marta. The deputy tried so hard not to snicker that he snorted, the rough sound echoing off the gory walls.

"You got something to say to me, little lady?" Barnes growled.

I didn't blink. "I believe I just did, Sheriff."

His face went a shade of reddish brown just shy of the blood-smeared walls. "I don't need help from a broad. Go on back wherever you came from and tell Baxter to send me a real cop."

"One hundred and twenty-seven murder cases cleared. The only perfect homicide record in the state." My voice had enough ice in it to freeze the Gulf of Mexico, channeling a perfect impression of Ruth McClellan. "How many murderers have you locked up?"

Barnes tried to make his lips work, but no words came out. His arm came up, one pudgy finger pointing at the door.

I shook my head slowly. "I try to be polite, Sheriff, because manners are an important cornerstone of our society and this job." I took a half-step closer to him. "But the minute I set foot in this house, this became my crime scene. This broad outranks you. Go on back to your office and find me a family member to inform. She told me Friday her mother is in a refugee camp in the Netherlands."

"How dare you, you little bi—" Spit flew off his lips with the words, and I stepped to one side.

"Milt." The coroner stepped in before he got the insult out, taking the sheriff by the arm. "Let's go."

Barnes rounded on her, a fresh round of swearing apparently ready on his lips, but something in the woman's flat, quiet expression stopped him. He sucked in a shuddering breath and shook his head, his color returning to something healthier. "She can't just...I'm not going to let..." he sputtered.

"She just did, Sheriff. Let's go before you get yourself in trouble."

My brow furrowed but Barnes turned and followed her out.

"Nice to meet you, ma'am." The deputy started for the door. "Sorry about him."

"Where do you think you're going, Officer?" I asked.

He paused. "I. Well, I thought I was going with Sheriff Barnes, ma'am. I do work for him."

"Not today you don't." I pointed at the walls and a camera lying on the coffee table. "That's your camera?"

"Yes, ma'am."

"Get images—good ones—of every bit of this room. And check the carpet carefully."

"For?"

"Bring me anything you find."

"Yes, ma'am."

"The JP, she'll be back for Marta, right?" I asked.

"Oh yeah. She's the sheriff's sister. Keeps him in line as much as anyone can."

Glad someone did, I went to the kitchen, turning the overhead light on and scanning the floor for marks in the sallow, jaundiced glow.

Nothing. I checked the door. Clean entry, and I'd seen the gloves in the video, so I didn't need to bother checking for prints.

I moved to the hulking vintage gold fridge that was probably older than I was.

Neat shelves organized by food group, with sodas and juices on the top shelf, milk, cream, four kinds of cheese, and butter on the second, colorful veggies on the next down, and half a smoked brisket wrapped in plastic wrap next to a package of deli turkey on the bottom. I peered into the solid white door bins. Nothing out of the ordinary. Just four different kinds of pickles.

I swung the door shut and opened the freezer, stumbling backward so fast I nearly sprawled across the floor on my ass, a scream sticking in my throat and coming out as a whimper.

Moving to the side, I planted a boot on the door and kicked it shut with enough force to rattle the whole fridge before I dug my phone out of my pocket and rang Graham's.

"I can't get anything out of these people but side eye," he said by way of hello. "The minute I walk over, everyone shuts right up. My charm isn't even working on the ladies."

"I'm pretty sure Samson's head is in her freezer," I countered.

"Oh, shit."

"Yep. That about covers it."

22

————

"So the thing with the pig from YouTube is somehow connected to this?"

The deputy's name was Craig Foster. He didn't bat an eyelash as he watched Graham carry what we assumed to be Samson's head out to Miranda Sherman's Escalade in a shiny new Igloo cooler that still had the price tag hanging from the handle. Kelsey Marie said her dad bought it to bring steaks home from a butcher he liked in the stockyards, but forgot to put it in his pickup when he left for Fort Worth. Jim would be able to tell us with some certainty if the wounds to the animal's neck made it a likely match.

"I mean, this family's prized pet was butchered and then their maid is similarly murdered not even three days later? This sure seems like a safe assumption."

"But why the pig and the housekeeper, though?" His hand went to his scruffy goatee, his brow furrowing with deep thought.

"Excellent question," I said. "The why is usually the quickest route to the who in a murder investigation."

"Have you really solved every one you've ever worked?"

"I have."

"Wow." His eyes lit up. "I've always wanted to be a homicide investigator."

"You have good instincts for it," I said.

"I do?"

"The first hurdle is being able to walk the scene without getting sick, and you cleared that one."

"I guess growing up in the sticks gives a person that advantage. One of my earliest memories is of watching my granny wring a chicken's neck. Gross doesn't bother me."

"If I might offer some advice: y'all get maybe one homicide every decade around these parts. If you want to catch murderers, you have to work where they do."

"I can't. It's my dad." Craig shuffled one boot along the outlines of the flower pattern on Marta's linoleum. "He worked the meat packing plant for a lot of years, but he got sick right after I got out of high school, and Sheriff Barnes, he knew my granddad for a long time, back to their ball-playing days, and so he hired me as a favor to my dad. Said I could support my pop and get some experience instead of a fancy college criminal justice degree."

"I'm sorry about your dad. How is he?"

"He has about nine months, according to the doc." Craig's voice caught.

"How old are you, Craig?"

"Twenty. On February second."

Nineteen. This was a nineteen-year-old kid watching calmly and asking me questions while a woman lay decomposing in a blood-smeared room on the other side of the wall.

I pulled a card from my hip pocket. "My cell is on the back. Call me if there's ever anything I can do to help you out. I was a Travis County deputy back in the day, and my fiancé is a commander there."

His jaw loosened, but didn't fall. "I—wow—thank you. Thank you so much."

Graham appeared in the doorway, nodding to me. "Snow is starting to melt as it warms up. You good here?"

"Almost. I'd like to have a look around the rest of the house and then I'll be out and we'll call Jim about the pig's head?"

"On Sunday. He's going to love us."

"Lucky for us, he already does." I turned to Craig. "Deputy Foster, TCSO Commander Graham Hardin."

Craig stuck out one hand and pumped Graham's like fresh Texas crude was going to spew out of his armpit. "Good to meet you, commander sir," he said.

Graham shot me a glance and returned the sentiment.

"Craig is interested in a career in homicide," I said. "He'll be twenty next month and he's been quite helpful here this morning."

Graham raised his eyebrows. "Outstanding. Let us know if we can do anything for you, Deputy."

"Yes sir, thank you, sir."

Graham flashed a grin. "This isn't the Marine Corps, kid. I appreciate the sentiment, but I'm just Hardin."

Craig folded his hands behind his back as Graham turned for the door.

"I'm headed back to Kelsey Marie. I locked the car, but I'm not sure I trust her to stay put for long."

"I'm more sure by the minute there's someone in this town who can't be trusted to be anywhere near that girl," I said, waving a hand toward the front room. "You watched the whole video in the car?"

"I did. I wish I hadn't. And I'm disturbed by the number of views it had when I looked at it."

"They yanked it already. And I don't want to have to tell her that her channel was suspended, but it's gone."

"I suppose this one goes beyond a warning."

"Her guy will straighten it out for her tomorrow," I said. "And for now, she doesn't have her phone. But we shouldn't leave her alone too long."

"On it." Graham turned to the door.

I waved for Craig to follow me to the hallway off the kitchen, where doors led to the bedrooms and bathrooms. "Most murders are committed by someone who knew the victim," I explained. "So the first thing you want to do is learn as much about the deceased as you possibly can."

"Snoop through their stuff," he said, nodding.

"Investigate their murder sounds better." I laughed, opening the door at the end of the hall and stepping into Marta's modest, tidy bedroom. "But yeah, basically. Don't overlook anything, but pay close attention to photos, books, mail, and especially..." I crossed the room. "...nightstand drawers. Most folks keep things in there that are special in some way— sometimes it's something they want to hide, sometimes it's mementos, sometimes it's medication, and sometimes you find stuff they'd probably rather nobody see. But this is always a decent place to start."

I pulled Marta's nightstand open and crouched, rifling carefully through the contents. A tube of IcyHot, a stack of greeting cards, four business cards, and a thumb drive memory stick.

"Why would you put a thumb drive in your nightstand?" Craig asked.

I shrugged and looked around for a laptop, but didn't see one. "You have gloves or evidence bags?" I wasn't too worried about prints because the murderer had gloves on in the video, but it never hurts to run them.

Craig patted his puffy McCulloch County Sheriff's Office

coat and reached into the inside pocket, producing a clear baggie with an orange "EVIDENCE" seal on the front.

"Thanks." I pulled it inside out and grabbed the thumb drive, sealing the bag before I tucked it in my pocket.

Pulling the business cards out, I flipped through them. Doctor, insurance agent, car salesman...private investigator?

I snapped photos with my phone and replaced all but the last one, sticking it in my pocket and moving to the greeting cards.

Five signed *Mama*, but no envelope or return address. "Her mother sent this in September." I waved the most recent card at Craig. "Doesn't say where to find her, but she's alive somewhere and deserves to know her child is dead."

"Wow, you really can learn a lot about a person from digging through their nightstand."

"Paying attention to the small things often ends up being the way to break a case wide open," I said. "Even stuff that doesn't look like it matters at the time. I've lost count of how many times I've come back to something I didn't understand when I first saw it, only to figure out later it was the key to the whole damned thing."

"I feel like I ought to be taking notes." He pulled out a pad and pen and scribbled for a minute. "Thanks. Really."

I closed the drawer and moved to the dresser.

Neat rolls of socks and plain white underwear alongside a worn, brown leather-covered Bible and a rosary in the top drawer, T-shirts in the second one, pajamas in the third. Nothing underneath or out of place.

The small reach-in closet was equally organized, with skirts, slacks, and jeans in the right-hand half organized by color, and blouses and sweaters the same on the left. A canvas over-the-door rack held four pairs of shoes: white sneakers, black sneakers, taupe pumps, and blue Crocs. I checked the other compartments in the shoe organizer and found five scarves, two more rosaries, eighty-seven cents, and a key.

I added the key to the evidence bag and moved the clothes side to side. No objects, hidden panels, or loose floorboards.

"She's really organized," Craig said.

"I suppose when your job is to keep other people's houses clean, a natural tendency to be tidy is helpful."

"Any idea what the key is for?"

"Nope. But sometimes when they're in a weird place like that, they're worth looking closer at."

I left the bedroom and moved to the bathroom. It was tiny, with a sink, toilet, and tub all in a row, a set of recessed shelves built into the wall that held linens, and an old-fashioned gas heater in the wall opposite the toilet.

I peeked in the drawers and the lone cabinet and rifled through her towels.

"Just a bathroom," I said. "But all told, this wasn't a waste of our time."

"Pardon the possibly stupid question, but why do all this investigation if she was killed because of something to do with the family she worked for?" Craig asked. "I mean, if you find out what happened to the pig, you know what happened here, too, right?"

"The scene investigation is often about getting to the why." I stepped around the JP without comment, relieved to see that she was back and Marta's remains had been placed in a body bag while we searched. "There's definitely a reason someone killed the Shermans' pet and then their housekeeper. I just don't know what it is yet."

He scribbled more notes. "Yes, ma'am. Thank you."

"Speaking of dead animals, I heard another pig was killed around these parts a few days before Samson," I said. "Would you know anything about that?"

"Oh sure." The words tripped on an eager wave, his tone saying he was excited to have something to share. "Pretty messy scene out there, from what we heard. Owners were upset when they called it in—said someone got him with a sledgehammer." He paused, leaning closer. "Right between his eyes." He stood back and shrugged. "No leads so far, but I can let you know if we turn something up."

"And nobody heard anything? Pigs are loud, especially in chorus. The other animals didn't kick up a fuss?"

"No, ma'am, that's a cattle farm. Clive was the only pig they owned," Craig said.

Adding that to my notes, I opened the front door and held it for Foster before I stepped outside and straight into a middle-aged man in a thick parka.

"Miss McClellan, Pete Zampras, the *Brady Star-Eagle*." He stuck out one hand, using the other to pull a pen from the unruly tuft of silvery-black hair jailbreaking out between his glasses and his ear. "Sheriff Barnes said you were the point person on this investigation. Seemed none too happy about it."

A reporter. I took a deep breath. So the sheriff wasn't going to play nicely, then. Fine.

"Nice to meet you, Mr. Zampras," I said. "I'm sorry to say you came all the way over here in the cold for no reason. The Rangers don't comment on open investigations."

"No, you only comment on open investigations when it's helpful to you," he said, twisting his lips to one side. "But I understand that. The thing is, I believe it would indeed be beneficial for you to work with me. I didn't come all the way over here—I walked. Because I live right there." He pointed to a green house with white trim next door.

He was suddenly a lot more interesting.

"You see anything the past couple of days?"

He waved a hand at the closed blinds in his Marta-facing windows. "I didn't. But I knew her. I'm aware of your personal history with the press, but I don't come with a TV camera. I've run the paper in this one-horse town since my father died and left it to me, and his father before him. I don't give two small shits about a scoop, because I am the news around here. But I care about this fucker who chopped up my neighbor being sent away for the rest of his days. I'm going to report the story to the extent that I need to so I can scare folks into locking their goddamn doors and keeping themselves safe. You're not from here, and Milt doesn't like you. If you're going to find out what happened to Marta, you're going to need folks to talk to you. And I know everyone."

He didn't move aside. "I can help."

I bit the inside of my cheek.

Work with a reporter.

The universe has a goddamned twisted sense of humor on occasion, but at least it wasn't Skye Morrow this time.

I stuck out my hand.

"Nice to meet you, Mr. Zampras. I'm Faith."

23

Courthouse Square in Brady holds, in addition to the court-house, a law office, the newspaper building, a saloon, a barbershop, a handful of precious little shops, and a cafe.

"Kelsey Marie swears by the biscuits and gravy," Graham said as we tucked into a table at the latter with Pete, me sitting opposite the two men so I could see Kelsey Marie, who had hopped onto a counter stool and begun chatting with the waitress.

"Edith's biscuits are the stuff of local legend—guarantee they're the butteriest, flakiest you've ever had anywhere." Pete put a hand up and signaled to the waitress. She patted the counter and squeezed Kelsey Marie's hand before rushing over with a pad in her hand.

"Morning, Pete." She didn't look at us.

"Maggie," he said. "This here's Ray and Delores McClellan's granddaughter and her partner, Commander Hardin."

Maggie turned an arched eyebrow on us. "That a fact? Dee McClellan was one of my Granny May's dearest friends."

"She was a fine lady who loved this community," I said.

"What brings you out here? Can't say anybody was shocked your daddy sold their place. Piece of work, that one."

"He is that."

"Faith here is a Texas Ranger. Helped send her old man away, in fact."

The raised eyebrow settled back next to its mate, her lips pursing with a grunt.

"I'm on special assignment. Currently looking out for Kelsey Marie"—I pointed to her seat at the counter—"and investigating a murder."

I laid a bit of emphasis on the last word. When people are scared, they're more likely to talk.

Maggie lowered her pen. "Damned fine woman, Marta. You wouldn't find a kinder soul or a harder worker anywhere."

Pete snapped his fingers. "She worked here before she went out to the Sherman place, didn't she?"

"For ten years. You could've eaten off this floor any hour of the day, and the stroganoff we had on the menu then was our most popular seller after Edith's biscuits."

I made a mental note of that. "When did she leave?"

"Three years ago this May," Maggie said. "We had some pissed off customers for a while. Lucky for Edith, we got a couple kids who do all right mopping and cleaning, and folks have gotten over missing the stroganoff."

"I'm sure this will come as a shock to the whole town."

"People are downright scared," Maggie said. "And it takes a lot to scare country folks. Thanks for watching over Kelsey Marie," she added. "She's had a rough year, that poor girl."

I blinked. "Like before last week?"

Maggie's eyes hooded, sliding to Kelsey Marie and then back to me. "What can I bring y'all?"

So my granny's memory would get me past the cold shoulder, but I still didn't belong. Check.

"Three rounds of biscuits and gravy with bacon, and some coffee?" Pete asked.

"Give my bacon to him, please." I pointed to Graham.

"Happy to take that one for the team." He grinned.

"Be right back with your coffee." She disappeared and returned with three mugs and a carafe.

I poured a cup and handed it to Pete. "Thanks for that."

"She'll tell half the town you had kin who were part of the community before sundown," he said. "But it's only going to get you so far."

"So I saw. Do you know what she was talking about? When she said Kelsey Marie's had a rough year? From what I've heard, aside from losing her pet, the kid has a pretty charmed life."

He turned to look at her before he seemed to think better of it. "Probably best not to talk about that here."

It's almost always about secrets. And I tend to underestimate how many of those a teenage girl can have.

I sipped my coffee. "So tell me what you know about the sheriff."

Pete fiddled with a fork. "He's not a bad guy. He does have some bad habits."

"I've heard about his drinking. More than that?"

"Maybe you might want to check the books at the horse track."

That's why he needed Jeff Sherman's money. He was a drinker and a gambler. Noted.

"But he's been reelected four times," I said.

"He's one of us. The job suits him—he comes and goes as he pleases, he sleeps off the booze on his office couch, and he doesn't have to do much but write tickets and referee things like water disputes. Or at least he hasn't until now. He's loud and a tad belligerent, which makes him handy for breaking up brawls at the saloon. He's got his faults, but he's never been bad at the job."

"Until now."

"Until now," Pete agreed.

"Is there any chance he knows something or has evidence that I'll need?"

Pete sipped his coffee. "You pissed him off and you're wondering if you're going to regret that."

"He was an asshole, but yes, I'm wondering if I'm going to need him to figure this out."

"Nah," Pete said. "I work around him on the regular, you can too."

"Work around him for what sort of things?"

"We had a deputy for a long while, got fired a couple years back. Milt said he was driving his cruiser while intoxicated, which is something Milt himself has been known to do."

"So why'd he get fired then?"

"Milt's the kind of guy whose bad habits have a tendency to pile on one another. Gambling led to drinking and the combination of the two led to a constant shortage of money. The job offers creative ways to make it up."

"Kickbacks," I said.

"Exactly. So the deputy found out the sheriff was taking payoffs, and the sheriff got rid of him."

"And you put this in the paper?"

Pete tipped his head to one side. "I didn't say that. I said I worked around Milt to find out what really happened."

"So why not run it, then?" Reporters live to break stories, regardless of who their story is going to hurt. At least, every one I've ever known does.

"This is a small town. My job is as much to protect folks as it is to inform them, and sometimes that means deciding what they need to know and what they don't. Milt won more than ninety percent of the vote in the last election. Folks here know his faults, or most of them, anyway—I wasn't the only person in town who knew what Deputy Brandt uncovered, after all, it was just that Milt thought I was. Nobody's going to recall him." He turned and pointed to the wall, a series of yellowed newspaper clippings of sports stories showcased in black wood frames. "He's still a local hero, forty years after he took the high school football team to its one and only state championship. People trust him. Nothing I print is going to change that."

"So people here are okay with having a sheriff who takes bribes to ignore things that put their families in danger?"

"You're missing the point." Pete moved his mug when Maggie returned to set plates in front of us.

"Thank you," I said to her. Then, to Pete, "What is the point I'm missing?"

"They wouldn't believe me if I did print it. Working in a place like this, you learn what your readers are willing to tolerate. And nobody in this town is going to believe that Milt is anything other than the upstanding hero they see him to be. Not enough to matter anyway."

"Then why would he care enough to fire the deputy?" Graham asked.

"Because his image matters to him." Pete pointed to the photo on the wall, a young Milt Barnes with a huge trophy hoisted high, riding on the shoulders of a pair of linemen who looked like twin refrigerators. "He knows people love him, and he thrives on it. He drinks on the quiet and gambles three counties over because he thinks he's hiding his faults. For whatever reason, he has no idea that he could damn near get away with murder around these parts, the public is so far on his side."

"Does he just think you don't put stuff about him in the paper because he's doing a good job hiding it, then?" I asked.

"Exactly."

I stabbed the biscuit on my plate and shoveled a bite into my mouth, where it promptly melted, undoubtedly the best I'd ever eaten. Not that I would've admitted that to my granny, Lord rest her.

Eating gave me time to think. I could unpack the case of the morally-conscious reporter later—right now we had more pressing things to understand. Before this tiny town started racking up a body count.

24

"So how well did you know Marta?"

Stuffed full of biscuits and gravy and coffee, I stepped through the door Graham held open and out into glaring Texas sunshine. The snowdrifts were already down by half, though still deeper than I'd ever seen them.

We stepped out of the way of the door, waiting for Kelsey Marie to come out of the restroom.

"She was a real nice lady," Pete said. "So proud, the day she moved into that house. I helped her carry furniture in because she didn't have anyone there to lend a hand. She kept the yard up herself in the summers and she liked to play music while she cooked on her days off—Maggie's right about her skills in the kitchen, it always smelled like heaven if her windows were open and the breeze was right on Saturday afternoons."

"And you're sure you didn't notice anything suspicious around her house last night? Even something small?"

"Saturday is press day for the Sunday edition. I worked until after eleven. Her house was dark when I got home."

"The sheriff was already gone?"

"He was there last night?"

"Don't you have a scanner app?" I asked. "We were told it was a welfare check call."

Pete's jaw dropped. "Oh hell, I saw that one but I figured it was out at the nursing home again, that's usually where those come from. And I was busy, so I didn't click it."

"Any regular visitors that came and went?"

"She had a boyfriend." Something in his tone drew my eyes sideways. A boyfriend he didn't care for, it sounded like. I waited for him to elaborate.

"Guy had been coming around since...probably Thanksgiving. Went real quick from weekly dates to sleeping over a few times a week." He wasn't even trying to hide his dour tone, but I couldn't tell if it was jealousy or something more sinister.

"So who was he?" I prodded.

"That's the thing. I don't know. And I know everyone."

Boy, mistrust of outsiders runs deep in this town. When I was a little girl and visiting my grandparents, I never noticed it, because if we went to town I was always with one of them, and like Pete, they knew everyone.

"Could you tell if he was white or black or Hispanic?" Graham asked.

"Dark skin, black hair, stocky guy. I think she was right about as tall as he was. I assumed he was Mexican."

Maybe a new hand on an area ranch. We were getting on toward slaughtering time.

Maybe someone interested in Marta because of Kelsey Marie, though.

"Did you ever see anyone from the Sherman family at her house? Or did anyone bother her because of Kelsey Marie's YouTube channel?" I asked.

"Why would the Shermans come to her house?" He shot me an are-you-stupid look. "She spent her whole life out there waiting on them." He kicked at a snow drift, a chunk breaking off and splattering on the concrete. "Nobody around here really regards Kelsey Marie as anything but—"

He shut up when she opened the front door of the diner and stepped outside.

"Thanks for waiting."

The road had a few patches of concrete showing through the snow, the sun inching higher in the sky and beating down hard enough to make me question how long I'd need my coat. The shops along the street were starting to open, proprietors scraping the sidewalk with yard shovels because nobody in central Texas had cause to own one made for snow.

"Pete!" The nearest scraping stopped and a stout man in a plaid shirt and green suspenders hooked to his dark Levi's raised his arm. "I got that hunting knife you were asking about back in stock. Just yesterday."

Pete kept walking, throwing the guy a nod. "Much obliged, Walter. I'll be by after it just as soon as I'm wrapped up here."

"Sure thing." Walter's tone dropped as he returned to scooping snow out from in front of his shop's front door. Skipper's Sports and Outdoors, the sign hanging next to the door read.

"Did you get enough to eat?" I asked Kelsey Marie.

"Not big on food lately. But I'm good, thanks." She smiled. "It's been a while since anyone cared enough to ask."

I patted her shoulder as she climbed into the backseat of the Escalade.

Pete milled about awkwardly. He shifted his eyes to Kelsey Marie, staring out the other window in the back seat.

"That vehicle is quiet as a church on Saturday night—she can't hear you."

"Everybody in town heard about her hog, and the other one up the road, too, but nobody cared. I know a lot of folks kinda found it funny. People getting famous on YouTube is...

well, the kid has had a hell of a time. She's got like, fans, all over the world, but she's almost been shunned here."

Graham leaned on the hood of the car. "Why?"

"I don't want to say folks are being snobbish, but...I can't exactly think of a better word to use. Like, they think she got too big for her britches. She thinks she's famous, but they don't. That kind of a thing."

"So the twenty-first century and all its trappings haven't exactly landed here," I said. "Fair enough."

Pete waved one arm. "Anyway. That horror show last night wasn't a hog slaughter." His Adam's apple bobbed with a hard swallow. "And he just walked right into her house. I need folks to lock doors. So I will run enough of the story to scare them. But not enough to interfere with your investigation." He handed me a card. "My cell is on there. Call if you need me."

Graham snorted as he opened the car door for me. "Better watch it, man, you'll give McClellan some faith in the concept of a free press."

The roads were clearing nicely by the time I started the Escalade, aiming for Cleetus's garage, which Kelsey Marie said was three blocks south of the square.

The place looked like someone picked it right up off the set of *The Andy Griffith Show* and plunked it down in Central Texas, in full color and complete with a full-service gas island.

I parked the Escalade and hopped down, spotting a short, round man in faded blue coveralls, a socket wrench and a shop rag hanging out of his back pocket.

He turned and raised one hand to shade his eyes, the toothpick hanging out one side of his mouth twisting with every flex of his jaw.

He might've been near Kelsey Marie's house last night, but his height and shape disqualified him from my suspect list.

"Morning, miss," he called. "What can I do for you and that..." He walked closer. "That Cadillac belongs to Miranda Sherman."

"It does indeed. The sheriff says it's possible you picked up my truck from in front of the Sherman place last night." I stuck out one hand. "Faith McClellan, Texas Rangers."

"McClellan. Like Ray McClellan?"

"My granddaddy." I flashed a pageant-bright smile, folding my hands behind my back.

"Good eye for horses and cars, Ray. And a damned fine poker player. Always said there was a reason his boy did well in politics. Well. Until lately...." He floundered, hunting for words that would start to dig him out of the pit of awkward.

I waved a hand. "My father isn't a whole lot like Grandaddy. Or me, for that matter."

"Well then. Let's talk about that pickup. Aggie Maroon, is it?"

Not on purpose, but the way he grinned when he said it, I wasn't telling him that. "Yes sir it is. An F-150."

"I'll tell you what. No charge for you, Ranger McClellan. My money says you'll probably figure out who's running all over the place hacking up folks and their animals before Milt Barnes gets good and sober. So you come on and take your truck home. You got the keys?"

I held them up.

"Works for me." He waved for me to follow him. "I went out last night thinking I'd probably need to rescue some poor souls who got caught by that storm. Blew right the hell up out of nowhere, didn't it? Like a damned tornado, but cold and wet. A real pain in the ass. But yours was the only stuck vehicle I saw, and you'd left by the time I got there."

My truck sat at an angle, still hooked to the tow behind the garage. Cleetus went to work setting it free. "Sorry if I inconvenienced you, ma'am. I could've left it when I figured out you weren't in it, but it was sitting out there and I didn't want it to get hit; them roads were awful slick."

My brow furrowed. "But then why didn't you take Kelsey Marie's Porsche?"

He dropped a metal hook into the remaining snow and grunted, peering up at me with squinted eyes.

"Why didn't I what?"

"The Porsche. It was in the drift not far from my truck."

He pursed his lips. "Uh. No. No, there wasn't anything else out there. Not when I picked this one up."

"Did you see a vehicle coming down the Shermans' driveway while you were there?"

He shook his head. "But I mean, who could see much of anything in that storm?"

"And what about on your way back? Did you pass anyone coming out of town?"

"Nope. Folks around here hunker down when it snows even a little bit. And I ain't never seen this much snow in all my days."

I watched him circle the truck to unhook something from the other side. "How long you figure it took you to hook this up and get gone last night?"

"Probably fifteen minutes? I can do it in good weather in ten, but the snow slowed me down."

"And you didn't see another car? In fifteen minutes?"

"No ma'am. I mean, there could'a been one, I guess, if it wasn't too near to the road. The way the wind was blowing and as thick as that snow was, it's not off the reservation to think I just didn't notice. I don't guess."

He didn't sound convinced. But I had seen Kelsey Marie's

Porsche out there covered in snow with my own eyes—and touched it with my own hands—the night before.

I just couldn't figure out how both things could be true.

I swung up into the truck, stashing the evidence bag from Marta's house in the glove compartment, and started the engine, waving as I drove around front. I stopped near the Escalade, motioning for Graham to put his window down. "You want to drive that one back to the Sherman place, we'll drop it off and take her with us?"

"Take her with us...where?" Graham furrowed his brow. Kelsey Marie stared out the window like we weren't talking about her.

"Work, home...wherever we're going. The deputy is only a deputy here because he has a dying father to care for and the sheriff is a drunk who probably wouldn't take orders from us in the first place, which would leave her alone, afraid of her father's gun collection, in the middle of nowhere. That's unacceptable."

Graham sighed. "How the hell are we going to solve a murder while we babysit?"

I stared at Kelsey Marie, who was watching a cardinal flit from bare branch to bare branch in a live oak next to the garage.

"No idea. But we are going to figure it out."

25

From Brady to Austin, babysitting was easy.

Kelsey Marie dug an ancient hot pink iPod out of her dresser when we dropped the Escalade off at the house, and she rode in my tiny back seat in silence, earbuds securely in place and her head occasionally bobbing to the music.

"Jim's meeting us at the lab." I kept my voice low. "She doesn't know anything yet?"

"Nope. Who knew a broken phone would come in so handy?"

"I picked up a few things from Marta's home that could be useful."

"Besides the pig's head?"

Kelsey Marie didn't give any indication of having heard.

"Flash drive in her night table drawer, a key in the shoe rack on the back of her closet door."

"You think there's a reason someone killed the maid that's not just that she was the Shermans' maid?"

I shrugged. "The video was so brutal. I think the killer was pissed at her."

"Or the killer is a psychopath who likes watching blood spray." He muttered that time.

"Yeah maybe. But my thing is statistically more likely."

"And easier to find."

I turned on the stereo and faded the speakers to the back for an extra layer of sound protection. "The folks in town are about how I expected them to be."

"The thing with the newspaper guy and the hunting knife he ordered was weird timing," Graham said.

"I'm trying to avoid letting my natural prejudices against reporters come into play, so I'm glad you said that and not me. But also, it's the country. Folks hunt. And I didn't pick up any signs that he was lying."

"So, assuming that's Samson's head in the trunk, how did it wind up where we found it?"

There was the question that was troubling me the most about the whole morning. It was easy to assume the killer put the pig's head in Marta's freezer for a lot of reasons. But the killer hadn't carried it in on camera. So a little nagging voice kept wanting to wonder if Marta had the head because she killed the pig. It wasn't impossible, and the eye-for-an-eye country mentality combined with the video of Samson's death could well be why Marta was dead. I didn't have enough information yet to rule anything out.

"I'm not sure of a single thing about this yet. But we'll get there."

Miles passed silently, each of us lost in our thoughts, Kelsey Marie lost in her music.

I needed a goddamn whiteboard. There was too much going on here for me to keep the different paths and suspects and connections straight.

We had plenty at Rangers HQ. We also had a conference room with a thick door and a break room with vending machines and tables. And there was hardly ever anyone there on Sunday.

Plus, I still needed to talk to Archie. Oddly fitting that this conversation would come in the middle of a murder investigation.

I plucked my phone from the cupholder and touched his name in the favorites list.

"Hey there, girl," he said by way of hello. "You two make it through the storm all right?"

"We're fine. Things in Brady are not."

"That bad, huh?"

"The murder Sheriff Barnes called you about was the housekeeper for the people with the murdered hog. And it wasn't your garden-variety murder."

"So your guy is moving up the food chain. That was quick."

"Seems so, yeah."

"You need me?"

"I could use another brain if you don't mind meeting me at the office in about an hour. I need to stop by the lab first."

"See you then."

"We'll have company," I added, almost as an afterthought.

"Animal or human? I'm likely to ask you that from now on, you know."

I smirked. "The girl. From the YouTube channel. I couldn't leave her there alone, her parents are both out of town. I just meant that we'll need a place for her to hang out at the office, so that we can talk about the case without being worried we'll emotionally scar her or something."

"She's a teenager with her own YouTube channel. Isn't her cell phone all the distraction we need?"

"Broken."

"Oh. Well then, a spare laptop and a Netflix password?"

"Maybe. See you in a bit, Archie."

I returned the phone to the cupholder and Graham caught my hand in his. "You ask him yet?"

"I'm going to do it today. Tired of waiting. I should've learned a long time ago that perfect moments and my life don't cross paths that often."

"Oh, I think we've had our share."

I squeezed Graham's hand. "You're just the Lord's way of making up for all my shitty ones, Graham."

His thumb brushed across my ring. "And I intend to keep it that way."

It took Jim twenty-three minutes to finish grunting and poking and squinting through a magnifier and declare the pig's head almost certainly Samson's.

"How can you do that in less than a half hour? You're like some sort of autopsy wizard."

He coughed over a laugh. "Been in the damned lab too many years, McClellan. It's all in the details." He waved one arm, beckoning. "See this splintering on the bone here?" He handed me a magnifier and adjusted the light over the table.

I leaned down, pulling the glass down in front of my eyes.

A tiny web of cracks snaked down one side of the vertebrae, fanning out where the bone got wider.

"I see it."

He turned to the next table, where the rest of Samson overflowed the gurney. "Now here." He pulled tissue back with gloved hands and exposed the top of the vertebrae.

Same splintering, but in mirror image.

"It's from where the axe hit it. The blow came from above, but slightly more forceful on the left side. So unless they've taken to beheading hogs execution-style on a large scale out there, this is pieces of the same pig."

I stepped back, pulling off the magnifier. "So how in the hell did his head end up in Marta's freezer?"

"Who's Marta?"

"The teenager who raised this guy? Marta is her family's housekeeper."

"And you found this in her freezer?"

"I found it because I was searching her house after she was murdered last night."

"Oh. Shit." Jim flipped the overhead light off and laid his magnifier on the side table. "So we're not just dealing with a dead animal anymore."

"We are not. Where do victims from McCulloch County go?"

"They'll bring her here. You want me to take the autopsy, I'm guessing?"

"Well, if it makes you feel better, there's not much blood left. Most of it was sprayed all over her living room by way of a heart puncture and a ripped carotid."

"Holy Jesus." His brow furrowed. "What the hell is going on out there? That's like slasher movie shit—it doesn't even happen here. There can't be but ten thousand people in the whole damned county."

"Everyone knows everyone."

"Clearly there's somebody who's an exception to that."

I started to nod and then stopped, pointing a finger. "Yes!" I was a little too forceful about my excitement.

"Why is that exciting?"

"Because I didn't think about it that way before. I realize small communities like that aren't like the city. Everyone knows everyone. The sheriff and the newspaper guy seriously know everyone. But maybe what we're looking for is someone people don't know very well. Or at least, that could be the place I ought to start."

"Much easier needle to find in that sort of a haystack," Jim agreed. "I'll let you know when I get the human variety remains. Marta, you said?"

"Marta Milosevic. Believe me, you'll recognize her by the Freddy Kruger MO."

"Where're you headed now?"

"Headquarters. Archie is meeting us to help comb through what we know so far. I need a whiteboard and a plan."

"You always get your man, McClellan. This won't be any different."

"I never take it for granted. Procedure, thoroughness, and attention to detail. Every little thing, no matter how little. Every single time."

"And the talking to corpses. That's what makes you special."

"Damn right." I tossed my gloves into the trash can by the door and waved as I let myself out.

Jim was too busy putting Samson's head on the gurney with the rest of him so he could wheel the whole thing back to cold storage to notice.

At least I had one answer to show for my morning. Maybe Marta had killed Samson. Without more information, I couldn't be sure. But either way, now we had a homicide on our hands, and my job here wasn't about the pig anymore.

It was about who killed Marta. And keeping Kelsey Marie safe until we found out.

26

"Milt Barnes doesn't like you," Archie said without looking up from his laptop.

"Milt Barnes is a bigoted old drunk who has a Ruth McClellan-sized closet positively bursting with skeletons," I said.

"He rang my phone half an hour ago telling me to send him someone else."

Graham snickered as he ushered Kelsey Marie toward the break room in the back of the building. "That went over well, I'm sure."

"Someone older and more male than me, I assume?"

"One would think, though I will give him that he didn't specifically say that. Did you make his crew physically ill by playing a video of the murder for them? And where in the Sam Hill did you get such a thing?"

I craned my neck back toward the hallway, but Kelsey Marie was out of sight by then. "The killer filmed it, and then posted it on Kelsey Marie's YouTube channel. Same as with the pig."

"Sweet cartwheeling Jesus. Is it still up?"

"Graham reported it with his LEO credentials when he first saw it. It cut out at the end when I played it for Barnes because they pulled it down. And her channel has been suspended now, which we haven't told her."

"So you saw this happen, in a manner of speaking."

"Which shortcuts the crime scene investigation part of it, because we know where the killer went and that they wore gloves the whole time."

"Got a bead on size? Any kind of description?"

"It's hard to tell because both videos show a figure in a shapeless black robe, and the camera angle distorts proportions. But we did some measuring at the scene of the first murder yesterday, and from the shadows we think we're looking for someone between five ten and six two."

"Male? Female?"

"I don't know," I said. "Right now, it could be anyone from Kelsey Marie's stepbrother to her dad, to...the freaking dog catcher for all I know." I paused. "Yesterday in Fort Worth, Kelsey Marie's father met a young woman in a parking garage at the old Tandy towers. We heard him tell her to stay away from his family."

"Worth following," Archie said.

"But we haven't yet, because she took off while we were chasing him after he punched her out. And the evening only got weirder from there."

"Damn, you have had an interesting weekend."

"You don't know the half of it. I am running on caffeine and adrenaline. I need a whiteboard and a computer and to talk this through with you and Graham. I'm pretty sure we're racing the clock until this creep picks another victim."

"Faith. Sit." He waved one hand at the chair next to his. "Get a mint. Breathe. I get the sense of urgency and I know why you feel the need to protect the girl, but we have resources for things like this. And we will get to the bottom of it."

I dropped into the chair and blew out a long, slow breath, plucking a mint from the star-shaped crystal candy dish on his desk.

"I know," I said with a slight lisp around the candy. "This whole week has just turned into such a whirlwind. I just need a pause. Time to think, to get the facts straight and figure out the most likely path to the killer." I tapped the end of the pen on the edge of the desk. "But first, there's something I have to ask you."

"I hope by now it goes without saying that I'll help with whatever you need. Call in favors, get information, tell old Milt to fuck off." He winked. "Say the word."

"How about walking me down the aisle? You up for helping with that?" His sharp inhale told me Ruth hadn't ruined my surprise.

"Faith." Archie swallowed hard, his Adam's apple bobbing and his voice catching.

"I had this whole plan." The words rushed out on top of each other, my fingers tightening around his. "We were supposed to go to lunch yesterday, nice place, good food, music...I was going to ask you then. But then Miss Donnie called and I had to go check out this damned dead pig. And anyhow, I know this isn't as nice as that, but I'm hoping you'll say yes, even if I did just blurt it at you at work."

A sound ripped from his throat, unnatural for him, I couldn't even tell if it was a laugh or a sob. "Why would you ever think I might say anything but yes?"

A tear escaped his left eye and he didn't even let go of my hand to try to brush it away.

My lips curled into a soft smile.

"Because of Chuck," I said. "You have to know he's going to be..." I paused, shaking my head. "This is why I would've totally talked Graham into hopping a plane to Vegas if his mother weren't so excited about seeing her baby boy get married. I don't even want to think about what the Governor is going to do." I barked a short laugh. "I watched a video of a nice woman I'd spoken to not forty-eight hours earlier being slasher movie slaughtered this morning while I stood in the room with her body, Archie, and I'm more afraid of what kind of fit Chuck McClellan is going to throw when he's not the center of attention at my wedding. I still can't believe Graham thinks he's okay with marrying into my batshit crazy family circus."

"Well first, you need to consider the fact that Chuck is in a federal prison cell until his trial, thanks to his little jaunt to the Bahamas for Christmas."

"For now. The wedding isn't for another two and a half months. He knows a lot of people who could change that between now and then."

"Fine. Let's play devil's advocate and say he gets himself out. So what? Are you going to invite him to the wedding?"

I shook my head. Graham and I had talked about it for weeks, with Graham reassuring me that he wouldn't mind. But I minded. I didn't want the Governor anywhere near our special day.

"So even if he does hear about it through the lead-up press, he's not invited. We'll have a couple officers standing security at the doors. Even if he decided to try to crash— which I don't think he will, he'd consider it beneath him— he'll never make it past a Rangers protection detail."

"The press?" I bypassed the rest of his argument largely because it made sense. The Governor was a bastard, but he wasn't the boogeyman. Worst case, security would catch him at the door. And two cops who do what Graham and I do for a living probably need some level of security anyway.

But I wasn't counting on needing protection from the paparazzi. "Why would the press give half a flying fuck about the fact that I'm getting married? I'm not a movie star. I'm not even a Kelsey Marie Sherman level YouTube star."

"But you *are* a former Miss Texas whose father was once the governor, who catches killers for a living, and you're marrying a onetime local college sports hero who is a hero cop in his own right. The story writes itself. Even Skye loves the occasional feel-good headline. Trust me: the press is going to give many, many fucks. Some of them may in fact have wings."

I pinched the bridge of my nose. He was right. I couldn't believe I hadn't thought of that.

Maybe Graham's mom could go with us to Vegas.

Except there were a dozen more reasons that would never work, not the least of them the man on the other side of this desk, looking at me the way I'd always imagined a real dad would.

"It's going to be a beautiful day, you have my word," Archie said. "And I would be honored to be such a special part of it."

"Thanks, Arch." I coughed to cover the fact that I choked up on the two simple words.

"I'm proud of you, girl. You've been through an awful lot of bullshit to still believe in happily ever after. You deserve to be happy more than maybe anyone I've ever known."

"I'm trying. It's like I'm almost afraid of it, though that may not even make any sense. Like, when I'm with Graham and we're cooking or working or watching football or bouncing ideas and cases off each other, things are so easy. And I'll stop every once in a while and look around, waiting for the big heavy boot to drop on my head. All my life, when things started to get good, the universe needed to balance itself, and so something went to hell. I think that's why I'm so afraid of this wedding nonsense. Way too much potential for shoes to just be raining from the goddamn sky. But I'm stuck now. I found the dress."

"Your mother told me. In fact, she's told me little else in the past couple of days. Come on," Archie jerked his chin at Graham, who returned from the hallway with two Diet Dr Peppers for them and one regular one for me. "Let's get Faith a board and figure out what the hell is going on out in McCulloch County before anyone else dies."

Clive.

Samson.

Marta.

I underlined the victims on the whiteboard in the conference room, drawing a timeline above their names—Clive last Friday, Samson Tuesday, Marta Saturday.

"So the obvious connection between these two"—I drew short lines out from Samson and Marta—"is the Sherman family. With Kelsey Marie leading that list."

Graham leaned back in a chair across the room, his feet up on the table and his fingers laced behind his head. "How about the first pig? You said that kid you saw from Kelsey Marie's 4H club last night told you people didn't like her because nobody got to raise a hog for the stock show this year. What if we've been ignoring that part of the story when it was important? If it was our guy, why did someone kill that pig before they killed Samson?"

"The first victim is usually someone the killer knows," Archie said.

I snorted. "We're talking about farm animals, Arch."

"I'm aware. And I feel about as ridiculous as you'd think after decades of hunting the kind of folks who slaughter people, but I'm willing to jump and go with it, so I'll thank the two of you to follow along. When you wash away all the weird —and I'll grant you there's a whole lot of weird—this seems to suggest that you've got yourself a serial. Three victims, similar MO in at least two of the cases, and escalating levels of gore. I mean, you're the psychobabble expert, Faith. What does that tell you?"

He was right, as usual. Even including the animals— maybe especially, when you got right down to it—this had all the trappings of a textbook serial killer. It was just that I didn't usually make it to the scene for the animal murders in cases like this one, so I hadn't paid that first one enough mind. Animals are usually practice for the main event, but nobody ever calls the police until it's humans that are dying. Until Miss Donnie called me.

"My attention has been focused on Samson and Kelsey Marie, but I did ask Deputy Foster about Clive. He said the owner had called the SO, pretty upset, told the dispatcher Clive was two years old, and somebody got him between the eyes with a sledgehammer." I wrinkled my nose as I spoke. "Messy, was the word he used. I suspect he was understating it."

"And the other animals didn't make enough racket to wake anyone while this was going on? It was just the one hog slaughtered?" Archie asked.

"The place is a cattle farm. Craig said the pig was a one-off; he was the only head of swine on the property." I grabbed my marker, scribbling on the board. "Dammit. So they were both being raised alone, most of their time spent around humans. I can't believe I didn't catch it when he said that." I pulled my notebook from my back pocket. "I even wrote it down, and it went right the hell out of my head. I wonder if Clive was also a pet?"

"What was the couple's name?" Graham asked. "The folks who owned that place?"

I flipped through my notes, coming up empty.

Holding up one finger, I pulled out my phone and queued up the recording of my conversation with my granny's old friend. "She told me who the other pig belonged to."

We listened in bits and pieces as I forwarded through the conversation.

"Her husband watched me play?" Graham asked, grinning.

"She said they were so sad when you got hurt. And that means I went too far." I backed the recording up.

"You remember Marvin DeWitt?" Miss Donnie's voice chirped from the speaker on my iPhone.

DeWitt. The name rang a bell, but not a big enough one for me to know why.

"You don't remember Marvin DeWitt, do you?" Archie asked.

"She said he used to fancy himself the mayor," I said. "That's what she said next. And that they cooked their dead pig. Served it at the town's kickoff celebration for the stock show."

Graham pulled Archie's laptop across the table and flipped it open, looking for public records on Mr. DeWitt. "Let's see what kind of connections we can make here," he said.

Archie and I turned back to the board while he typed.

"Where are the girl's parents? They're connected to the housekeeper and the famous pig, too." Archie didn't even shake his head that time. You get used to talking about a famous pig after a while, no matter how crazy it sounds when you first mention it.

"The mom is..." I paused, staring at the shut door.

Archie backed across the room and opened it, looking around. "All clear." He shut it again.

"She's gone. The kid thinks—at least mostly thinks—that she's on vacation with the half- brother who's her son from before she and the dad got together, but the dad was pretty blitzed when I caught up with him at his hotel last night and he told me she left them. He swore he didn't know where she went, and as of yesterday she hadn't used any of her credit cards."

"We'll put out an all-points on her vehicle," Archie said. "Hell, for all we know, she might be in danger, as well. Where'd you find her dad?"

"He was up in Fort Worth at the stock show yesterday. Kelsey Marie said he had business to do."

"But you caught him drinking in his hotel room."

"He's at the Worthington. And that's not all we caught him doing. Like I said, he met up with a young woman in an abandoned parking garage, and promptly punched her out such that she was briefly unconscious. But he didn't mention her, and even as drunk as he was, I couldn't risk asking him and letting on that I'd been following him. If he tells me to stay away from Kelsey Marie and she gets hurt..." I let the sentence trail, shaking my head.

"Understood." Archie waved a hand. "Captain Jones up at Fort Worth SWAT is an old buddy of mine. Give me this guy's room number, I'll send him by. Very personable, Jones. Holds their local record for confessions. If your guy knows anything, Jones will know it in a couple of hours."

"I don't want him hurt, Arch."

Archie raised both hands. "Of course not. Jones is all charm. Hand to God."

"That'd be great, thanks. Sherman's in the Johnson Suite."

Archie added it to his list.

I tapped Marta's name on the board.

"I can't shake the feeling that everything about her murder was deliberate."

"I'd say if you're going to butcher someone on camera, that's pretty deliberate, yeah." Archie took a seat at the table.

"Of course. But I mean everything. Like they used a cooking knife from her kitchen—picked it up on camera on the way in, and then stood there playing with the knife while she dozed in the recliner."

"Yeah, like the killer was totally unafraid," Graham said.

"Almost like he was hunting." I turned back to the board. "Kelsey Marie said her parents used her money to…"

"Buy Dustin a hunting lease," Graham finished.

I put a star by his name on the board.

"When you say the killer was playing with the knife—you mean like performing?" Archie asked.

"Exactly. The video of Samson was the same way—like a gruesome theater show. The killer collected blood and splashed it everywhere. And after he gutted Marta, he smeared her insides on the walls and tracked them over the carpet. Like he was showing off what he could get away with."

"Who does that?" Archie asked.

"Psychos," Graham said.

"Or melodramatic kids?" Archie asked. "Maybe the performances help narrow it down. Who gains from Kelsey Marie's YouTube channel being shut down?"

"Not her family," I said. "She supports them."

"Not her dad. Probably not her mom," Graham said. "But remember the news story about Dustin? He wouldn't have to clean up the pig shit anymore if the pig was dead and she didn't have a channel anymore."

"And if Marta saw him coming out of the barn when she got there to make Kelsey Marie's breakfast, maybe he killed her, too," I said. "We have to find this kid."

My phone buzzed and I checked the number on the screen.

"Miss Donnie?" I put it to my ear.

"I knew I had a bad feeling about this." Her voice quavered. "They're dead, Faith. Just like I was afraid of."

She'd heard about Marta. I took a deep breath, but paused before I got any words out. "Did you say 'they?' "

"Marvin and Edith DeWitt." Her voice broke. "The pastor called, said the sheriff found them this morning."

27

"No blood, no gore, no theatrics," I reported, putting my phone on the table after I ended my call with Craig Foster. "I asked that the bodies go to Jim for autopsy, but our deputy friend out there on the scene said the cause of death wasn't readily apparent. They're leaning natural causes at the moment."

Archie and Graham grunted as I added Marvin and Edith DeWitt's names to my board, under Clive's and linked by a question mark.

"So the question is whether or not they're right," Archie said. "No blood or gore doesn't fit with your other scenes, though."

"Not even a little."

"How'd they find them?" Graham asked.

"Welfare check," I said. "Mr. DeWitt's hunting buddies said he bailed on them yesterday and wasn't answering the phone today, they were concerned that something had happened to him in the snowstorm."

"So we don't know how long they've been dead," Archie said.

"Nope. Not until Jim gets to them. But Craig seemed to think they just...died. He said they were both elderly."

"Craig had never worked a scene until this morning, though," Graham said.

"I'm kind of surprised Milt didn't call to tell me to send help again," Archie said.

"When he tried that yesterday he got me." I grinned. "Maybe he's scared to?"

"He's too full of himself to be scared. He'd just shout and bluster some more and tell me to send him someone else."

"So that means he doesn't suspect foul play, either," I said, turning to Graham. "How old were they?"

He touched a few keys. "Sixty-eight and sixty-five. He was older."

"That's pretty young still, especially since it was both of them."

I drew a line under their names on the board.

"Folks were running generators because of power outages due to the storm. Could've been carbon monoxide."

"If that's true, it's the worst timing in the history of clocks," Archie said.

Graham drummed his fingers on the table, his eyes on the board. "How much did you find out about the young deputy this morning?"

"Nothing earth-shattering. He's super young, hired by the sheriff as a favor to his ailing father because Foster takes care of his dad. He says he wants to be a homicide investigator. He's smart, seemed like a good student, and certainly had the stomach for this line of work." I twirled the marker through my fingers.

"Which is great. Unless he could stomach the scene because he created it."

I froze mid-marker-flip. "I'm sorry?"

"I'm not hurling accusations, I'm just thinking. Not many people can see something like Marta's murder up close and personal without feeling ill. You said yourself the sheriff got sick," Graham said. "This nineteen-year-old kid did not—but he did get himself invited to shadow you through Marta's house, and now you're calling him for updates. He's got your trust. He's got the community's trust. He's the right height and build to match our killer, and he's young enough to think these grand performances for the camera are cool. We might ought to look a little harder at him before we bring him any further into our case."

I flipped the marker from one hand to the other.

I didn't want to think it, but he wasn't wrong.

I turned back to the board and added Craig's name on the left-hand side with Dustin's.

"Anything in the database on him?" I asked.

Graham tapped a few keys. Paused. Tapped a few more. "No information on anyone in the sheriff's office out there. Not the sheriff, not the deputy. Not even the dispatcher."

"If Barnes is into as much shady stuff as we think, secrecy tracks," I said.

"I'll pull a background check first thing in the morning." Archie scribbled himself a note. "If the deputy's got a record, we'll find it."

"Okay, so if we assume every dead person or animal on this board is connected, at least for the time being, there are still some weird things about the DeWitt situation."

"Such as?" Graham raised an eyebrow.

"A pig is a weird thing to have for a pet. Even out in the country where people have room to raise them."

"They're fiercely loyal," Graham said.

"They're also large and expensive to feed, and I read somewhere once that they'll eat people given the chance, which is more than a little horrifying. In livestock country, at the end of the day, they're either food or money. Which is a weird way to view a pet."

"So what's your point?"

"Miss Donnie talked about Clive in the same way she did about Samson, except she said he was ornery and no one would want his head." I tapped the marker on my thigh, drawing connecting lines under the pigs' names at the bottom of the board.

YouTube star under Samson.

Barbecue under Clive.

Cute names and solo habitats under both.

"He wasn't much of a pet if they ate him." Archie pointed to the board. "Can you imagine?"

"We weren't allowed to have pets as kids except our horses at the ranch, and I don't have time to properly care for one now. But if you're asking if I can imagine you eating your dog? Not in any universe, even one where people saw them as an acceptable dish."

"Exactly. And the other folks, the ones with the internet show, they didn't eat their pig even though he was dead anyway and they farm pigs and not cows."

"So the DeWitts likely weren't as bonded to Clive," Graham said.

"But he still had a name," Archie said.

I paused. "But was it their name?"

"Huh?" the guys said in unison.

I spun and started pacing the length of the room.

"Uh-oh," Archie grumbled.

Graham snickered. "Let her think."

"What if the DeWitts didn't name Clive? Like you said, who cooks and eats a pet with a name? I know when I was a kid, we named the horses and the barn cats on the ranch, but not the cows."

"Why would your grandmother's friend have told you the pig had a name?" Graham said.

I turned and walked toward the back wall. "Because she talked to someone who wasn't Marvin or Edith DeWitt about the pig and his death."

"Who?"

"Hard to say, bad news travels fast in places like that. But I can find out." I pulled out my phone and found her number in my calls from Friday.

The phone rang.

And rang.

I hung up after the tenth one.

"Nobody home?" Graham asked.

"She wouldn't have gone anywhere in this weather."

"Except out to her barn, or out to her hen house, or any number of places right there on her property," Archie said. "Calm down. We'll try her again in a bit. Let's hop back on this train of thought you were driving. If the DeWitts didn't name their pig, who might've?"

"A farmhand," I said just as Graham said, "Caretaker."

Archie put one index finger up. "What about a kid? That's who named the other one, right?"

Graham turned back to the computer. "The DeWitts have one son. He's older than I am..." He touched a few more keys. "Oh. Was older than I am. He and his wife died three years ago in a car accident." He opened another search window in public records and typed. "They had one daughter, fifteen. Plays basketball at the high school out there."

"And probably lives with her grandparents, right? Is she by any chance in the 4H?"

Search results turned up a website for the school 4H. A

link to Kelsey Marie's YouTube channel was the first—and largest—thing on the home page.

"There. Members." I pointed.

"I see it, Miss Patience," Graham grumbled.

"Yep. Olivia DeWitt," he read after he clicked the list.

I went back to the board and added her name under her grandparents', pulling my notebook out of my hip pocket and flipping back. "We gauged from the video of Samson's murder that the killer was between five ten and six two. The video of Marta's murder was tricky because of the camera angle, but it didn't look like the murderer there was more than about six one, and I could be being generous. You said Olivia plays basketball, Graham."

"Two seconds." He clicked the keyboard. "She's six feet even. Plays center."

"Now we're getting somewhere," Archie said.

"Where?" I resumed pacing. "Y'all think this child raised a pig at her grandparents' house, named him, got pissed that she couldn't show him because the teacher is up Kelsey Marie's ass, and then she killed her own pig before she butchered Samson in front of a camera and then recorded herself slicing up Marta?"

"Actually, I'd buy that." The words came from the doorway, freezing me mid-step.

"Olivia despises me." Kelsey Marie's voice caught on the last word.

I turned just as her tears breached the dam of her thick lashes. "What did you say about Marta?"

Dammit.

I crossed the room in three long strides, laying a hand on Kelsey Marie's arm. "I'm sorry, honey. I didn't want to scare you or make you sad."

"Someone..." She snuffled in a deep breath. "Oh my God. Someone killed Marta? Like killed her? I thought when the sheriff called looking for my dad that she like was in an accident or had a stroke or something."

"Did the sheriff happen to say anything else, Kelsey Marie?"

Why didn't I think of it when she'd told me about the phone call that morning? And

why was Barnes looking for Jeff Sherman, anyway?

Maybe because he wanted to tell him what happened—everyone in town likely knew Marta worked for the Shermans. Maybe he was looking for contact information for next of kin, though his contempt for the idea made me doubt it.

But what if he wanted to question him?

This was where my temper could occasionally get me in trouble. If I hadn't snapped at that old bastard, I'd probably already know why he was looking for Jeff Sherman when he called Kelsey Marie. As it stood now, we had yet another question added to our ever-growing pile of them.

"He said he needed to ask him some questions. And that Marta was dead." Kelsey Marie scrubbed at the end of her nose with her sweatshirt sleeve. "I told him my dad was in Fort Worth."

"Did he ask you to give your dad a message?" I asked.

Jeff Sherman couldn't be the person in those videos. Right? I closed my eyes and ran the pictures through my head on repeat. Sherman was as tall as Graham and nearly as wide. I couldn't say if the killer was a woman or a man—a little absurd and a whole fucking lot frustrating when I'd actually watched both crimes being committed in high resolution full color—and the camera angles made it hard to gauge size, but not impossible to land in a ballpark. My upper limit would have to be off by two or three inches for Kelsey Marie's dad to be the killer.

It wasn't likely.

But I couldn't say it was impossible, either.

I'd dismissed him as a true possibility when we did the height calculations the day before. But owing a shit ton of cash to the Dixie Mafia could be a powerful motive—though I still couldn't find a gain for Sherman in Samson's murder.

"He just said he'd catch up with him when he got home." She narrowed her eyes. "You don't think he wanted to like, *question him*, question him?" Her eyes popped wide. "My dad wouldn't hurt a fly. Like literally, he opens windows and shoos them out of the house. Drives my mother batshit crazy."

Um. The guy was a pig farmer. Hurting them goes with the territory.

I could tell Graham was thinking the same thing from the glance he shot me. I let it go. I don't suppose my grandfather had done the actual slaughtering himself, when you got right down to it.

"Of course not. Come have a seat and let's talk about Olivia."

Kelsey Marie's eyes nearly disappeared into slits at the mention of the other girl's name. "She's such a nasty bitch. She hates me, and she's made it her mission in life this year to make me miserable."

I pulled out a chair for her at the table, relieved to have her talking about something that wasn't her dad or their house-keeper. "Why didn't you tell me about her on Thursday? Or even yesterday?"

"Olivia is mean but she couldn't..." Kelsey Marie chewed on her lower lip. "I mean I guess I didn't ever think anyone I knew could be that mean until I heard what you were saying just now." Her lower lip trembled as more tears strained against her lashes. "What was it you said about her pig? The one she had out at her grandpa's? Someone hurt him, too?"

"So Clive was her pet?"

"She was raising one, I heard. He was about the same age as Samson, started off as a runt, too."

"Who told you that?"

"She got Dusty to ask me about having her and her pig as guests in a video. Like a playdate." Kelsey Marie huffed out a frustrated sigh. "Two hogs, who had never been around each other."

"I can infer that they might fight?" I asked.

"Exactly," Kelsey Marie said. "They don't always fight, but you get two who are used to being the center of attention in the same pen and you're pretty much daring them to. They could do some serious damage to each other, and what could we have done to stop it? I would've had to tranq them, and that carries its own set of risks."

"So you said no." I didn't bother with inflecting a question at the end.

"I told him to tell her she could get her own channel if she wanted her pig in a video, but she wasn't endangering Samson to get her like, twenty minutes of fame or whatever."

My brain flashed to the kid from the midway and his snide reference to "Queen Kelsey." Because the 4H kids from Brady were in Fort Worth for the weekend, too.

The young blonde woman from the parking garage.

I needed a picture of Olivia. But being smart about asking for one was probably prudent.

"Do you know if Olivia raised an animal for the stock show this year?" I asked.

"Everybody did. We were all going to go together."

"But you weren't going to sell Samson," I said. The winning stock usually goes to the highest bidder at the sale of champions auction, with the cash touted as college money for the kids who raise winning animals.

"Right. I wanted him to get his chance at the show, but then Daddy was going to buy him at the auction so he'd just go home with us and live out his days in his playpen." She started sniffling again.

"So was Olivia taking her pig to the show?"

Kelsey Marie shook her head. "I think she had decided to compete an angus heifer."

"Why would she do that if she had raised a pig from a baby?"

"Swine is a smaller category with a smaller payout," Kelsey Marie informed us. "Prize hogs go for like fifty grand at auction, but if you win in a cattle category you get six figures easy. Last year the overall grand champion sold for three hundred thousand. Her grandparents raise cattle. I guess she thought that was her best chance at winning big money."

I tapped one finger on the table, studying her. I have a pretty good bullshit radar—it's a benefit of years of listening to people spout manure during murder investigations. She wasn't tripping it. But something wasn't quite right, either.

The boy I'd met at the midway said nobody was allowed to compete against Kelsey Marie, by edict of the teacher. He hadn't said she knew about that, but I assumed she did, because...well. Because of the way he talked about her, and because fame, no matter the brand, makes folks act downright foolish.

If she knew, she wasn't letting on. Because she was embarrassed, or because she was afraid of us finding that out?

I couldn't tell. And I couldn't ask outright without risking pissing her off, which would make her more likely to do something foolish, like try to take off.

"Most schools like to spread out the categories the kids compete animals in, to give the widest shot at the most kids winning some scholarship money," Graham said.

"We have a lot of kids who won't be able to afford college without some kind of help," Kelsey Marie said. "I was thinking of starting a scholarship fund for 4H even before all this, but now I think a Samson Sherman scholarship ought to be a regular thing." She perked right back up.

"You two want to brainstorm on that while you pick up some lunch?" I said, standing and putting one hand on my stomach. "The biscuits were good this morning, but they're wearing off."

"Sure." Graham stood and waved Kelsey Marie to the door in front of him. "What do you feel like?"

"Can we go to a taco truck?" She grinned. "I see videos all the time, I'm dying to try one."

Graham chuckled. "Surely there's at least one in the city brave enough to be open today."

As soon as the door shut behind them, I grabbed the laptop and went back to the school's 4H site.

"What's up?" Archie asked.

"The girl, Olivia. Wondering if she's the girl I saw with Jeff Sherman in the garage yesterday. I'm hoping there's a club photo on this site."

"I thought you said the girl he punched was short," Archie said.

"She was shorter than Sherman, but he's a tall, lanky guy. Anyone whose hair I could see over his shoulder has to be as tall as I am—maybe taller."

The membership page took nearly a full minute to load.

"The internet has been spotty everywhere. Downed lines

because of the storm," Archie said. "But at least we have heat and lights."

True. I tapped my fingers on the edge of the keyboard, then tapped my foot.

Page up, I scrolled down and watched the photo at the bottom of the page load what seemed like one pixel at a time.

"They'll be back with food before we get a look at this picture. It was working fine ten minutes ago."

"Rolling outages," Archie said. "They say they might have to do that with power, too, if it gets below twenty tonight."

"Below twenty?" My eyes popped wide. "Nearly four decades here, and I've never seen a winter like this, and now it's coming for us with both barrels?"

"TV weather guy at Channel Two said it's going to dip below freezing the next three nights, but tonight will be the worst of it."

"Great." The photo snapped into clear relief on the screen before I could say anything else.

And there she was. I pulled my phone out and grabbed a photo to show Graham, but the blonde three people to the right of center in the back row was the girl we'd watched Jeff Sherman deck yesterday. I'd bet my granny's favorite quilt her name was Olivia DeWitt.

For the first time since I left Miss Donnie's house Thursday, I felt like I might know what was going on here. Which meant we needed to find Olivia before anyone else died.

28

Turns out, murder is a lot like a lie—it takes more murders to make sure no one finds out about the first one.

A true predator welcomes the opportunity to hunt. To hone skills. To learn how to make this kill better than the last.

Each death is easier. Each death carries a lesson. Each death brings a predator closer to the perfect murder.

The last kill.

No witnesses.

No links.

Just the thrill of winning the hunt.

And going on to hunt another day.

Maybe even in another place.

29

Cases can turn on a pinhead.

In one hour in front of a whiteboard, Olivia DeWitt had gone from a name we'd never even heard to our prime suspect.

This is also a main reason I love whiteboards.

"You saw this young woman in Fort Worth yesterday afternoon?" Archie asked.

"I did."

"Well then how would she have murdered the woman in Brady last night?"

"I mean, if she left immediately after we saw her get hit, she could've made it," I said. "Not with time to spare, maybe, but she could've made it back."

"It'd be clever to plan it for this weekend," Archie said. "Because everyone would think she was in Fort Worth."

"Smart. Hell, they had a good size group at the midway last night, and I'm not even sure I saw every kid who was there from that school. Kelsey Marie said their membership is way up from where it's ever been."

"Which makes it easy for one girl to be lost in the crowd."

"Exactly."

I stared at the photo.

"She was thin. And she's tall enough but not too tall. She asked to be on Kelsey Marie's YouTube channel and Kelsey Marie turned her down."

"Sounded to me like Kelsey Marie flat ass dismissed her."

I blew out a slow breath. "For some personality types, there's not much worse."

"It's a solid motive for killing Kelsey Marie's pig, for sure. Why kill the housekeeper, though?"

I crossed back to the board. "She knew something. Or Olivia thought she did."

"And her own pig?"

"To see if she could stomach it? Or throw suspicion away from herself? Or both?"

"And posting the videos?"

I waved at the door. "It's scaring the shit out of Kelsey Marie."

"Making her look bad, too, I'd imagine. I mean a lot of her audience is kids, right? How many will still be allowed to watch her after this?"

I hadn't thought about that. "And I think she gets paid based on how many views each video gets."

"There you go. Covers all the motive bases I can see."

"Now how the hell do we find Olivia? We don't even know for sure which city to look in."

"It's Sunday. They should wrap up with auctions and head home ahead of the roads refreezing, so in a few hours, she'll be in Brady either way."

I held up one finger and pulled out my phone, dialing the number on the back of Pete's card. "Hey, Pete, it's Faith McClellan with the Rangers," I said. "How's it going there?"

"My heat is working and none of the pipes have busted," he said. "What can I do for you?"

"I need to know everything you can tell me about Olivia DeWitt."

"Nice enough kid," he said. "She comes into the office twice a week and helps out with obits and calendar announcements and filing. Takes pictures at the high school stuff, too." His tone already sounded guarded.

Better than I'd hoped for, as long as I didn't let on why I wanted to know.

"What do you need with Olivia?" he asked.

"Just have some questions for her, she's in the 4H with Kelsey Marie and I'm trying to get a better line on what Kelsey Marie's life was like at school and who might've wanted to hurt or scare her. There are only a handful of girls in the club, and I heard Olivia was friends with Kelsey Marie's brother. Do you happen to have a number for her?" I was skating close to raising his suspicions, but I didn't have time to tiptoe more carefully around this than I already was.

"Yeah, I have her cell. I'll text it to you. Any leads yet?"

"Not really," I said. "There are a lot of possibilities to work through."

"Do you seriously believe someone could be trying to hurt Kelsey Marie Sherman?"

"Off the record?"

"Of course, if you want."

"I do, but it's not happening on my watch. Kelsey Marie is safe here with me. But if you come across anything that might help me figure out who has it out for her, I'd appreciate the inside scoop."

"Like I said, most folks around here are pretty indifferent to her. I'm not sure I could point to someone who would hurt her, and she does get points by doing good things for the community with the money she makes, but most people wouldn't go out of their way to help her. I've noticed that when she's not on social media, she's quiet. Almost like two different people: Internet Kelsey Marie, who is bright and engaging, and hometown Kelsey Marie, a quiet girl who likes animals and keeps to herself."

I jotted that down. It was a lot of pressure for a teenage girl, though the papers in her dad's study showed good motive for putting herself through the wringer to keep her family afloat financially.

"Thanks for your help."

"I'm doing my best. I've got a piece on Marta up on the paper's website, posted the link to every community group on Facebook. Hoping I can get people to lock their doors."

"A murder in the middle of a blizzard is a whole lot of local news for one weekend," I said.

"Power's back on out here," he said. "It was a transformer that blew; they got it back up and running about an hour ago now. I'll send Olivia's number." He paused for a beat. "Don't scare her. She's a good girl. Hasn't had a great year."

"Why not?"

"Having trouble finding her footing at school. She doesn't talk about it much, but it's weighing on her."

"Of course," I said just before the silence stretched into awkward territory.

I clicked the end circle and put the phone down, reaching for the computer and searching for the newspaper's site.

"Anything?" Archie said.

"She works at the local newspaper office after school. He's sending me her number. I just have to see something first."

I clicked the link for the home page from the Google results.

Sheriff reports county's first homicide in twelve years, with a subhead: *residents advised to lock doors, take precautions, Texas Rangers conducting local investigation.*

Archie leaned over my shoulder as I skimmed the short article, which only mentioned a "female victim" and a "gruesome crime scene" and quoted me as saying locals should act with caution until we'd made an arrest, which I had in fact told him that morning at the diner.

"I'll be damned," I muttered. "He didn't go for the blood and gore."

"Responsible journalism isn't dead," Archie said.

"Seems it just lives in the sticks." I closed the computer.

My phone buzzed with a text.

Pete sent Olivia's number.

I tapped one finger on the edge of the table. "How many friends you have in APD dispatch?"

"Enough. What're you up to?"

"Well, I can't just call this girl and ask where she is. She'll never tell me. I would advise her not to tell me if I was standing there when she took such a call. But I'm wondering if I can call through 911 dispatch and add her to the call, can they triangulate her? I don't need a pinpoint, just a ballpark."

"I like the way you think, McClellan. Let me find out what we can do. Everyone is on skeleton crews today because of the storm."

I reached for the computer again, typing in the password from my notes for Kelsey Marie's Instagram and scrolling messages. There were four hundred and thirty-one new ones. Since yesterday. Halfway down the page, I sat up straighter in the chair.

Looks like you're about to get what's coming to you. Nowhere to hide now, bitch. Time to die.

I grabbed my phone and took a photo, then clicked the commenter's handle.

Profile photo was a faceless figure in a dark hood.

Now what?

I went to the board and grabbed a red marker from the tray. Under Samson's name I added another bullet point: online stalker.

It seemed like a week ago that I'd looked up the accounts sending the disgusting messages through Kelsey Marie's Instagram. Several of them were from a single IP, and it was a McCulloch County address. Sam's address. But what if Sam didn't send the messages? How close were he and Olivia DeWitt? Anyone who could hack Kelsey Marie's YouTube could certainly figure out how to send messages from someone else's IP address to escape suspicion.

I went back to the computer and read through the profile. It was a generic user, location listed as USA, no identifying details, handle HavocWrkd. No activity on anything that wasn't on Kelsey Marie's page, which was also the only one they followed.

I scrolled back. This person had commented on every single thing Kelsey Marie had posted since last summer. The messages started off vaguely creepy, with one in July talking about her piercing blue eyes, and got worse as time went on. In mid-September, on a video of Samson learning to bat a lightweight ball up in the air with his snout, came the first threat.

I know where you sleep.

It had a string of replies that started with "*fuck right off this page, cretin,*" and ended with "*I'm calling the sheriff.*" I grabbed my notebook and jotted that down. Jeff Sherman would be the JDSherm12 who was calling the sheriff, and the initial defense comment came from ODW36.

Wait.

I clicked that profile.

Olivia DeWitt, starting center for the 3A regional champion Lady Yellowjackets.

Huh. Smart, especially if she was replying to her own comment. Talk about covering your bases.

I sat back in the chair, shuffling variables to a very messy equation around my head.

Whoever was doing this was smart. And they loathed Kelsey Marie. And they had access to her—and those she cared about.

The good thing about that was, it narrowed the scope of possible suspects significantly enough that good old-fashioned police work would get us to the answer.

All we had to do was work the case, and keep Kelsey Marie safe in the meantime.

Archie stuck his head around the corner and shot me a thumbs up. "Ready when you are."

Time to find Olivia DeWitt.

30

"Adding caller now." I tapped Olivia's number on my cell screen and turned off the speaker.

The ring came through as I put it to my ear.

"Teenagers don't answer calls from numbers they don't recognize," Archie said.

"This is the best plan I have at the moment. We could have ten more dead people by the time I get a warrant satisfied for Google to track her phone."

"Hello?" She sounded out of breath.

"Olivia?"

"Can I help you?" came the reply.

Archie, who was on the landline with APD dispatch, pointed a *we're rolling.*

"This is Faith McClellan, I'm an officer with the Texas Department of Public Safety." I kept my cadence slow and affected a drawl Ruth McClellan would smack me for speaking in, because every second I could keep her on the phone mattered at this point.

"Do you know what happened to them?" Her words were

cleaved in half by a sob. "I saw on Insta that someone was murdered yesterday."

She thought I was calling about her grandparents.

"The local authorities don't suspect foul play in your grandparents' case," I said. Hell, maybe she would tell me where she was. "I actually need to talk to you about another matter. Are you home right now?"

The three beeps in response meant the call had ended. "Dammit," I muttered, touching her number again.

Voicemail this time.

"They got her," Archie said, jotting something down and thanking the person on the other end of his call before he hung up. "And not in Fort Worth. Or Brady."

"Where, then?"

"According to this, she's here in Austin."

My brow furrowed. "Why?"

"Maybe because she knows Kelsey Marie is here?"

"How would she?" I asked. "Kelsey Marie's phone is broken."

"Didn't she have her computer in the break room to watch TV?" Archie asked.

"She did, but we haven't been here that long."

He shrugged, pointing to the conference room. "I'm out of theories, so let's just go find out. We mentioned car registrations for Kelsey Marie's mother, pull any for this girl's family as well. We'll put out an all-points on all the cars and see who we can turn up to talk to."

"There's not a car registered to Kelsey Marie's dad, so I assume they lease them. But I'm in for seeing what we can dig up." I turned back for the computer as Graham and Kelsey Marie came through the doors carrying grease-spotted white paper bags.

"I can't believe how fast that snow is melting," Graham

said. "It was easy to find a taco truck near the university campus."

"Welcome to Texas."

"The guy working there let me try samples of everything vegetarian so I could pick what I liked." Kelsey Marie bounced with excitement, pointing to a desk. "Can I sit here?"

It was nice to see her excited about something.

"I'm going to take mine in the conference room and work while I eat," I said.

"Will you stay with me?" Kelsey Marie looked up at Graham.

"Uh. Sure?" Graham nodded to Archie. "You going with Faith?"

"We have a lead." Archie pulled the chair out for him. "Join us when you're done eating?"

"Of course."

In the conference room with the door shut, I flipped the computer open and logged into the DPS site with my credentials. I ran a search first for Miranda Sherman.

No results found.

"Is the system down?" I asked.

Archie waved a hand at the screen. "Check my car."

I ran Archie's name and it returned his Crown Vic and his old Ford pickup.

"They must lease," I said. "They can't be registered to Kelsey Marie. She might pay for them, but she's a minor."

"What about the other kid? The brother? How old is he?"

I opened a new tab and went to vital records. "He's not Sherman's kid, Miranda was pregnant when he married her. Stand by."

I found the Shermans' marriage certificate and then searched with her maiden name for Dustin's birth certificate.

Bingo.

"Almost nineteen." I moved to go back to the other window, wondering why the hell they'd register their cars to a teenager, when my eye landed on something.

Pete Zampras was listed as the kid's father on his birth certificate. But his last name was Golden, Miranda's maiden name.

I pointed to the screen. "Small town. Everyone is connected to everyone else."

"Who is Pete Zampras?"

"Mr. Responsible Journalism."

"And he didn't tell you he was this boy's father?"

I shook my head. "Jeff and Kelsey Marie both said they didn't know who his father was. Jeff said she was 'just barely' pregnant when they started dating. Kelsey Marie is only 14 months younger than Dustin. I mean, he said Olivia DeWitt works in the newspaper office after school. If that's a regular thing with teenage girls and maybe he was a little too friendly with Kelsey Marie's mother 20 years ago... he probably wouldn't have been too much older than she was."

"Could explain why he's being so careful around this story," Archie said.

"It could also give him a massive grudge against Jeff Sherman. But I honestly think there's just as much chance he doesn't even know he has a kid."

I made a note and went back to the vehicle title search, typing in Dustin Golden.

"I'll be damned," I said, when all five vehicles popped onto my screen. "Kelsey Marie's Porsche, Jeff's truck, the Escalade we took to town to get my truck back." I skimmed the list. The other two vehicles were a Mustang Cobra and a BMW 228i convertible.

Like we thought, they were in the Mustang. Which probably meant the tire ruts at the hunting lease were theirs. I copied the personalized plate—FASTR1—and passed it to Archie. "This one."

Back on the search screen, I searched for vehicles registered to the DeWitts.

A late model Buick and a 2003 Honda Civic. My money was on the Honda for a teenager. I jotted the tag number on a Post-it. "Try this for Olivia DeWitt."

He took them both and went out the door just as Graham came in.

"She's all settled with the TV." He exhaled. "And I am worn the hell out. Is this what it's going to be like having a kid?"

I tipped my head to one side and stared, words sticking in my throat. We hadn't talked about that.

"You good?" He slung one arm around my shoulders and dropped a kiss on top of my head. "You must be running on caffeine and stubbornness by now."

"Pretty much," I choked out.

"Archie's putting out an APB on vehicles belonging to Kelsey Marie's brother and the DeWitt girl." I pulled out my phone and touched the photos icon. "Who is the same girl Jeff Sherman decked in that parking garage yesterday."

Graham took the phone. "No shit? Sounds like a decent lead."

"We have to find her." I waved one hand at the closed door. "Kelsey Marie back in the break room?"

"Full of tacos and watching some Netflix show about a boarding school."

"Her half-brother's father is the guy from the local paper there in town."

"Pete?" His brows went up. "Interesting he didn't mention that."

"I'm not sure he knows."

"Huh. How did you find out?"

"Kid's birth certificate."

"Wouldn't the state notify him if he was listed on the birth certificate?"

"I don't actually know," I said. "On the one hand, you'd think so. On the other, I guess if she wanted child support the court would notify him of the petition."

I clicked a new window open and ran a search of the county court filings. "Nothing on child support." I lowered myself slowly to a seat.

"But something else?" Graham asked.

"There are two suits against the newspaper for bad debts, with him named as a defendant." I clicked links up in new windows as Graham leaned to read over my shoulder.

"Both filed in the second half of last year," he said. "So he needs money."

"Money is always a good motive," I said. "Shit. I'll say this —if it's him, he was damned crafty about getting on my good side."

"And getting information. He knows we have Kelsey Marie with us."

"And that we're in Austin," I said, snapping my fingers. "Which could be how Olivia DeWitt found out we're here."

"Huh? You lost me."

"She's here in Austin," I said. "Archie and I figured out how to use 911 to triangulate her phone, and she's in the city somewhere."

Archie stuck his head in the door. "Found Olivia." He shrugged into his jacket. "Hardin, you staying with the girl?"

"Do I have a choice? We can't take her to check out a suspect."

"How do we bring said suspect in for questioning with her here?" I hadn't thought of that until that second.

"Go see what she knows. If you need to bring her in, let me

know," Graham said. "And tell me what I can do while y'all are gone."

"Don't let Kelsey Marie die, and see what else you can find in the county court records."

"About who?" he asked.

"All of them," I said. "If Pete is hiding stuff, the rest of them might be, too. Check everyone from Sheriff Barnes to Miranda Sherman. Maybe if there's trouble to be found it will help narrow our search."

"I'm on it." He went to the table and plopped down in front of the laptop. "Y'all be safe out there."

31

"How did they find her so fast?" I asked.

"She's at a coffee shop. Patrol car in the parking lot saw the APB and called it right in."

I glanced around. "Holy hell, Graham wasn't kidding." The snow was nearly gone, a few piles clinging to the ground in the shade the only evidence of the crazy storm, save that everything was soaked.

"Welcome to Texas, where Jack Frost gets run out of town on a rail by full-on January spring."

I snorted. "Winter doesn't like us, Arch."

"They're still saying it's going to freeze tonight."

"I'm just going to keep hoping they're as wrong as they usually are about that."

"For now, I'm hoping we're right about this kid."

He turned into the parking lot at a tiny pink brick coffee house I'd never heard of and cut the engine, pointing to Olivia's Honda.

"We're playing this as a coincidence?" I asked.

"It might be the easiest way to get her to talk."

"Whatever you say." She was a kid. She probably wouldn't

think to question us showing up.

We walked into the shop talking a little louder than necessary about football, going straight to the counter to order.

I pulled cash out of my pocket while the woman behind the counter set our coffee down, waving the money away and pointing to our badges. "First responders never pay here," she said.

"Much obliged, ma'am," Archie said, tipping his hat.

I dropped a five into the tip jar and took my drink. "Thank you."

We chose the table next to Olivia's. She sat with her long legs folded up crisscross-style in the ladder-back wooden chair, tapping away at her laptop keyboard. There was no way to see what she was doing without practically climbing into her lap.

"Olivia?" I asked.

"Subtle." I just barely heard Archie so I knew the kid couldn't have, but I swiped at him with my boot under the table anyway. We were out of time for subtle.

She raised weary, red-rimmed eyes to meet mine over the top of her computer screen. "Do I know you?"

I stood and slid into the second seat at her table without waiting to be asked. "Faith McClellan. We spoke on the phone this morning, but I think we got cut off."

"Oh." Her eyes popped wide. "My phone, uh, it died."

I glanced around. "Is the rest of the 4H here too? I thought y'all were up at the stock show. Could've sworn I saw you in Fort Worth yesterday."

Tears welled and spilled over in half a blink. "Look, I know you saw me yesterday with Kelsey Marie's dad," she said. "I wasn't as knocked out as you thought, I just didn't want to talk to you." She closed her computer and moved to get up. "I still don't."

Archie stood and turned, blocking her exit. "I'm afraid I'm going to have to ask you to keep your seat." He kept his voice low, casting a quick glance around the room.

"Am I like under arrest or something?" She put the computer down and tugged on a strand of her hair.

"Not yet," Archie said.

I flicked a glance at him. We'd practically need a signed confession or a video of her without the hood to take a minor in without a guardian present. He was betting she didn't know that.

She sank back into her chair, still pulling at her hair.

Archie was usually right.

I leaned both elbows on the table, curving my lips into a half-smile. "Why did you sneak off to meet Mr. Sherman yesterday, Olivia?" I kept my voice low. There were a half dozen other people, mostly college students, in the shop, and while they probably didn't care what we were talking about, I wasn't practiced in the art of grilling a suspect in a public place.

"Because I'm stupid, apparently." Two tears rolled down her cheeks and she swiped at them with her sleeve, wincing when she caught the bruise covering her left orbital. "I thought that bastard might actually keep his word. I should've known the whole fucking family was full of lying pricks."

Archie turned his chair around and scooted it up to the table. "Lying about what?"

"He said he was going to pay for me to go to college." She sniffled. "Grandaddy can't afford that, he's spent all his money on nurses for Granny since she got sick, and I worked so hard with Clive to get that best in show scholarship, and then they told me I couldn't enter him because it wouldn't be fair to Kelsey Marie."

That was the second time someone had said that, but

Kelsey Marie didn't seem to know anything about it. "Who said that?"

"Mrs. Owensby," she said. "She said Kelsey Marie couldn't enter Samson because she didn't want to sell him."

I pulled out a notebook and jotted that down, keeping Kelsey Marie's contradiction to myself for the moment.

"And that made you mad?"

"Well sure. It made everyone mad. My granddaddy said the teacher could go straight to hell, I'd never seen him so worked up. He called an old friend up in Fort Worth and I was going to enter Clive anyway."

Oh. My. I gripped my pen tighter to keep my voice in check. "Did anyone know that?"

"Fucking Dustin Golden. That bastard. He killed my pig." Her lower lip trembled and more tears fell, spattering little dark spots on the wood tabletop in front of her.

"What?" I didn't mean for that to bust out of my throat so sharp or so loud. "Can you prove that?"

"I have photos. From the security camera Grandaddy had installed at Christmas. It was Dusty's Mustang in our driveway, and he snuck up into the barn in a robe with a hood."

Holy shit. "And you'd told him you were entering Clive in the stock show?"

"I did no such thing. I don't know where he found out, and Mr. Sherman wouldn't tell me. He just said he was sorry and he'd pay the scholarship himself. And then Granddaddy cooked Clive for the kickoff party, and I didn't even get to say goodbye. I know people said he was ornery, but he was mine."

She sniffled. "So I was supposed to go meet Sherman yesterday to get a check and take him the pictures, but instead he hit me and took off with the photos." She waved a hand at the angry purple bruise that spread from her temple to her nose and winced. "I couldn't go back to the hotel with my friends like this. And I couldn't go home until Granddaddy would be in bed. I drove back and hung out at the newspaper office until the storm started, and then I snuck in my bathroom window and went to my room. I didn't think Granddaddy knew I was in the house." She buried her face in her sleeves and sobbed. "Turned out I was right."

Archie and I exchanged a glance. He believed her. And—though I'd seen the theatrical predisposition of our killer in HD color—I did, too.

I patted her shoulder. That was a shitty week for anyone, let alone a teenager. "I'm so sorry for your loss."

"I saw them there this morning and I just had to get out of the house. I called the sheriff and told him I was in Fort Worth and they wouldn't answer the phone and I was worried." She peeked at me between splayed fingers. "I know you shouldn't lie to the police, but I wasn't supposed to be there. And I couldn't help them."

"We'll worry about whether that's important later," Archie said. "For right now, do you happen to have copies of those photos?"

She flipped her computer open. "Sherman wanted me to delete them, but now I'm real glad I didn't. Coach always says the best offense is good defense."

She turned the screen around. A grainy night vision photo filled the screen, an orange and black Mustang with a tall figure next to it, a black robe puddling on the ground around his feet, an axe gripped in one hand.

"Do you have one of Dustin's face?"

She blinked hard a couple of times. "Well, no." She swiped right. "See, he had this hood on. But that"—she touched the corner of the screen—"is definitely his class ring."

I peered at it.

Maybe.

"Can you send me those?" We could have cyber work some computer magic to enhance the image of the ring.

"Anyway, his dad said it was him."

"Did he?" Archie didn't sound confrontational, but I knew he was trying to make her consider her words.

"Well. He was going to pay me, wasn't he?"

That part was hard to argue with.

I opened her email program and sent the five images she had on the laptop to myself before I handed her computer back. "Where are you going to stay tonight, sweetie?"

She shrugged. "I don't want to go home."

"I don't think that's a great idea, but I'm wondering if you have a friend you can stay with."

She twisted her mouth to one side. "I could go to Sam's house, I guess. He didn't go with 4H to Fort Worth, and his mom is a great cook."

"I think I met him," I said. "You two are friends?"

"He's my boyfriend. Some of the time. But his mom will let me stay; she loves me."

Based on Sam's parents being home and the story she'd just told us, I was okay with that plan. I had a different idea about our killer than I'd expected to leave here with, though.

I handed her a card. "My cell is on the back. The roads are fine now; you head there and text me when you're safe, please."

Archie tipped his hat. "Drive safely, young lady," he said.

"Thank you," she said. "Do you think Dustin will have to go to jail for killing Clive? That's not really murder, but I don't know what to call it."

"Cruelty to animals," I said. "That's the short answer, though we could probably find other charges, too. And my best answer is that I'm not sure of anything right now."

"Except that we need to find Dustin and his mother?" Archie muttered.

I bobbed my head because he hadn't talked loud enough for her to hear him.

She got halfway to the door and turned back. "My grand-parents. What you said before...you were telling the truth? Nobody hurt them?"

I shook my head. "Nobody hurt them. At least not according to my source in the sheriff's office out there. They're working on the details, but he was pretty certain it wasn't foul play."

She ducked out the door. We watched her drive off. I dropped my cold coffee in the trash can next to the door on my way out.

Back in the car, Archie started the engine and the heater before he turned to me. "Jeff Sherman?"

Funny that we both skipped over Dustin and went right to Jeff.

"Got to be a reason he was willing to pay her off to keep the stepson out of trouble," I agreed. "I'm wondering if Dustin isn't going to tell us he chopped Clive up because Jeff told him to. I suppose Miranda's leaving might've made Jeff feel like he wasn't responsible for cleaning up Dustin's messes anymore, and that's why he backed out of the deal he made Olivia."

"But why kill her pig?"

"To be sure she couldn't compete against Kelsey Marie? What's weird, though, is that Kelsey Marie thought she was going to show Samson and her dad was going to buy him at auction to keep him as her pet. Yet I believed Olivia when she said the teacher told her otherwise."

"Maybe Sherman didn't have the cash to make that bid and so he killed her hog himself?" Archie mused.

"It seems short-sighted given that Kelsey Marie was

supporting the family with her YouTube income," I said. "But people don't always consider the big picture in moments of desperation."

"You make it sound like he'd have to be insane. How much can the kid actually be making?"

"Two hundred grand a month, plus profit from merchandise sales."

"No shit?" Archie let out a long whistle. "We're in the wrong line of work."

"It's almost obscene," I said. "A teenage girl paying off her dad's debts to the Dixie Mafia and holding together an entire family enterprise."

"Was she, though?" Archie tapped one finger on his chin.

"Was she what?"

"Paying off his debts to Dennis Laveaux? You said he borrowed a hundred grand the year before her channel took off. And she's raking in cash from the advertising on the channel and from merchandising, right?"

I pulled out my phone and flipped through photos until I found the farm ledgers I'd snapped photos of in Sherman's study as Archie talked.

"It's easy to assume that when people have a truckload of cash coming in, they're financially secure. But in two years, Sherman would owe Laveaux more than a hundred grand in interest alone at the shark rates they charge. And that would be in addition to whatever other credit he maxed out before he got desperate enough to go to a guy like that."

I heard the last bit as background noise, my eyes scanning ledger pages from last winter. "Quick math here has a hundred fifty grand coming in last January, with ten of that from the farm operations and twenty-four of it from *High on the Hog* merchandise sales. But there's about a hundred and sixty in expenses."

"So even with everything Kelsey Marie had coming in, they were still in the red."

I kept going through the pages. "Yep. Until October. That's the first time more came in than went out. And it's been that way since."

My eyes keyed on a line item in very small print, on the last day of each month. Labeled DLE, they started out at fifteen thousand and change in the months money was tight, and went to twenty-five, then thirty, then fifty thousand in the most recent months. "I'd bet this is Sherman trying to get Laveaux paid off, right here. He's probably making a dent."

"All the more reason for him to want the hog alive and entertaining people, though. Isn't it?" Archie said.

"Do we know anyone in Laveaux's organization?"

"Not that we're supposed to talk about."

"See if you can find out what Sherman's status with them is. The Oxy in Dustin's room and Sherman's admission that he paid off the sheriff might track with working off debts to the Dixie Mafia."

"It's enough to check out, especially with his involvement and these photos of his stepson," Archie agreed, reaching for his phone.

"Why don't we go ahead and get Fort Worth to pick Sherman up, too? Just in case someone tips him off that we're asking Laveaux's outfit about him. I'll drive back up there if I have to. He's got some questions to answer." I sighed. "What are we going to do with Kelsey Marie?"

"Put her in a hotel. Tell Hardin we need that big kid on his command and another good deputy to stand guard."

I'd sat in a hotel room with Jeff Sherman the night before and thought I was getting inside information from a drunk.

Had I gotten played instead?

32

Archie's friend Captain Jones at FWPD SWAT was a little miffed at being asked to pick up a suspect, but he owed Archie a favor, so he said he'd call us when he had Sherman ready to talk. Another call, and we had a supplier for the Oxy—which the local kingpin was under the impression Sherman had been distributing himself. Kelsey Marie's dad was in way deeper with the Dixie Mafia than a single loan. Deep enough that Archie's informant said he'd have to do some judicious asking around and call us back if we needed the full story.

We definitely did.

A third phone call from the parking lot, and Graham was on his way to put Kelsey Marie in a second-floor room at a DoubleTree near the university campus with Deputy Bolton and another officer outside her door. He promised to leave her laptop in Bolton's care, so she wouldn't be tempted to get online and see any of the awful comments cropping up by the hundreds every hour on her social media. Screencaps of Marta's death had gone viral faster than they could be squashed, and the blowback was intense. Kelsey Marie would have to deal with the fallout at some point, but today wasn't the day.

I told Graham we'd see him in a bit and put the phone in Archie's cupholder as he started the car.

"Back to the office to circle up with Hardin?"

"And start over with my board? I guess. I believed Olivia. While those photos wouldn't stand up in court to convict Dustin of killing her hog, I get why she thinks he did it."

"And the boy's stepfather offering to pay her off doesn't exactly scream innocence." Archie turned onto the expressway just as a wide chunk of snow fell from the bridge to our left and shattered, sending chunks skidding across both lanes.

The world fell into slow motion.

Archie's years of emergency driver training kicked in and he swerved to the shoulder, applying the brakes slowly and bringing us to a stop about a hundred yards clear of the ice. My head swiveled to track the scene as I grabbed blindly for the radio handset.

The pickup in the center lane hit a tire-size chunk and skidded into a spin. A red convertible smashed into the back driver's side of the truck, sending it spinning the other way. A deep horn sounded from a tractor-trailer in the left lane, the driver realizing half a second too late he couldn't stop. He tried to turn and his rig jackknifed, teetering on two tires before settling back to the ground.

"Faith McClellan, Texas DPS Rangers division, multi-vehicle accident on Northbound Capital Expressway just before 15th Street." I kept my voice flat as I recited pertinent information into the radio. "Request marked units, para-medics, and AFD assistance."

"Holy shit." Archie scrambled out of the car, running back

down the shoulder like he was still a college football player, not an aging cop with a shitty right knee.

I checked the side mirror for oncoming traffic and followed, pausing to grab a handful of flares from the trunk. Racing toward the scene, my eyes stuck on flames coming from under the hood of the pickup at the front end of the mess that racked up six vehicles before reaching a gap that allowed other drivers to stop.

Traffic backed up quickly, motorists honking and putting flashers on before exiting their cars in the middle of the freeway. Everyone had a phone in their hand, some calling for help and others taking video.

I popped the flares and spaced them out across the road behind the last car, a mangled mess half-lodged under the semi-trailer, which had twisted about as far as physics would allow without fully jackknifing.

Archie had beelined for the pickup, and was working the driver's door with a crowbar he'd snagged from a tool chest in the bed. On the other side of the spiderweb of cracks in the window, the driver was slumped over the wheel, blood trickling from his left ear.

Shit.

The first rule of working an accident scene is smart distribution of resources.

I knew it backward and forward—a stint with the highway patrol is required for commission to the Rangers. We had two officers and six damaged vehicles.

I turned to the crowd, which was inching closer to the flares. Cupping my hands around my mouth, I screamed, "Anyone a doctor or a nurse?"

A sea of heads shook, then began slowly parting from the divider wall. A petite blonde in yoga gear and sneakers, her blue parka unzipped, flew out of an Audi convertible and hopped the wall marking the southbound side of the expressway to come running. "Dr. Jodi Lindstrom, University Memorial general surgery. How do I help?"

Praise Jesus. My own real life Meredith Grey.

"Faith McClellan, Texas Rangers. We're still assessing, my partner and I were just driving through and narrowly missed getting caught up in this." I pointed to Archie. "He's working on getting to a guy who's bleeding from the ear. And I think this vehicle under the semi is the next one to triage."

A man in a gray jogging suit with a thick shock of matching hair stumbled from the red convertible, one hand covering his temple.

"Why don't you take him and let me see how stable this situation might be?" I asked.

She offered a thumbs-up and jogged toward the convertible's driver, moving his hand and pressing hers back down in its place when blood spurted from his head.

The first strains of sirens howled as I reached the car pinned beneath the trailer. It was a black Mustang. I didn't see the orange racing stripes until I was ass-deep on hands and knees under the trailer.

"Holy shit. No way," I muttered, wincing as a shard of shattered glass worked its way into my palm. I pulled a flashlight from my pocket and tried to choose my hand placement as carefully as I could.

"Hello?" I called. "Can anyone hear me?"

"Help!" A male voice, faint but panicked, from the driver's side. I thought.

"That's why I'm here," I said. "And more help is on the way. Do you smell gasoline from where you are?"

"No. I can't...move. My head is stuck between the steering wheel and the windshield."

"Is there anyone in the vehicle with you?"

"She's...oh God, she's not moving. Hey. Hey! Wake up! Hey, she's not waking up. There's a lot of blood. Oh my God. Oh my God, please get me out of here!" His voice got higher with every panicked word.

Fuck. "I need you to stay calm for me," I said. "I'm coming. What's your name?"

No answer.

"Hello? Are you still with me?"

Silence.

Shit.

"Hey, Officer?" Dr. Lindstrom's voice came from behind me. "Can I help?"

"There's a woman on the other side of this vehicle. He said she's not responsive before he stopped answering me. I'm not sure this trailer is stable, and someone should also check on the driver of the rig."

"I did, he has a broken rib and a few facial lacs. He'll be fine. Can you see into the car from where you are?"

"Not yet. And I'm slicing my hands all to hell on the glass." I wriggled forward, dropping from my knees to my stomach and hoping my coat was thick enough to ward off the glass. The whole rig was precariously perched, with at least two of the passenger side tires on the trailer blown from the jack-knife, so the further I went, the tighter the space. And the more pancaked the Mustang.

"Almost to the window," I called to Dr. Lindstrom, turning my head to crane for a look.

Sliding closer, I pointed the light at the jagged maw of glass where the driver's window used to be.

And almost wished I hadn't.

The guy's neck was hyperextended and twisted in a gruesome way that had me wondering how he'd been talking at all. Not that I could holler that back to the doctor—not worth the risk he might come to and hear me. Causing accident victims to panic is never a wise move.

I worked the light around. "If you can hear me, I need you to hold perfectly still," I called.

The roof of the car had caved, tighter toward the front, shattering the windshield and cutting the headroom almost to the tops of the headrests. I couldn't see around him to the passenger side. His shoulders were pinned to the seat by the belt, but it looked like his head had been thrown forward just before the roof caved, and he'd been looking at his passenger.

I tapped lightly on the doorframe with the light. "Hello?"

Nothing.

"I'm coming back your way, Doc."

Clearing the trailer, I stood carefully, the warmth running over my fingers in the cold air telling me I didn't want to look at my hands.

Rounding the back of the Mustang, I checked the plates instead.

FASTR1

This was Dustin Golden's car. What the hell were the odds?

"Fuck me," I muttered. We'd found him—yay! But also, he might be dead, which wasn't so helpful.

Archie appeared at my elbow as Dr. Lindstrom reached for my hand.

"Can I just take a look?" she asked.

I kept my eyes on Archie, ignoring the stinging fire in my palm as she picked glass out of it. "That's Dustin Golden in there. With his neck twisted all to fuck and his mother bleeding out." I jerked my head. "Look at the plate."

"I'll be goddamned." He had to shout it over the sirens, which were just the other side of the crowd, finally. The longest minutes in my life are ones I've spent waiting for fire and EMS to arrive on an accident scene.

It took another minute and a half for a pair of firefighters to get to us.

"You in charge?" They looked from one of us to the other.

"Next please," Dr. Lindstrom said, letting go of my right hand and starting on the left.

I nodded to the firefighters. "Faith McClellan and Archie Baxter, Texas Rangers. We have two vics pinned in this vehicle, one with severe injuries to the neck and head, one with unknown injuries, both non-responsive, though the driver was talking to me until a few minutes ago."

"Joe Herrera and Samantha Johnson, AFD. We'll get them out," Johnson said, turning to Dr. Lindstrom. "And you are?"

"Jodi Lindstrom, general surgery at University Memorial."

"Excellent," Herrera said. "Looks like we're going to need you, can you stay?"

"As long as I'm needed," Lindstrom said.

Johnson turned, pointing to the trailer. "Can we move this, or do we need a crane?"

"The tires on the far side are out. At least some of them are. They blew when it tried to turn," I said.

"So the car wedged in there like that is likely the only thing keeping it upright," Herrera said. "How about the rig? The driver clear?"

"Yeah, the doc checked him out already, he's back there." I tipped my head to the shoulder of the road where the other victims, including Archie's bleeding ear from the pickup, were all huddled together, some talking on their phones, others staring at the Mustang, probably feeling selfish for being so thankful they were walking around the shoulder and not pinned under an 18-wheeler.

"We can't pull the car out," I said. "It's wedged in too

tightly and the driver's neck injuries are too severe to risk jarring him like that."

"What do you think? Tip it?" Herrera asked Johnson.

She pointed to my hands. "You were under there?"

"I was."

"Is the car more than halfway under the trailer?"

"No."

"Did you smell any gas?"

"I did not."

She patted Herrera's shoulder. "Tip it."

"Officers, can you take out the rest of those far side tires for us?" he asked as Johnson jogged toward the crowd.

"Folks, I'm going to need you to return to your vehicles now, please," she called. "Return to your vehicles and move them to the shoulders so we can get the trucks through. Thank you for your cooperation."

Archie and I exchanged a glance.

"You want us to shoot out the tires on the far side of this rig?" I asked.

"It will lean it back sufficiently to allow us to use jacks to tip it over. That way we can get to the victims in the vehicle, and as long as the car isn't more than halfway under, everything we do will relieve pressure on the roof, not add it."

"You need someone over there telling the kid in the driver's seat not to move if he suddenly has space to," I said. "His name is Dustin."

"On it," Herrera said.

"Let's get all these people out of here, y'all," Archie said.

"Outstanding." Herrera grinned. "Yes sir."

Johnson pulled a fire engine up, followed by a second engine and an ambulance. Archie waved the ambulance to the front of the wreckage, herding the other accident victims that way. When the ambulance stopped and the medics got out to begin tending injuries, everyone was well out of line with the trailer.

Herrera and a burly firefighter with a beard so long and thick it belonged on Santa Claus hauled a comically large hydraulic jack out of the back of one engine and placed it near the trailer.

"Do your thing, Officers."

Archie and I jogged to the other side of the trailer.

"We're really going to do this?"

"You want those people out of the car?"

I shook my head. "Discharging our weapons in the middle of the freeway. Not on my list this morning."

"That's why we love the job."

I drew my weapon and planted my feet. He moved to the other end of the trailer and did the same.

My palms protested squeezing anything. I did it anyway.

There were six tires that weren't already flat. I fired into the two closest to me and watched them deflate. Two shots from Archie. We met in the middle, nodding and each taking a third shot.

The trailer sank to the road, massive puddles of rubber spreading under the wheels.

"Go, go, go!" Herrera's voice came from the other side, and Archie grabbed my sleeve and tugged me to the front of the rig.

"Just in case they go too fast," he said.

I holstered my Sig and we moved back, watching the massive jack tilt the trailer higher and higher.

When it crashed to the dividing wall and we could see daylight above the Mustang, Herrera called a halt.

"Medics!" Johnson hollered.

They fanned out around the car. We followed, hanging several yards back and watching.

My phone buzzed in my pocket. I whimpered pulling it free. My palms were free of the big chunks of glass—but also of bandages.

"Get someone to fix that." Archie scowled at me.

"In a minute." I smiled. "It's Graham." I put the phone to my ear. "We got hung up," I said.

"Are you bleeding?" he asked.

"Uh. As a matter of fact, I am. I'm also now curious as to how you knew that."

"Did you just shoot three tires out from under a semi?"

"Oh shit."

I spun, looking for the news van.

Not on this side.

Jogging back to the nose of the rig, I leaned around and spotted it.

"Goddamn her." I swore into the phone, glaring at Skye Morrow from the other side of the freeway.

"She's live, don't punch her," Graham said.

"What the fuck does she care about a car crash anyway?" I grumbled, walking back to Archie. "I thought she was a bigshot investigative reporter."

"Anchor said she was southbound on the freeway in her van when she saw the scene and stopped. They sent a chopper too."

"So the lieutenant will get a multi-angle view of me killing giant tires. Great."

"What's going on there? And what happened to your hands?"

"I found the rest of Kelsey Marie's family," I said. "But they're pinned in the Mustang under the trailer. They needed to tip the trailer up to get them out. So we helped it tip. Anything going on there?"

"I pulled the flash drive from Marta Milosevic's night table out of the glovebox and looked at it."

"You're my hero. What'd you find?"

"A single spreadsheet file. Lots of big numbers, no labels. But I can imagine that we're dealing with dollars and not like, tubes of toothpaste. It's a lot of money, making that assumption."

"Just different amounts? Weird." And possibly not all that useful.

"Dates and amounts. Maybe account numbers. I'm working on it. You take care of yourself and see what you can get out of the mom and the stepbrother."

"We gotta get them out of this fucking car alive first."

"Be safe, baby. See you soon."

I hung up and turned to find Archie waiting with a fresh-faced paramedic who couldn't possibly be out of high school.

"This is Drake. He's going to fix your hands. Cooperate please." Archie pinched his lips into a stern line.

"Thanks." I held my hands out, palms up. "Have at it, Drake."

He worked quickly, using a magnifier and tweezers to clean up the rest of the glass and wrapping everything in cool, soft layers of gauze.

"Thanks," I said.

"Happy to help." He closed the lid on his first aid tackle box and hustled back to his ambulance.

I turned to Archie. "Skye is here. We were on TV."

He groaned. "Great. I'm shocked that your mother hasn't called me."

"Oh, I bet she has. Your phone is in the car."

"Shit."

Metal on metal squealed as the firefighters peeled the mangled roof of the car back.

A squad of medics rushed for the car with backboards and neck braces ready, Dr. Lindstrom standing back to call out orders and check the victims.

In less than three minutes, they had both strapped to boards. "They're breathing," Johnson called to the doctor, flashing a thumbs up.

Lindstrom approached the scene with Herrera's okay, going to the driver first. She leaned in to examine him and then turned to Herrera and waved her hands as she talked, but I couldn't make out what she was saying. The firefighters lifted the board onto a waiting gurney and took off for the ambulance.

Johnson and her team stepped back as Lindstrom approached the passenger and my hand closed around Archie's arm.

"Is she...?" He let the question hang in the air.

I nodded, my eyes on the bloody but definitely African American woman on the backboard.

That was not Kelsey Marie's mother.

So where the hell was Miranda Sherman?

33

First rule of an average homicide investigation: the easy answers are usually the right ones. When the answers get harder to come by, it means the case isn't average.

"Well shit. Was the guy in the ambulance even Dustin?" I pointed to the Mustang. "That's Dustin's car. Why isn't anything ever easy?"

"Let them clear their scene and we'll ask about ID," Archie said. "But yeah, my kingdom for one decent lead. It's like being in that nightmare where every time you can see the end of the maze, the walls move." He bumped my arm with his shoulder. "And you thought you were doing an easy favor for your granny's old friend."

"Teach me to have a big head. I walked out of her house thinking this was beneath me, and you'd laugh at me."

"I laughed a little." He chuckled. "But as usual, you have an eye for when something's not right."

"I suppose at least the dead woman and drunk-ass sheriff means for right now this takes priority for me. If I had to work another case during the day tomorrow, I'd lose my mind."

Johnson waved one arm in a "wrap it up" signal, her crew

turning to pack up and a fleet of tow trucks waiting for a go-ahead. An APD patrolman in a traffic vest stepped out to wave them into position when the firefighters had cleared.

Archie and I jogged over to the tow driver examining the Mustang. "So it turns out, we have an all-points out on this vehicle," Archie said after introducing himself. "We're going to need to check the vehicle for ID on the people they pulled out of it before it's loaded up."

The guy shrugged and waved a hand at the car. "Go for it, man. I'm not sure how you're going to get into it, but you're welcome to try."

Archie and I surveyed the car. "I can fit through this passenger side opening without too much trouble, I think," I said.

He peered in, judging for himself. "Is that a handbag on the floor?"

Sure was. I leaned in through a twisted, cut, and peeled door and snagged the handle.

The purple Kate Spade wallet inside had three credit cards and a driver's license. "Serena McCombs, home address in Beeville, DOB 8-19-99."

"So now we need to know how she knows Dustin Golden?" I tucked the wallet back inside the purse and passed it to Archie.

"I'm more concerned with where his mother is, truthfully, but maybe this young woman could help with that, too." I turned back to the wreckage of Dustin's prized possession. So Miranda took her son and left, but she didn't go far.

Stretching my spine and leaning on tiptoe, I opened the car's center console and rummaged. "No phone, but I got another wallet." I slid back out and flipped it open, looking for a hotel room key card. I found nine credit cards and a whole slot full of business cards.

"That's a lot of plastic for a 19-year-old kid," I said.

"I mean, he does own five cars," Archie quipped.

"This is weird even for rich people. And from what I've been able to gather, the parents aren't the breadwinners in their house, Kelsey Marie is."

"So they're probably doing some shady tax shit because she can't write them off as dependents, but they can write her off."

"I should've thought of that. Lord knows I grew up around enough discussions of dodging income taxes."

I pulled the Amex card out. "Uh. Dalton Boyd?" I handed that card to Archie and went to the next. "Dalton Boyd."

Business card. "Dalton Boyd, senior buyer specialist at Keller Williams Realty."

The card had a photo. I stared.

Broad shoulders. Shaggy blond hair.

"Shit, Archie, this might be the guy who was driving. I didn't see his face, but I'm thinking from the back he'd look similar enough to Kelsey Marie's brother that I wouldn't have noticed it wasn't him." I passed him the card.

"But this is definitely Golden's car."

"That's his plate. According to our records."

"So why is this real estate hotshot driving it too fast to stop behind a pileup?" Archie waved a hand. "He was the last car that hit, and he had to be going pretty damn fast to lodge that far under the back of this trailer."

"Maybe he's helping Miranda find a new home? And the kid loaned him the car?"

"Maybe. But I think we ought to go ask him."

34

Our badges did jack shit for getting information out of the desk nurse, who waved a HIPAA document in my face and told me to come back with a warrant in a tone so snide she was lucky Archie got me away from the desk while she still had all her teeth, injured hands be damned.

"Thank you, ma'am." He tipped his hat and I swallowed what I wanted to say.

"She could tell us where they are if she wanted to," I muttered.

"We don't need her to." Archie steered me to a set of double doors leading to a hallway that connected this wing to the rest of the hospital. "That doctor got out of her car in her workout clothes on a Sunday afternoon to help us, and she stayed to pull these people out of the car. She's in the building, I guarantee it. The surgical floor here is four. Let's go find her."

I walked faster toward the lobby and the elevators. He was a good cop, but the thing I still needed to learn from him the most was patience. I was better than just about anyone at being dogged in my pursuit of an answer, but Archie was a master of looking at every angle to a problem, which gave him multiple paths to a solution.

We stepped out of the elevator on the fourth floor and almost walked into a tall, dark-haired guy in a white coat and gray scrubs.

"Excuse me," I said, moving to step around him.

"Wow, those are some impressive bandages," he said, bending his knees to catch my eye.

"It looks worse than it is," I said. "The paramedic was overly enthusiastic."

"Can I have a look?" he asked through a bright white smile.

Archie snorted behind me, but the doctor ignored him. His coat said his name was Chris Gilroy, M.D.

More than one way to skin a cat...or to find an accident victim.

"I'm okay, though I appreciate that. What I need right now is to speak to Dr. Jodi Lindstrom. Do you think you could help me find her?"

"Can I ask what she can do that I can't?"

He had self-confidence, I'd give him that. Probably handy in his profession.

"Help me find an accident victim that I need to interview in connection to a homicide case," I said. "Faith McClellan, Texas Rangers. I'd shake your hand, but..." I waved my gauze mitt.

"Nice to meet you, Ranger...McClellan. As in?" He raised his eyebrows.

"As much as I wish it weren't. This is my partner, Archie Baxter."

"I see. Let me find Jodi for you."

"Tell that poor guy he doesn't have a chance," Archie said as soon as the doctor was out of earshot.

"I'll be nice about it as soon as I find Dr. Lindstrom," I said. "This way we don't have to risk any more surly nurses."

"Surely there's not more than one that bad in this building."

"Why chance it?" I whispered as Dr. Chris headed back toward us.

"She is in an emergency laparotomy on an MVA victim." He clasped his hands together in front of him. "So...you sure you don't want me to take a look at the hands? I'm very good at my job."

"And what exactly is that?" I asked.

"I'm head of cosmetic surgery," he said.

"I don't suppose there's a better person to have check my hands out, then."

"Right this way." He waved us into an empty room and held up one finger. "I'll be right back. Y'all have a seat."

"Faith." Archie's voice dripped exasperation.

"We have to wait for the other doctor anyway, and I can't very well function properly with my hands like this. Maybe he's better at bandaging. Call Graham and see what kind of headway he made with that flash drive. I feel like we're getting close to figuring out what the hell is happening here, and if we can just get a handle on the situation, it's an easy jump to who killed Marta."

"Your definition of an 'easy jump' is on par with Evel Knievel's."

"Please call Graham."

"Shall I tell him about the handsome doctor?"

I snorted. "He's quite secure in the knowledge that he has no competition."

"I'll be right outside." Archie pulled out his phone as Dr. Chris came back in carrying a metal tray full of unpleasant-looking sharp things.

He rolled a stool over and sat down, putting the tray on a table and pulling another toward me. "Let's have a look."

I laid my left hand on the table and gritted my teeth when he got down to pulling the gauze pads loose.

My hand kind of looked like someone went at it with a meat tenderizing hammer. Gross.

"How did you do this?" He pulled on a headband with a magnifier and a light and flicked the light on.

"Crawling over glass shards to try to get the victims in that totaled car."

"And you kept going even though it was doing this to your hands?"

"I wanted to get them out of the car. I had reason to believe they might have information about a homicide case."

"You are some kind of determined, Officer." He glanced up and smiled. "Let's start by getting the rest of the glass out of here, and then we'll irrigate it with some warm saline."

Picking over my palm, he noticed my ring. "Too late to the party to ask you to get some coffee?"

"I'm afraid so."

"He's a lucky man."

"I don't deserve him," I said.

"Some of these need sutures. When did this happen?"

"About two hours ago?"

He reached for the other tray, turning back with a small basin and a bag of saline, which he popped one end off of and squeezed over my hand into the bucket. "I'll re-dress it when I'm done here. Leave the bandages for 24 hours—I'd recommend wearing latex gloves and using hand sanitizer on them when you need to—then wash the cuts with warm water and replace the gauze. I'll show you how to make it more tolerable."

I watched his fingers as he sewed up three of the biggest

gashes in the meat of my palm. He was good—I could hardly see the sutures, which boded well for any scars. "Thanks for your help," I said.

"Of course." He clipped off the last thread and moved on to fix up my right hand, using gauze and tape to wrap my palms in a much more svelte fashion and putting antibiotic cream and Band-Aids on the finger cuts.

Archie stuck his head back in. "I think we've got something."

"Homicide, huh?" Dr. Chris swiveled his head between us. "That sounds fascinating."

"It's usually not dull," I said. "Though I'm sure your job is the same."

"Eh. Not today, anyway. Officer, it's been a pleasure." He grabbed a pair of latex gloves and held them open one at a time while I slid my hands in. "All set." He handed me the box. "Change them as needed, and stay safe out there."

"Thank you, Doctor."

"I'll see if Jodi's out of her OR yet."

Archie held the door for Dr. Chris as he ducked out of the room, then shut it behind him.

"That spreadsheet is indeed full of account numbers—the offshore kind, and the dollar values listed look like there's been a shit ton of money moving between them."

"Nice. But do we know for who? Or why?"

Archie shook his head. "Graham is working on that. He's got my guy at the State Department tracking down the accounts' owners. When we know whose name the accounts are in, it might just crack the whole damned thing."

"We're finally getting somewhere." I tapped one foot. "Marta was a refugee, you know. From Albania. Her mother is in the Netherlands. You think she was trying to get cash to buy her mom a way into the U.S.?"

"Maybe. We'll know more in a few hours."

A knock sounded at the door and Jodi Lindstrom poked her head into the room. "Dr. Gilroy said you wanted to see me?" she asked.

"We need to speak with the folks they pulled out of that Mustang this afternoon."

"That might prove a little difficult. She's in recovery coming out of anesthesia and he died on the table about twenty-five minutes ago."

I sucked in a sharp breath.

"Were you able to get an ID on him?"

She flipped the lid on the tablet in her hands.

"Dalton Boyd, 31, lives in South Austin." She tapped the screen a few times. "He was talking while they pulled him out. Kept asking about his girl and saying he was sorry, that she told him he should slow down but he just got the car and wanted to show off."

"Got the car?" I leaned forward. "You're sure that's what he said? Not borrowed it?"

"I'm sure. She was bleeding so badly I thought they'd have to sedate him on the ride in. But then he just passed out in the ambulance, and neuro took him straight into the OR when we got here. I've been working on her, but I checked on him when I got out of surgery because I know she's going to be asking about him when she wakes up." Her lips turned down at the corners. "I'm not looking forward to telling her we couldn't save him."

"We understand."

"I'd imagine you do, yeah."

Her phone bleated and she looked down at it. "Speaking of..."

"Dr. Lindstrom, could we come with you?" I asked. "I know the timing is not ideal, but we have an active murder investigation and a probability that lives could be in danger, and I need to know what she knows about where her friend got that car."

She tipped her head to one side and studied me. "Yeah. Okay."

"Thank you."

Archie fell into step beside me at the door. "You think Dustin sold his car? Maybe they needed cash?"

"I think someone did. And I'm beginning to think it seems like Jeff Sherman has an awful lot of secrets, and I'm not sure how much we can trust anything he told me."

Serena McCombs was too groggy for anything she told us to stand for a warrant, but I didn't need a warrant. I needed to know what the hell was happening with the Sherman family, because instinct and experience were combining to tell me I had misjudged this situation on at least one level.

Dr. Lindstrom, who'd agreed to stay quiet while we asked about the car, checked machines and IV bags and tapped notes into her charting tablet.

"Did Dalton buy that car recently, Serena?" I asked.

"Are you a different doctor?" she asked, her eyes on my gloved hands.

"No, I'm not a doctor, my name is Faith. I'm looking for the last person who owned the car you were in today. Did Dalton buy it recently?"

"Day before yesterday. I was with him."

"From a teenager, or maybe a woman?"

She shook her head, grimacing. "Ouch. No, no. It was a big guy. Older, like maybe my dad's age. Thick drawl." She pointed at Archie. "Same hat."

Jeff Sherman. Archie met my eyes over her bed while Dr. Lindstrom watched, her eyes wide.

"Did he get a copy of the title?"

"We took it to the DMV processing center, but they said it was Friday and they would get to it Monday," she said. "I told Dalton that was a lot of cash to fork over without making sure the title was in his name, but I swear, we didn't steal it. They have the signed paper at the DMV office on East Parmer."

"Thank you. You rest and feel better, Serena."

Archie and I backed away, not hurrying until we were out of her eyeline.

"That son of a bitch," I swore under my breath.

"We don't know anything for sure."

"We know enough for maybe," I said. "I didn't get the faintest inkling that something was off with him. Goddammit. This wedding shit is messing up my asshole radar. People who work in that industry are way too fake."

"Let me see if Jones was able to find him," Archie said as we stepped onto the elevator.

"So what, he found out the wife was leaving him and he killed her?" I mused, punching the L button harder than my injured finger appreciated.

"And the boy?" Archie looked skeptical.

"Maybe the kid came home early and saw it. Maybe he used that vehicle to dump their bodies. We've seen all this before, Archie."

He shrugged. "Wouldn't be the weirdest thing. It's usually someone they know. But we don't have shit to prove the woman and her son are dead. You said the kid was the local Oxy dealer. Maybe she's lying low to keep him out of trouble?"

"But that's actually bugged me all weekend, too. Why would a teenage boy leave home for good, moving out, and leave not only his main source of income, but all of his clothes? She still had plenty of stuff hanging neatly in the closet, too, come to think of it." I stomped a foot. "I should've noticed that before now. Sherman told me she'd left him more than 36 hours ago. I'm good at noticing the details. It shouldn't have taken me this long to get to the idea that his word was the only evidence they left voluntarily." I shook my head. "My gut says they're dead, Arch."

"Never disregard the gut," Archie said in a practiced tone. "But do always work the case."

He touched his phone screen a few times and put it to his ear. "Jones, it's Baxter again. Any luck on the pickup I asked for?"

He was quiet for a minute. "I see. Thanks, man. Stay on the traffic cams and let me know if you find him." He put the phone back in his pocket, shaking his head, and he followed me off the elevator.

"I have to get to Kelsey Marie," I said.

"Hardin has two deputies outside her door. I don't care who this guy is, he's not getting past that Bolton kid. Boy missed a calling as a professional wrestler."

"It's her dad," I said, pulling out my phone to call Graham. "He wouldn't have to get past anyone. All he has to do is track her laptop and call the hotel. She'll go to him."

35

"Jones said the room had been cleaned by the time he got the damned manager at the hotel to tell him Sherman had checked out," Archie seethed as he dodged in and out of traffic, speeding toward the DoubleTree where Kelsey Marie was sleeping, no sign of visitors, according to Bolton. "Jones banged on the door for ten minutes, until the manager sent someone up there, and then they gave him this bullshit runaround.

"This Sherman guy had to have paid them off. There's discretion because of some sort of celebrity adjacent status, but it's never that hard to get hotel personnel to talk when you wave a badge. It was thirty minutes of 'oh the computer crashed' and 'you can't enter a guest room without a warrant, so let's just wait for it to reboot...' By the time Jones found out he was gone and got into the room, nobody could've told he'd ever been there. Parking lot feed shows his truck turning left out of the valet drive. That's all we've got. They're following traffic cam feeds in the area to see if they can pick up his truck and track him, but the weight of the snow knocked a lot of them offline, so it's patchy."

"Of course." I drummed my fingers on my thigh, my thoughts on Marta. "So say for the sake of argument that we've found the magic rock here, and Jeff Sherman killed his wife and maybe also his stepson, and that's why we haven't been able to find them. How does that link to the pigs and Marta? The numbers in her spreadsheet—were they her accounts? Was she blackmailing him?"

"Hardin said there was almost two million total accounted for there. So if it was blackmail, he paid big time to keep her quiet."

"And then there's the whole fact that he was in Fort Worth when she died." I sighed. "Nothing here fits neatly. Every time I think I have a bead on what's going on, there's a hole because someone has an alibi."

"You did say the videos you saw showed someone of above average height, but not outlandishly so. And thin. Could it actually be this guy?"

I tipped my head to one side and leaned back in my seat when the light changed. "Maybe? The height thing would be easy to be off by a few inches because of the camera angle, especially on the video in Samson's pen because the lighting was crazy. It's true I disregarded Sherman as a suspect based on his size, but that could've been a mistake. I mean, I even said the figure at Marta's looked shorter than the one from the video of Samson. So I'm willing to give that I started out with a faulty guess on that." I paused. "Wait. His boots."

"Pardon?"

"Every time I've seen Jeff Sherman, he had boots on. Nice ones. I never looked at the heels, but they could be high enough to make him look too tall to be the person in these videos."

"Clever."

I sat forward in my seat, warming to the theory. "And

Sherman isn't scrawny or anything, but he's had a puffy jacket on every time I've ever seen him, and his jeans are relaxed, cowboy style, like yours. He might be thin enough to fit. Especially with the weird camera angle. I'd say it's definitely not impossible."

"It's enough to keep trying to find him."

I stared out the window. "I'm still stuck on the pig. Why would he kill Samson?"

"I mean, talk about cutting off your nose to spite your face. The pig was literally a cash cow...uh...pet...for the family. Why would Sherman kill it, no matter how mad he was?"

"I'm not any help there. No idea. Cover, maybe? To make it look like it was someone else?"

"It did almost work, if that was the idea."

It was like the world's most complicated equation, and I had everything almost balanced, but I kept finding overlooked variables out of place.

No matter. Right then my biggest concern was making sure Kelsey Marie was safe. We could ask more questions of or about her dad when I had confirmed that.

I unbuckled my seat belt at the parking lot entrance and jumped out of the car before Archie had it completely stopped in the portico at the front of the hotel, sprinting for the doors.

The elevator covered five floors, and Christmas came faster than it did.

I stepped off on two and ran to Bolton, gesturing to the door. "Open it."

"I don't have the key," he said. "The commander said you were on your way, but I'm telling you, she's asleep. She said she was going to bed and it's been quiet ever since."

"I need to see that for myself, Bolton. How are you guarding a witness and you don't have the room key?"

"It's..." He frowned. "She's a teenage girl. I didn't feel right about having a key."

"Oh, for fuck's sake."

I looked at my gloved and bandaged hands and pointed to the door. "Knock. Loud."

He raised one Hulk-sized fist and pounded so hard the heavy hotel door rattled in the frame.

"That ought to do it." I leaned toward the door. "Kelsey Marie! It's Faith, please open the door."

I pressed my ear to it.

Silence.

"Again," I said.

Bolton obliged.

The door to the next room over opened. "Do you mind? I'm trying to work," a disheveled man in a rumpled button-down and khakis asked, glaring through his square, black-rimmed glasses.

"So sorry, sir," Bolton said. "Police emergency."

"We won't be loud for long," I said, my eyes still on the door. "Kelsey Marie!"

The guy disappeared into his room, muttering about the caliber of guests here going downhill.

I waited for a thirty count. Still nothing.

"I'm going to get a key."

I tapped my foot through the elevator ride and ran to the desk, flashing my badge at the clerk. "I need a key to room 247."

"Can I have your name, please?"

"Faith...Hardin." It felt a little weird on my tongue, but I knew Graham had booked the room so that would be the last name they had on file.

"Oh sure, Mrs. Hardin. I just need to see your ID."

I patted my pockets and made a face. "I'm pretty sure it's in the room."

It was. I just didn't say which room.

She looked around and smiled, leaning in. "I'm sure it's you." She winked.

Key in hand, I charged back down the hall to Bolton. "Still nothing?" I asked as I shoved the key into the slot on the door.

"No ma'am."

I flung the door wide, not sure what I was even expecting. Bolton and his partner had been outside all day, the other guy was just gone to dinner. Jeff Sherman wasn't in there.

But neither was his daughter. The phone lay off the hook on the table next to the bed, the covers rumpled.

My stomach twisted as I checked the small closet and the bathroom before I noticed the balcony. She wasn't out there, either, but that's how she left.

Sometimes I fucking hate being right.

36

"Her bag is gone too." I pointed to a slowly-slushifying snow-bank with a crater in the top of it just under and to the left of the balcony. "Her dad called her and she jumped off the balcony and left with him."

"Why the hell would she do that?" Archie asked, opening and checking drawers.

"It's her father. She trusts him. He could've told her any kind of outlandish bullshit. 'Your mom is hurt, I know what happened to Samson,' anything that would've given him a plausible reason to convince her she needed to jump ten feet to the ground rather than deal with Bolton and try to get permission to leave."

"So something urgent."

"Right."

"Dammit!" Graham slammed a fist into the top of the dresser.

I put one hand on his shoulder. "We'll find her."

"How? Who the fuck knows where he took her?"

I turned to Archie. "Can you go back to APD for another

all-points, this one on his truck? She's only seventeen; we can put out an Amber Alert, too."

"On it." He pulled out his phone and tapped a text. "Oh hey...Fort Worth has traffic cam footage of him merging onto southbound 35W about four hours ago."

"Nice." I let my chin drop to my chest. "I shouldn't have let her out of my sight."

"We'll find her," Graham reassured me. "I agree that the thing about the wife and the stepson and the car is weird. Maybe even damning. But we also don't know anything for sure. He's her father. It's possible he's trying to keep her safe. I mean, if he was going to hurt her, wouldn't he have done it already? She was asleep in his house every night, right?"

He was right. I needed to slow down and look at the facts —what we actually knew, not what I suspected. My instinct is good after so many cleared cases, but it's not infallible. And right then all I knew was Sherman lied to me about the car his wife and her son took when they left; he then sold said car and forged the kid's signature on the title; he assaulted Olivia DeWitt after—according to her—trying to buy her silence because she said Dustin killed her pig; and he was headed toward Austin the last time traffic cameras could give us his whereabouts.

Kelsey Marie was gone, and I couldn't think of anyone she would leave with other than her father because she was right-fully scared shitless after the week she'd had.

It all seemed like it ought to add up to trouble.

But maybe there were variables to this equation I didn't see yet.

Taking a deep breath, I raised my head as Archie hung up from calling in the APB and the Amber Alert to Austin PD. "Going out shortly."

By the time we cleared the hotel room, everyone's phone blared with the Amber Alert. I checked their information. All correct. "Now we wait?"

"Let's go back to the office. We'll go over what we have and make sure we haven't missed something. Someone will find them, Faith. They always do."

It was whether or not we'd find them in time that had my heart rate up.

Hands on my hips, I surveyed the whiteboard in the conference room at headquarters.

"We still don't know what happened to the DeWitts."

"Sheriff said he didn't suspect foul play."

"I'm not sure I trust him to be a good judge of that." I tapped a marker on my thigh, looking at the lines I'd drawn between Clive the pig and Dustin Golden, and then to Miranda Sherman.

Jeff Sherman's name had taken over the center of the board, with lines webbing out to connect him to most of the victims and locations. The more I thought about it, the more I thought I'd missed a whole fucking lot when the guy was right under my nose.

My eyes kept going back to Samson. Why would Sherman hurt a pig that made him so much money?

"Say something is off about the DeWitts. Just for the sake of argument. What if Jeff Sherman killed the people and someone else killed the pigs?" I asked.

"Didn't the other girl—Olivia, right?—say that Dustin killed her pig? What if he killed Kelsey Marie's pig too?"

"Why would he do that, though?" I asked, tapping the marker faster before I whirled and started pacing.

"Jealousy? She was the famous sibling," Archie said.

"But again, the timeline is off." Graham pointed to the top of the board. "Wasn't he already gone before they died?"

The fucking timeline was my problem with the whole damn case. I stared at it, letting the letters go soft and unfocused, looking for what we weren't seeing.

It was right there. The smallest possible detail, and I had seen it—or not seen it, when you got right down to it—with my own two eyes. I snapped my fingers and spun to face Archie and Graham.

"Everyone has told us they were gone. But that's part of the simple beauty of this whole thing, isn't it?" I touched the timeline. "According to this, Jeff couldn't have killed Marta because he was in Fort Worth all weekend. He made himself an alibi—we even went up there and verified it ourselves."

"Why do I think you're about to tell us how this guy was in two places at once?"

I pointed at Archie. "Because I kind of am. Marta left the Sherman house Friday night for her weekend off. Kelsey Marie said her dad left Friday morning for Fort Worth, and we saw him in Fort Worth on Saturday. Marta's body was found thanks to a welfare check Saturday night, and all Craig could tell me about that was the caller was male, the dispatcher said it sounded like he had a cold, and he hung up without leaving his name. The sheriff went and found the body, the video was posted Sunday morning. A nice tight timeline. But the killer made a mistake."

Archie and Graham stared at me.

"Which was?" Archie asked after a long pause.

"You always dampen my big reveals," I grouched. "I only watched the video of her death once before it came down, but it was dark out, same as when I was leaving Sherman's room in Fort Worth, which he was in at the time."

"So he couldn't have killed her."

I shook my head, grabbing an eraser and moving her name backward on my timeline. "False. There was no snow. In the exterior shot of her house at the beginning of that video, it was dark. And it wasn't snowing."

"Holy shit, she died on Friday," Graham said.

"She died on Friday." I pointed at him, so excited I was half tempted to dance a little jig. If Marta died Friday evening, the whole thing worked. "I was thrown off because the scene didn't smell like she'd been dead long when I got there this morning."

"Because he gutted the body, right?" Archie winced. "Gross, by the way."

"You didn't have to watch it," Graham said.

"Sherman left his house, went there, waited for her to come home, killed her and then drove to Fort Worth." I put a star by his name on the board. "Archie, see if APD can run traffic cams from Friday for his truck. He didn't get to Fort Worth until after dark. I'm sure of it."

"He's crafty," Graham said. "Those videos had us looking for a kid all this time, because of the melodrama of it. Just this afternoon we were convinced it was Olivia DeWitt."

I snapped my fingers. "Which is quite possibly exactly what he was going for. If she's arrested for a series of gruesome murders, even if she tells on Dustin, who's going to listen to her? And it gets a competitor for Kelsey Marie out of the way before the start of her senior year, too."

"I don't hate this theory the deeper we dig into it," Graham agreed.

Archie pulled his phone out and tapped at the screen. "Especially when you add this." He brandished the phone. "My contact inside the Dixie Mafia says Dennis Laveaux himself had an appointment with Sherman today. A big deal going down."

My hand went to my throat as Graham shot out of his chair.

"You don't think..." Archie let it trail as the hand holding his phone dropped to his side.

"Yeah. Yeah, I do." I hurled the marker at the wall, where it left a black dot on the beige paint and flopped unsatisfyingly to the carpet. "He wasn't worried about competition for Kelsey Marie and Samson, he was worried about controlling the story so he didn't get caught."

I paced. "What a piece of work this asshole is. He had me convinced I ought to feel sorry for him last night, for crying out loud. And all along, he was playing us all. He's killed everyone close to Kelsey Marie, he got millions of views and made hundreds of thousands of dollars hamming up two murders for what turned out to be a disturbed YouTube audience, and now..." My chin dropped to my chest.

"We failed her," I whispered. "He's going to sell his own daughter to Dennis Laveaux. Who probably has some internet sicko with deep pockets waiting to get his hands on her. And we might have already missed it."

Graham crossed the room to put a hand on my shoulder.

Archie's phone rang before he could offer a comment.

"Hey, Retha," he said, snapping his fingers and miming writing. Graham retrieved my marker and tossed it to him.

Archie moved to the board. "Main near Sixth at 3:40, 87 north at 4:25, and State 71 at 5:02. Got it. Thank you so much. Hey listen, can y'all check for the same vehicle, but on Friday? We think he'd have been headed out of McCulloch County to Fort Worth. Morning and evening, please. Thank you."

He hung up. "We might not be too late. Two Amber calls and a traffic cam in the middle," he said. "They'll let us know about Friday when they find something. So now all we need is a map."

I stared at the words, snatching my coat off the back of a chair and shrugging it back on.

"That's the way to my grandparents' place. He took her home."

37

Everything is clear in the rearview, Faith.

It was one of Charity's favorite things to tell me. Whenever I was bothered by the fact that I felt like I should've seen something coming, she reminded me that I can be too hard on myself.

Better than twenty years after she died, I still needed to hear it every once in a while.

"Why make the videos?" I asked as Graham turned Archie's Crown Vic onto Highway 87 northwest of the city. My truck was low on gas and Archie's the guy who fills up when his needle dips below three quarters of a tank. "Like, I can almost see how he might've killed the wife and maybe even the stepson, but why Samson? And why post the videos to Kelsey Marie's channel?"

"Well, first of all, I think that would answer the question of how someone posted the videos to her channel and changed her password and all that shit, because it's her dad. He probably has the passwords, right?"

"Yeah, I'd imagine so."

"And if he's auctioning his daughter off to the Dixie Mafia's highest bidder, he wouldn't need Samson anymore."

"True. Though now I'm wondering, what if like you said before, Sherman didn't kill Samson? Marta had his head. If she was blackmailing Sherman, then what if she killed the pig?"

"Why would she do that?"

"To show him she was serious? To threaten his income? Archie's guy at the State Department said she grew up pretty poor in rural Albania; it's plausible she could slaughter a pig. And twenty bucks says she was barred from Dustin's room because she found his stash. There was plenty of blackmail material to be had in that house if she was smart about her evidence."

I nodded, staring out the window as the fields, most of the snow gone, blurred by. "And maybe Sherman killed her because she killed the pig? Revenge, plus an out for the blackmail."

My phone buzzed in the cupholder and I snatched it up when I saw Jim's name.

"What've you got?" I asked.

"Tox screens back on the humans that gave me a weird idea."

"I like your weird ideas most of the time," I said. "So were any of the people ODs?"

"I don't think these concentrations would've killed anyone but the older couple. But the maid definitely had enough on board to knock her out. Kind of like the pig. But that's not the weirdest thing."

"Oh, Lord. I'm almost afraid to ask, Jim."

"Well, Samson here had quite a close-to-last supper. See, the buildup of this Oxy in the DeWitt couple was the kind I see when a junkie ODs on the stuff. There were no traces of pills in their guts, but they had high levels in the blood. They also had none of the other physical markers of drug addiction—his heart was probably in better condition than mine is. Got me thinking about the tox level in old Samson here and wondering about the pig of theirs you said they barbecued."

"But that was a community event. Nobody else died," I said.

"Bet you a steak dinner—because I know I'm right—that if someone checks their fridge they'll find leftovers these folks have been eating on all week."

"So they overdosed themselves on opioids by eating Clive?" I asked.

"With no tolerance built up in their systems it wouldn't even be that hard," Jim said. "It's been a week."

"But you said the weird thing was what Samson ate."

"I'm getting there. So then I got to thinking about Samson and whether I'd find pills in his gut, which I thought I would based on his tox results. And I did. But that wasn't the most interesting thing I found. Farm pigs are generally vegetarians, but his whole gut is clogged with meat," Jim said. "Like, he might've died of a bowel obstruction from all this if he hadn't been killed."

"What kind of meat?"

"Hard to say, other than something with fur. Dark fur, shaggy by the looks of this."

"So he ate another animal?"

"A decent size one. Did they have a big dog?"

"Not that anyone told me. But if I can find Kelsey Marie alive, I'll ask her."

"Good deal. Watch yourself, McClellan."

"Thanks for your help, Jim. Have a good night."

"I'll call you if I find anything else weird here."

I hung up.

"Jim thinks Samson ate a dog. Or rather, he said he ate some kind of animal. But that most people feed pigs a vegetarian diet. He said this much meat might have caused a bowel obstruction."

"Kelsey Marie said the pig was a vegan like her," Graham said. "Remember? She made a big thing out of that. And how people would eat him and she didn't know if she could run a pig farm."

"Would a pig just eat another animal?"

"If it saw the other animal as prey, yeah. Their jaws are strong enough to crush bone. It's just that they're big and slow, so they're not seen as dangerous."

"Can we go faster?" I asked. I wasn't even sure why I was more unsettled by what Jim had said, but something about it made my skin crawl.

"I'm going ninety now," Graham said.

"It's an open road. Are we going to get pulled over or something?"

"We're getting there. You won't do anyone any good if we both die in a fiery crash on the way."

"It's getting dark," I said.

"So? You want to call the sheriff's office? They might still beat us there."

I shook my head. "If Sherman is dangerous and something happens to Craig, I won't ever forgive myself. I told you he was a good kid."

Graham patted my knee. "I'll get us there. And when I do, you have to remember that we have a theory. Use caution, yes, but let the man talk before you start shooting."

"When have I ever forgotten that?" I shot him a sideways glare. "Mansplaining isn't a good look for you. That was actually a little offensive."

"I'm not trying to mansplain." Graham laughed. "And I'm

sorry if it sounded like I was. I'm not sure I've ever seen you so antsy about much of anything, and I just want to make sure we're checking all our regular boxes. That's all."

There was the Graham Hardin I knew and loved. The methods had to be followed. Boxes checked, I's dotted, T's crossed. But in perfect fairness, he was a stickler for it because it worked, which I knew.

I watched miles go by for nearly an hour.

"I won't fly off the handle," I said when he turned onto 71.

"I know." He put on the signal to turn on the Shermans' land. I caught a deep breath when I spotted Jeff's silver pickup.

"I'm holding you to that," Graham said as he cut the engine and I opened my door.

38

We heard the screams as we ran toward the house.

"Graham!" My voice high with panic, I unsnapped my holster and drew my weapon. He kept stride with me, gun in his right hand, until we got to the front porch.

"On three." He counted, and I tried the door latch.

The heavy doors swung wide, another scream reverberating off the walls.

"Stop where you are!" I called, relieved that it came out more commanding than shrill. "Mr. Sherman, the house is surrounded. Put both hands on the back of your head and make your way to the foyer."

Running footsteps stopped Graham and me in our tracks. We exchanged a glance and raised our weapons, planting our feet and resting our fingers on the trigger guards. I couldn't even feel my patched-up hands through the adrenaline.

"Stop, Mr. Sherman," I called.

The footsteps faltered, followed by sobs as Kelsey Marie staggered into the foyer, dropping a Ruger semiautomatic pistol at her feet and collapsing into a heap on the floor.

I jammed my weapon back into its holster and hurried to

kneel next to her, gasping when she raised her head. Blood poured from a slash across her right cheek, a flap of skin loose, and matching trickles trailed from her nose and upper lip. "My God. Graham, can we have something—anything—to stop this bleeding?"

He ran for the kitchen and returned with a roll of paper towels. I ripped off a long strand and wadded it up, touching Kelsey Marie's shoulder. "Lean your head back for me, sweetie," I said.

She plopped it into my lap, blood dripping over her eye and back toward my jeans.

I pressed the towels first against the side of her face and then directly over the cut, my eyes on the gun. "Honey, is your dad here?"

She sobbed harder, the blood picking up again as her head moved under the towels.

"Hold still," I said. "It's going to be okay."

"My face," she said. "It hurts. Is it bad?"

"I met the best plastic surgeon in Austin today," I said. "I bet he can make it like it never happened."

I looked up at Graham and then back at the blood soaking the towels. I couldn't help her if she bled out on the way to Austin. "They don't have a hospital out here. We need a doctor. Kelsey Marie, where does the doctor live?"

"Almost to town. A big Victorian-looking house with porches." She stumbled over the words, but got them out.

"You can get him faster than 911 will help us out here," I told Graham. "We can take her to Austin for care as long as she doesn't need immediate help for this before the drive."

"I'm not leaving you here." Graham's eyes popped wide. "Are you kidding?"

"My dad," Kelsey Marie squeaked. "He's dead. He tried to kill me. He said with Samson gone he didn't have use for me anymore and he needed my money." The last word was swallowed up by sobs.

Several hitching breaths later, she wiped at her left eye with the back of one hand. "He said my mom and Dustin were waiting for me on the other side. And I could see my damned pig again. That's what he said. He had a knife. He swung and got my cheek, and then he chased me toward the kitchen and tackled me, and I smashed my face into the floor.

"Where'd you get the gun?" I glanced at it.

"That's the one he keeps in the kitchen," she said. "There's a handgun stashed somewhere in every room in this house. I kicked him in the face and got up and got to the gun before he got back to me."

Her face crumpled and the blood rushed again, soaking through the wad of towels. "I loved my daddy. And I shot him. Shot him dead."

She let out a piercing wail riddled with an anguish I hadn't even seen often in my job.

I brushed her hair off her forehead and shushed her. "You did what you had to do. It was self-defense. And it's over now."

"Can we go?" she sniffled. "I don't want to be here with him...looking at me. I'm so sorry, Daddy."

I waved a hand at Graham.

"The local authorities are going to want the scene processed," I said. "I can help them with that, but not with her bleeding like this."

I reached for my phone, dialing Craig.

Voicemail.

I left a message and shot an imploring glance at Graham. "Please?"

He looked around before he got out the keys. "She's okay. And I'll be right back with reinforcements."

Kelsey Marie groped with one hand, pressing the nearly

saturated mess of bloody paper to her face. "Like this?" she asked.

"Yeah, but let's change it out."

I pulled off more towels and helped her get a hold on them and sit up. The bleeding slowed.

Keeping her behind me, I went to the living room and peered over the leather sectional toward the kitchen.

Jeff was dead all right. Wide blue eyes stared, unseeing, at the fireplace. Blood seeped out of him and into a dark circle on the polished hardwood floor.

Two neat holes, both in the vicinity of his heart, marred the front of his jacket. No pulse.

At least she was a good shot under pressure.

"Can we...could we go in the kitchen? Maybe get some coffee, or some hot chocolate? If we have to wait here, I'd like to do it away from him." Her voice caught on the end of the last word.

"Of course." I turned back, herding her toward the kitchen. "I can get it, if you'll tell me how to work this thing." I pointed to the coffee machine.

Sniffling still, she tried for a brave half-smile. It almost worked. "Is this the kind of stuff you see, like every day?"

"Not every day. But way more days than most people," I said.

"How do you do it?" She pulled milk from the fridge and bumped the door with her hip to close it.

"I focus on the people I'm trying to help. The victims. Their families."

"Anything for when the victims are their families?" She started the coffee machine and turned back, her lower lip quivering. Switching the hand holding the paper towels, she shook her other arm out. "I keep thinking this must be a bad dream, and I'll wake up in a minute."

"I'm so sorry, Kelsey Marie."

"Don't be," she said. "You promised me you wouldn't let anything happen to me, and you kept your word."

"I suppose." I waved one hand at her face. "I'm not sure that counts."

"This can be fixed, like you said." She sighed. "My dad. How the fuck does this even happen? I'm so stupid. I called him from the hotel to tell him I was safe; I knew he'd be worried because I didn't have my phone. He said he needed to talk to me about my mom and he was coming to get me. I told him the deputies wouldn't let me leave and he told me to jump off the balcony. So I did. Just like that, without a second thought." She blinked hard. "He was so quiet all the way out here, like he was mad at me, but I couldn't figure out why. He didn't say anything about Mom, and when I asked he just told me to shut my filthy mouth." She sniffled, pulling in a shuddering breath.

"You don't have to—" I began.

She waved her free hand in front of her face. "I do, though," she wailed.

I raised both hands. "Okay."

"We came into the house and he started yelling at me, about being stupid and pissing off Olivia DeWitt, and about her stupid pig getting killed before Samson, and my mom having an affair—I guess that was my fault, too." She sobbed, lowering her head as tears rained onto the counter from the side of her face that wasn't bleeding.

"Did he ever have trouble with his temper or try to hurt you before tonight?" I asked.

"Never. He had his hunting knife in his pocket, and he started tossing it back and forth in his hands."

Like the video from Marta's murder. Which she hadn't seen. Box checked.

"He said my mother was a cheating whore and her bastard kid was no good, and he knew I'd be just like her so he was going to put me out of my misery." She hitched in a long breath. "When he lunged at me, he swung his arm back and slashed at my throat. I ducked, and he got my face instead. I ran, but he tackled me. And then I got the gun. Holy crap, I got the gun and I shot my own father." She cried silently, leaning forward but still pressing on the facial wound.

"It wasn't your fault, Kelsey Marie," I said. "Your dad was sick." Even if the wife was a heat-of-the-moment crime, three more murders weren't. I just wished Sherman had lived for me to book him.

Catching her breath, Kelsey Marie wiped at her eyes and switched her hands back. "How long do I have to keep pressing on this, anyway?"

I crossed the kitchen. "Let me see?"

I moved the towels back gingerly, still holding my hand under the gash from the front of the makeshift dressing.

It was red, and it looked horrifying, but the gap between skin and muscle looked smaller, and the bleeding had stopped.

"I think maybe we're okay here." I slowly pulled the paper towels away.

The wound was angry and red, but not as deep as I'd first feared. Facial lacerations are good about offering plenty of bloody drama. Dr. Chris better actually be as good as his ego told him he was.

I swallowed hard and smiled as she handed me the red cup. "Thanks."

She went to the sink to wash her hands and set about making her own drink.

I picked up the towel she'd used to dry her hands and went to hang it back up, when something brown caught my eye. I put it through the handle on the dishwasher and picked at the flecks.

I didn't have a microscope or a lab test, but that looked like dried blood.

A lot of dried blood.

A paring knife with a gleaming blade lay on the counter next to the sink, water droplets clinging from a recent rinse.

I looked back at Kelsey Marie, who was squirting whipped cream into the top of her latte with her right hand.

The cut went from left to right across her right cheek.

Jeff Sherman was left-handed. I could see him in my head, holding his whiskey glass in that hotel room in Fort Worth.

I let my eyes fall shut for a long blink. If he'd slashed forward at her face like she said, the cut would start wide at her cheekbone and taper toward her nose.

It did not.

If, on the other hand, right-handed Kelsey Marie slashed her own face with the paring knife after she shot her father, the cut would look...well, just exactly like it did.

Holy shit.

I read everything about this case a hundred and eighty degrees wrong.

39

The first murder is almost always an accident. Even predators have to live and function in society. The gifts required lie dormant until a tipping point, when control is lost.

A new skill is found—and it is a skill. Just a misunderstood one.

The ability to face down death, to beat it back, is celebrated.

The ability to give over to pure rage and become death himself is more rare. Just as brave in its own way.

But darker. More mysterious.

We don't celebrate it. We fear it. Lock it away.

Pretend it doesn't exist so we can sleep at night.

So when a predator is born, it's often a surprise.

A blur of blinding anger.

A flash of quick motion.

And a flood of warm, red blood.

Most humans don't like to think about how close they could come to crossing that line. Nearly everyone drawing breath has a motive that would push them right over it. Revenge is the most common one.

But even through rage, horror and remorse bloom. For most people.

When the blood gushes and leaves only a cold void, a calculation of how to survive, a plan for disposing of the prey —the almost instant realization that hogs eat humans when given the chance, for instance—a true predator comes into their own.

New eyes see the world through a different lens. Everyone and everything could be prey.

Most are too easy. A true predator doesn't want simplicity. It's insulting.

We hunt challenging strength and speed. Devise creative ways to dispose of remains. Every success brings a rush. And the desire for a new challenge.

Until we meet another predator—one who may be more clever. One who is our equal.

Even if they don't realize what's playing out, they have a chance of winning.

That's the real test of a predator—can you face an equal and be the last one standing?

It's true survival of the fittest.

40

I slid along the counter toward the sink, looking down but trying not to be too obvious about it.

An adrenaline rush warmed my cheeks. I'd been wrong about this case twice already, but since she was the last member of the Sherman family standing, I didn't think I was wrong this time.

I needed to be sure, though.

"Officer? You okay?" she asked behind me.

I spun to face her with a wide, fool-the-judges smile pasted on my face. I'd spent a lot of years wishing I could wrench my childhood back from the blood-red talons of pageant hell, but damned if the ability to offer a genuine, warm smile in any circumstance doesn't come in handy in this line of work way more frequently than I ever would've thought.

"I'm good," I said, raising my mug. "Thanks for the latte. It's amazing."

My phone buzzed a text arrival and I pulled it out.

Archie: *Cyber managed to get into Kelsey Marie's cloud account per your request from yesterday. They found recently uploaded video footage of Marta's murder that was taken with*

Kelsey Marie's cell, plus some videos of someone in that black hooded cape, talking through a synthesizer about getting away with murder. Weird stuff, I'm watching now. Whoever this is keeps talking about true predators. She could be working with her dad. Proceed with caution on arrival.

That's why she smashed her phone. I slid mine back into my pocket.

Looked around the kitchen.

"Kelsey Marie?" I spun.

Like every other damn thing about this case, I was about half a second too late.

I tried to move, but my arms and legs felt like they weighed a thousand pounds each. Blinking, I glanced around.

I was in the Shermans' living room, Jeff still dead on the floor but at a different angle, about five feet away from my left foot, which—along with all my other limbs—was tied to a chair. My head felt big, every inch of it throbbing like she'd swung an anvil at me in the kitchen instead of a cast iron skillet.

Shit.

"Kelsey Marie, what are you doing?" I kept panic out of my voice with some superhuman power I didn't know I had, twisting my head, trying to see where her voice was coming from before I noticed the camera on the table in front of me, pointed at me.

I swallowed hard.

She leaned in from my right, wearing the cloak from the videos, her face completely obscured by a thin panel of black cloth sewn between the sides of the hood. "Boo!"

I flinched backward before I could stop myself.

She laughed and stepped around me, squatting in front of me with a butcher knife in her right hand. "I thought I'd start off by giving us matching scars."

My nostrils flared with a deep breath as I nodded slightly toward the camera. "Are you recording this? How do you think you're going to get away with something you put on film?"

"The finished cut won't have sound—nobody wants to hear us yakking, and my job is to give people what they want. Do you know how many followers I've gained since I put the video of Samson's murder on *High on the Hog*? I thought I'd lose people for sure, but I had to do it so you'd feel sorry for me, and instead..." She threw her arms wide. "It turns out the movies have been right all this time. People love violence. Never thought I'd be glad I forgot to turn off my motion sensors the night Samson died." She stopped in front of me and touched the knife to the tip of my nose. "I'm always in for giving my viewers what they want. It's why they love me."

"YouTube isn't going to love this," I said.

"I've moved beyond YouTube. The dark web is so much more entrepreneurial, Ranger. You should check it out. Do you know how many people get off on stuff like this? And how much they'll pay for it?" She moved behind me.

"Money's not as good yet, and bitcoin is weird, but based on what I saw this weekend, the money will pick up. And I'll figure out the currency thing."

"You think your viewers want to watch me die?"

"They sure loved watching Marta die. I got the most adoring fan letters. And you know what I didn't get? One single perv talking about what he wants to do to me."

"I bet not. They'd be crazy to insult someone who could do what you've done here."

Kelsey Marie wrinkled her nose at Jeff. "He was too hard. I didn't get a video. Quick and dirty, and kind of sad, and there's no entertainment in that. But you...oh, me and you are going to have some fun."

First rule of a hostage situation: get them talking and keep them that way. A terrorist who's running their mouth is way less likely to start killing people.

"Does that mean Samson wasn't hard?"

"Of course Samson was hard," she snapped. "He was necessary. A sad casualty. I fed him Miranda's corpse and two days later he bit me." She pulled up the cavernous robe sleeve to reveal a wide bandage on her arm. "Survival of the fittest. I couldn't wait for him to turn on me. He was the most difficult thing about all this—didn't you see me when you first came over here? I loved Samson, I wouldn't have hurt him unless I had to. What kind of monster do you think I am?"

"The kind who literally smeared Marta's guts all over her living room wall." It came out almost before I thought it.

She jumped toward me, knife raised, the skin flopping against her face making a small slurping sound that made my stomach turn. "Marta had it coming. She was snooping in things I warned her she didn't want to know, and she didn't listen." She froze, bringing the knife down and behind her back. "You are not going to get me to kill you quick and easy, Ranger. Nice try."

"I wasn't trying, believe me. Kelsey Marie, how could you do this? Why would you do this?" I thought she needed protection, for fuck's sake. Boy, did she play me like a golden fiddle.

She flipped the knife back to her other hand. "Didn't you tell me you were good at this?"

I swallowed a smartass retort, seeing as how she had a large knife and I was restrained and had no idea where my gun had gone.

"Enlighten me."

"My mother was cheating on my dad. She even programmed her fucking boyfriend's birthday as the password for my light systems in the barn. My light systems." Her thin lips twisted into a snarl. "Like that wasn't bad enough, the bitch was stealing from me, planning to take off with her boy toy. Stealing." She shouted it for emphasis when my face didn't give her the reaction she wanted. "From her own daughter! After I gave her a very nice life—me! With my talent! She had every single car we owned including mine put in Dusty's name. So they could take them or sell them if they wanted."

"But your dad sold Dustin's car just the other day."

"Sure he did, because I brought it back and showed him what she did. He was good and pissed and said two could play that game." She flashed a grin. "Just like I knew he would. And you thought he killed everyone. Just like I knew you would."

"Brought it back from where?"

"Where I took Dusty's body in it."

I was still missing several parts of the story. Deep breath. She liked performing. Just lead her. Graham would be back if I could just keep her talking.

"So you killed your mother. And told your dad she left?"

"I killed her because she lied to me. Told me she wasn't stealing from me when I had a whole spreadsheet showing the money she was moving from my accounts into ones she'd set up for herself. I wasn't going to like, murder her, I just wanted her to stop fucking Sam and give my money back and not break up our family." She sniffled and tipped her head back, blinking hard. "But then she started lying and I lost my temper and my knitting needles were right there, and...it was over so fast, and she bled so much." She waved a hand in front of her face. "I didn't mean to."

Sweet Jesus. Sam, like her son's friend?

"*I'm Sam. The boyfriend?*" he'd said.

Seemed he didn't mean Kelsey Marie after all.

Later. Right then, Kelsey Marie was still waving the butcher knife like a fan, spilling her own guts like I was her therapist, not someone she was trying to murder. Teenagers.

"My dad wasn't here. He was out of town, and Dustin was supposed to be staying at Sam's house for the night. Perfect timing, because I could be sure neither of them would be around. So I drug her out to the barn and put her in the trough. I knew Samson would pick her clean as soon as he figured out she wasn't moving."

Meat in the pig's intestines. My stomach lurched.

"Your mom isn't the only person who watches a lot of crime TV shows," was all I said.

"*How to Get Away with Murder* is the best show in the history of TV. And I thought that before I was trying to do it, too."

Wow. Moving on.

"But the boys didn't stay at Sam's?" I guessed.

"Fucking Dustin. He was cutting a drug deal out by my barn," she said. "He saw me."

"But he didn't call the sheriff."

"The sheriff hates Dusty, and Dusty hated him. He hated everything but money, when you get right down to it. He watched everything and waited two days—two whole days—to come tell me he wanted one and a half million dollars to keep my secret."

"And you didn't want to pay him?"

"Would you?"

"It seems like maybe it would've been the easiest thing to do," I said, looking around.

"Well, I'll tell you, I thought so at first, too. I told him I'd get it for him. But then I got to thinking about it and I realized two things: he would always know my secret and it wouldn't stop at that one and a half million, and I've never liked Dustin. He's a dick. I loved my mother and I was okay a few hours after she died. So I killed him instead. Didn't even cry that time.

"I just loaded him into his stupid precious Mustang and carted him out to the middle of nowhere, that stupid hunting lease. They used my money to buy Dusty a place to murder more defenseless animals. So that's where he'll stay. I cleaned his body like a deer and put the meat in the curing house. Once it's done I'll go back and bury it, and it won't stink. Nobody will ever find him, those woods go on for miles.

"It was perfect. Everybody knows Milt Barnes couldn't catch a murderer who was in the process of cutting Milt Barnes up, so I figured that was it. I'd get a new pig this spring and just start over, you know? My followers would love a baby. Until you showed up here, talking about your perfect arrest record, and I knew I had to make way sure my tracks were covered. I went back to get the car and convinced my dad that my mom wasn't ever coming back and he needed to sell it."

"But Marta took your flash drive with the evidence that your mom was stealing from you because she thought something was fishy about your story that Miranda took off."

Kelsey Marie pointed the knife at me. "Yep. She wanted me to pay to get her mother into the U.S. Six hundred grand. I told her it wouldn't be worth it, mothers are a pain in the ass. She didn't agree. So did you find my thumb drive, then? I looked through all her stuff in the kitchen, that's where she practically lived no matter which house she was in, but I didn't see it."

"Night table."

"Ah."

What the hell was I doing?

"Kelsey Marie, you need to let me go. Murdering a peace officer is a capital offense in Texas."

"But they can't convict Jeff there—he's dead. And when you're dead too, Commander Hardin will come back to find me passed out over there"—she pointed with the knife—"and I'll explain that my aim was off—I hate guns, remember? So Jeff got up after the commander left. By the time I got back in here, it was too late to save you. It's perfect."

"But if you're supposed to take him down again in that scene, how are you going to explain postmortem wounds on him?"

"I'm not. He wasn't dead, that doesn't mean he didn't keep bleeding. I tripped on the rug and hit my head and when I came to, he was over there dead and you were here dead." She checked her watch. Adjusted the camera. "We're about out of time here. Ready? This is my first video with prey that's awake. See, the more I saw of you, the more I thought you were going to figure me out eventually, so I needed to get you alone and tie up this one"—she flicked the blade, air whooshing close to my cheek—"last loose end."

She turned the camera on.

Turned back to me and straightened the hood.

Raised the knife.

41

Two quick shots split the air, and something heavy and wet fell on me, pain ripping through my side.

I opened my eyes to see Deputy Craig clenching his service weapon, his eyes wide.

"Faith!" Graham's voice came from the foyer. "What the hell was that?"

He sprinted in, his gorgeous mossy eyes going wide.

"I was wrong," I said. "Kelsey Marie did it."

Graham pulled her off me and dropped her to the floor, kneeling to check a pulse and close her eyes before he threw a glance at Craig. "Nice shooting, kid."

Turning back to me, he furrowed his brow, gesturing to my predicament. "Where's your gun?"

I tried to shrug. "Get me loose? She clocked me with a skillet. Just as I was figuring out she killed her dad and cut her own face."

"Jesus."

Craig appeared at Graham's shoulder with a utility knife. I flexed my fingers and toes when the ties popped loose, looking down at my shirt, where a red stain was spreading over my ribs courtesy of the knife that sank into my side when Kelsey Marie fell on me. "Oh."

"Doctor is coming," Graham said. "That's what took so long. He wanted to drive himself, and he's not exactly moving at top pace these days."

"He can be as slow as he wants," I said. "I'm going to be damned glad to see him."

I tried to stand and Graham put a hand on my shoulder. "Wait there."

Happy to oblige.

Deputy Craig came out of the Sherman family murders with a huge TikTok following, thanks to Kelsey Marie's last act being live-streamed because she hit the wrong button on her expensive wifi-enabled camera. She must've missed the TV episode about how it's impossible to cover all your cyber tracks, no matter how clever you are.

Craig parlayed his newfound fifteen minutes into a crowd-funded college fund for himself and a private nurse for his dad. He was in Austin studying criminal justice, with a job waiting for him with the DPS upon graduation. Lieutenant Boone was a little more thankful than I would've expected that I didn't die.

Jeff Sherman actually had been in Fort Worth looking at a horse—for Dennis Laveaux to buy a prize Palomino yearling his daughter wanted. Guys like Laveaux aren't generally welcomed into auctions by most reputable ranchers thanks to fears about money laundering and federal indictments. Archie's contact said Laveaux's lawyers were already pursuing any barely-legal avenues to recouping the rest of what Sherman owed him from the estate. I'd warned Jeff

Sherman's sister—as his only surviving relative—that she didn't want to tangle with Laveaux. I hoped she was a good listener.

Miss Donnie was back to leaving her doors unlocked, and she'd sent me a huge bouquet and a ham with a note both apologizing and thanking me for my help.

"This ham is mighty tasty," Archie called from the kitchen, where he was carving it. "We're sure it's not loaded with anything that's going to poison us?"

"Miss Donnie's pigs are drug free," I said. The DeWitts had kept the leftovers from the stock show barbecue, and felt like my grandparents had about wasting food, evidently. The toxins had built up in their systems until they died shortly after the last dinner they ate. Olivia was only spared because she didn't want to eat her pet pig. "As are most of the people in McCulloch County these days, without Dustin Golden to deal to them."

"We solved the case and saved a whole town. Not bad for a weekend." Graham rested his cheek on my hair, ruffling Archie's dog's fur.

My mother appeared in the kitchen doorway, wearing an apron.

An apron. Ruth McClellan. "Dinner's almost ready."

Archie put his arms around her from behind. "We eat in front of the TV when football is on."

Her mouth gaped open and she turned.

I smiled, snuggling closer to Graham, a look I'd never seen on my mother's face. They were good for each other.

"The funeral was yesterday," I said under my breath as my mother left the room. "They buried the whole family in a mausoleum at the local cemetery after Craig and old Milt found Dustin's body near their cabin. Except Kelsey Marie. Jeff's sister wouldn't allow it. Pete had a story about it in his paper. A remarkable tasteful one. That guy is going to change my blanket opinion of journalists."

"So what happened to Kelsey Marie, then? She was just a kid."

"She did a whole lot of damage. Her remains were remanded to the county; they'll inter them at a cemetery where they can get a charity to cover the plot, or commandeer one."

"What a ride." He put one finger under my chin and tipped my face up for a kiss. "I'm glad you're okay. I may never leave you alone again."

"I'm glad Craig checked his voicemail and is a clean shot," I said. "And that's about all the thought I want to give that part of it. Hey—Olivia got a scholarship from the stock show endowment after word got out about what happened to her pig. And her YouTube channel about her journey to vet school is picking up followers who miss Samson and Kelsey Marie."

"The video of you almost dying was up to twelve million views last time I checked." Graham scowled. "Every time one site removes it, someone puts it up somewhere else. People are sick."

"I'm sure people thought it was a role play at first," I said.

"Well no one should anymore."

"It'll fade eventually."

"You've gotten some pretty gross letters because of it," he reminded me.

"I got those when we arrested the Governor, too. And before that because of a dozen other cases that put my picture in the paper. These will go away, too."

"Seriously. Never leaving you alone again."

I tipped my head back for a quick kiss. "Fine by me."

I cleared my throat when Ruth and Archie came in. "Speaking of those awful letters, I've been thinking we might ought to consider moving the wedding. Something smaller, more private. No news coverage."

Ruth looked like I'd pulled my gun on her, every ounce of color draining from her face. "You cannot be serious, Faith Lorraine."

Archie leaned in between the two of us. "If I may, ladies," he said. "What if we keep the plans as they are, and the Rangers provide whatever level of security we deem overkill?" He winked at me. "I'm told folks today have a short attention span, and we do have six more weeks."

I glanced at Graham.

"Whatever you want, Faith."

"Thanks, Arch." I reached for my margarita and patted Tyler's head as I fed him a piece of ham from the platter Archie had put on the coffee table.

"It's going to be a beautiful wedding," Ruth said. "I just got the samples of the hand-lettered invitations yesterday."

Archie listened to her talk and I chewed a piece of ham and leaned back into Graham's warm arms, smiling at Archie's goofy lovestruck expression, the dog, the game, and even my nicely-healing most recent set of war wounds.

Ruth could have her beautiful wedding.

We had a beautiful life.

NO LOVE LOST: Faith McClellan #5

**FROM AMAZON CHARTS BESTSELLING AUTHOR
LYNDEE WALKER**

A trail of dead bodies throws Texas Ranger Faith McClellan
into a race to catch a serial killer obsessed with stealing
organs...

The Rangers are running an active shooter simulation in an
empty mall when they find a young woman's body, wrapped in
plastic in a mechanical closet. When the medical examiner
discovers that this woman is missing several organs, it is Faith's
first clue that this is not your average murder.

Soon, Faith discovers a trail of bodies matching the killer's
M.O., all stored in remote indoor locations, all with organs
removed, each one closer to the last. With the missing organs
affecting the decomposition timeline, it's almost impossible to
pinpoint the time of each murder, and the investigation takes
on a life of its own.

Faith will risk everything to put a stop to the murders—but
the killer is smarter than she thinks, and they won't hesitate to
cut down anyone who interferes with their lethal plan...

LOVE READING MYSTERIES & THRILLERS?

Never miss a new release! Sign up to receive exclusive updates from author LynDee Walker.

Join today at LynDeeWalker.com

As a thank you for signing up, you'll receive a free copy of *Fatal Features: A Nichelle Clarke Crime Thriller Novella*.

YOU MIGHT ALSO ENJOY...

The Nichelle Clarke Series

Front Page Fatality

Buried Leads

Small Town Spin

Devil in the Deadline

Cover Shot

Lethal Lifestyles

Deadly Politics

Hidden Victims

Dangerous Intent

The Faith McClellan Series

Fear No Truth

Leave No Stone

No Sin Unpunished

Nowhere to Hide

No Love Lost

Never miss a new release!

Sign up to receive exclusive updates from author LynDee Walker.

LynDeeWalker.com

As a thank you for signing up, you'll receive a free copy of
Fatal Features: A Nichelle Clarke Crime Thriller Novella.

ACKNOWLEDGMENTS

No matter how many times I do this, it never gets old—and I hope it stays that way. This book was a fun and often surprising one to write, and I loved being able to set part of it in my hometown—the actual places and events referenced were skimmed from my childhood memories, and I make no promises that they're entirely currently factual, but the spirit is definitely there for Faith.

Many thanks, as always, to my wonderful agent John Talbot, and to the fantastic team behind my books at Severn River Publishing. I so appreciate everything y'all do to make this job the most fun one I could hope for.

Cris Dukehart, your talent for bringing Faith and her friends to life consistently blows me away—thank you for lending your voice to this series.

I feel lucky every book that I get to work with Randall Klein, who uses his incredible gift of insight to really make my books sparkle.

Cara Quinlan, many thanks for cleaning up my messy manuscripts with your sharp eyes, and also for your kind words about my stories and characters.

Jennifer Hillier, Laura McHugh, S.A. Cosby, Jason Kasper, Brian Shea, Lisa Regan, and Hank Phillippi Ryan: thank you all so much for your kindness and generosity with your words and your time, and for your support and encouragement over the years. I maintain that the best thing about this writing gig is the wonderful people I get to call my friends.

Readers, please know that I appreciate every one of you and the hours you spend with my imaginary friends, and every message and email you send telling me they brighten your days inevitably brightens mine.

Special thanks this time to Jo Ben Whittenburg, who sent one of the earliest such messages about Faith after FEAR NO TRUTH was published, and has been generous with his kind words about each new novel in the series. I hope this one is your favorite yet.

As always, any mistakes are mine alone.

ABOUT THE AUTHOR

LynDee Walker is the national bestselling author of two crime fiction series featuring strong heroines and "twisty, absorbing" mysteries. Her first Nichelle Clarke crime thriller, FRONT PAGE FATALITY, was nominated for the Agatha Award for best first novel and is an Amazon Charts Bestseller. In 2018, she introduced readers to Texas Ranger Faith McClellan in FEAR NO TRUTH. Reviews have praised her work as "well-crafted, compelling, and fast-paced," and "an edge-of-your-seat ride" with "a spider web of twists and turns that will keep you reading until the end."

Before she started writing fiction, LynDee was an award-winning journalist who covered everything from ribbon cuttings to high level police corruption, and worked closely with the various law enforcement agencies that she reported on. Her work has appeared in newspapers and magazines across the U.S.

Aside from books, LynDee loves her family, her readers, travel, and coffee. She lives in Richmond, Virginia, where she is working on her next novel when she's not juggling laundry and children's sports schedules.

You can find LynDee online at www.lyndeewalker.com, and connect with her on Facebook at lyndeewalkerbooks or Twitter @LynDeeWalker.

9 781648 751363